THE FIELD TRIP

R.A. Andrade

Selladore Press
10246 Crouse Rd. #703
Hartland MI 48353

FAN
Andrade

ISBN-13: 978-0-9903254-2-0
ISBN-10: 0990325423

eBook ISBN-13: 978-0-9903254-3-7
eBook ISBN-10: 0990325431

Andrade, R.A.
The Field Trip / by R.A. Andrade – 1st ed.

Library of Congress Control Number: 2014920240

raandrade.com

Edits and layout by Judy Berlinski
Cover by 5 Avenues Design Firm

Printed in the United States of America

For my children Melissa, Donna, Ron, and Sandra

Chapter 1

Ross smiled when he read the familiar sign over the hangar office door, "IF YOU GOT THE ITCH WE CAN SCRATCH IT," wondering if the catchy phrase attracted or frightened potential students. He opened the door to a young woman's welcoming face behind the counter. "Hi Penny, is your dad around?"

"Hi Ross," she answered coyly, her eyes betraying delight. "I think he's just inside the hangar."

"No rush, I'm five minutes early."

Cupping her hands aside her mouth, she turned to the doorway and yelled, "Hey Dad! Time for Professor Barton's lesson!"

"Beautiful day," Ross said.

"Yeah, great weather for flying," she responded, a pale blush rising to her cheeks.

His fingers fidgeted on the countertop. After an awkward silence, he asked himself, *So what do I say now?* Taking a cue from her outfit, he asked, "You into yoga?"

Penny looked down at her powder blue T-shirt tucked into her jeans that read Silver Tree Yoga. Returning her eyes to his, she answered, "Just started last week. They gave me the shirt free."

I could use a coffee, he told himself. But instead he said, "The forecast is for possible showers later in the day."

"Heard that too," she responded too quickly, trying to keep the conversation going.

Rescuing Ross from his clumsy attempt to construct another sentence of dialogue, Ernie appeared through the open hangar doorway wiping his hands on a greasy rag. "Thanks Penny," he said to his daughter as she continued her vigil over Ross. "Ready to rock, Professor?"

Once outside, Ernie lightly grabbed Ross' arm and motioned with his head in the direction of the office. "Hey, my daughter seems to have a crush on you."

"Huh?"

"You never seem to talk about girls," Ernie tested. "Do you like women?"

"Yeah, I like women. I'm just not very good with them. I think I bore the living hell out of them."

"Just guessing, but I think Penny wants you to ask her out."

"I didn't think fathers told secrets about their daughters," Ross said, then added, "She has a great personality and seems very bright. You did a nice job raising her."

"She never said anything to me, but a father can tell. She's perkier on the days you have a lesson."

Shaking his head at the absurd idea Penny might like him, Ross asked, "It would be okay with you if I did?"

"Won't hold it against you," Ernie answered, peeking above the frame of his aviator sunglasses.

"But I've got to warn you, she probably won't want a second date. Now, can we get my lesson in?"

"Oh, sorry, just got sidetracked."

Halfway to the red and white Robinson R22 helicopter sitting on the asphalt pad, Ross stopped. "Ernie, this is going to be my last lesson for the summer. I'll pick it up again in the fall."

"If it's the two-eighty an hour, I could give you a break for a few months," Ernie offered. "You're my best student. Not many pick it up as fast as you have. And I've seen a lot since Desert Storm."

"No, the money would never stop me from flying. You know, I fell in love with helicopters when my father took me up in one a year before he died. I was fourteen. Ever since, I've read every book I could get my hands on about them. Even got to go up in some with a student in the National Guard. It's tight on my salary, but that's not the reason. I'm going to do some field research in New England."

Ernie brightened. "I see. Where 'bouts in New England?"

"Long Trail in Vermont," Ross answered.

A thoughtful look washed over Ernie. He stroked his chin, his mind working to bring up a memory of something he heard. Snapping his fingers, he announced, "Vermont . . . now I remember. One of my war buddies runs a fixed-wing school up there. Been some strange shit going on last couple of weeks."

"Strange shit?"

"Odd lights in the sky at night. And been seeing lots of military chopper activity during the day. Says it's really unusual."

"Probably just military exercises," Ross suggested.

"Could be, but this guy doesn't spook easily. Been through hell in the war. He's about to retire so he's not trying to drum up sightseeing business or anything like that. If he says it's strange shit, let me tell you, it's strange shit."

Not giving too much credence to the revelation, Ross thanked Ernie for the inside scoop and resumed walking toward the aircraft.

* * *

Ross ran through the external aircraft inspection while Ernie relaxed cross-legged against the plane and smoked his Camels. When complete, Ross nodded and the two climbed into the Robinson, popular for both training and livestock management. Once seated in the simple but functional cockpit behind the T-Bar cyclic control, Ross continued the preflight checklist under his instructor's watchful eye. Where typical helicopters had a cyclic control stick between the operator's legs, the R22 utilized what resembled a bicycle handlebar, easily reached from either seat. Ross started the four-cylinder Lycoming engine, and then read each of the gauges on the black, freestanding center pod and console. He gave thumbs up.

Satisfied all was as it should be, Ernie spoke loudly above the clatter of engine and rotor noise, "Okay, since you are going to be gone for a while, let's not do anything new today. I want to review everything you've learned so far. So let's take this puppy up and get the show on the road."

Twisting the throttle and pulling up on the collective stick to his left, a thrilling sensation overcame Ross as the helicopter rose smoothly off the pad. He sensed he had crossed a threshold like a child who just had the coordination come together for riding a bicycle. The synchronization of his hands and feet felt natural, causing the aircraft to move as if by will alone. Some of the elation faded when he remembered he might lose this hard-earned skill with a three-month hiatus.

Ernie tested Ross' capabilities for the next forty-five minutes, pushing the student hard to evaluate his reactions to quick demands. He knew the flight controls for the Robinson trainer were extremely sensitive, requiring skill to avoid overcorrecting. A student who could fly the R22 competently generally found operating a heavier helicopter easy by comparison.

"You're a natural for this," Ernie finally said. "Tower says some storm cells moving in faster than expected, so why don't we head back to the hangar and I'll describe what you'll learn next after your field trip."

"Not a field trip, a *research* trip," Ross corrected, moving the cyclic bar to the right and bringing the aircraft into a turn.

"Whatever you say Professor," Ernie said, smirking. "Hey, there's one of our other choppers to the west. Seems to be jumping around a lot. Move in for a closer look."

"Toward that huge bank of clouds, right?" Ross checked as he broke out of the sweeping turn and was startled to see that the thunderheads reached from just above ground level, rising to thousands of feet above them. He located the sister white and red Robinson, a dot growing in size against the clouds. It dropped in free-fall nearly one hundred feet, and then its plunge stopped abruptly as if yanked to a halt at the end of an invisible wire. Jumbled calls of distress filled his headset and he saw the tail of the aircraft wobble twice.

The nose angled down.

Time stopped.

Nothing moved.

Without warning, the helicopter plummeted to the earth.

"I'm taking control!" Ernie yelled, grabbing the cyclic and placing his feet on his own pedals. "I think they hit a wind shear." They both watched in horror as the other helicopter crashed through the roof of a large barn and disappeared from view as the old building collapsed over it. A haze of brown dust and debris colored the air above the site. A metallic "snap-twang" sound came from the floor of their cockpit.

"Oh, shit, something's wrong with my pedals. Ross, get us down there, fast."

Regaining control, the machine became an extension of Ross' body. He brought them to a heading straight for the barn. Ernie shouted for a rescue team above the noise of their chopper and the control tower chatter. Within minutes, they landed near the heap of aged lumber arranged like a monstrous pile of pick-up sticks. Both men opened their doors in unison and bounded into the scraggly, tall grass in a life or death race to the rubble.

"Anyone hear me?" Ernie yelled into the shambles.

A faint, unintelligible voice answered from deep within the demolished barn.

Ross immediately began climbing the disarray of planks while Ernie skirted the perimeter in search of an opening. "Rescue team should be here in just a few minutes," Ernie shouted up to Ross.

When Ross finally reached the top of the heap, he peered down between the boards and thought he could recognize a sliver of white fuselage paint. "I think I see it," he said. He studied the arrangement of the shattered wood and added, "I'm going down."

"Hold up. Wait for the rescue unit."

Spotting a slight haze below, and the unmistakable smell of fuel and smoke, Ross concluded, "Think I'd better get down there. Something may be burning."

Ernie looked up and began to argue, "Just wait, the . . ." but halted the plea when the professor disappeared from view. "Damn him," he swore, and then started to pick his way up the unstable boards to where he had last seen his student.

Weaving his body feet-first through the random gaps between the crisscrossing, aged wood, Ross realized the smell of smoke became stronger as he progressed. Exhilaration surged through him. Looking down between his legs, he could make out a wedge of white body paint just feet below him. "Anyone hear me?" he called.

"Hey, we're here," a muffled voice reached his ears.

Ross squirmed down through haphazard openings between planks with more urgency, ignoring caution as his feet felt for solid support. Dropping the last couple of feet to the crumpled helicopter, he brushed away splintered wooden debris revealing the side door window. He saw the two men laying against the far door that had become the lowest point in the craft. Also noticing a small pool of blood below the head of one, he quickly surmised they had unfastened their belts to either attempt to get out, or attend to the injury of the one.

He rapped on the plastic pane and both men's eyes darted to the window, adrenaline bursting through their bodies. One had a large open gash on his forehead, blood running into his eyes. Grasping the door handle, Ross pulled. Both men climbed through the cockpit, steadying their feet on the console and seat, and then pushed up on the door. The efforts of the three were ineffective.

Thickening smoke rising to his side and the fumes from the fuel increasing, Ross braced himself against a large beam, and then drove his heel into the window. The bounce of his foot off the plastic gave him immediate feedback as to the folly of the approach. From somewhere came the crackle of a fire, driving Ross' mind to create a means of rescue. His eyes danced across his surroundings in search of a makeshift tool.

One of the men trapped inside, detecting the smoke for the first time and projecting how it might adversely affect their survival, pounded feverishly on the window.

Ross saw a glint of shiny metal between the broken layers of barn planks. Hurriedly pushing some of the wood aside, he grinned, pinpointing one of the landing struts that had separated from the craft in the crash. Finding an end, he

7

wriggled it until it became free. When he made his way back to the window and looked in, he saw an ominous red glow faintly lighting the side of one of the men's face. Realizing they were all moments away from complete disaster, he motioned the men away and then drove the end of the strut into the window with all the strength his arms could muster. The pane broke. Working together, Ross and the men inside removed enough of the plastic for an opening large enough for passage. Reaching in, he helped each of them out of the cockpit, for the first time noticing rivulets of blood running down his own right forearm.

Flames shot up inside the aircraft and in sections of the surrounding debris. Sweat beaded on his forehead, the heat building around him. Knowing fuel detonation likely seconds away, Ross urged the men to climb faster.

When Ross emerged from the depths of the demolished barn after the two crash victims, he hurriedly waved Ernie off. "Fire!"

Grasping the significance of the simple word, Ernie and the others scampered off the rubble and ran across the field. Fully intending to join them, Ross instead found himself running directly to his training helicopter. He opened the door, jumped inside, twisted the throttle to get the rotors to speed and lifted off.

A thunderclap abruptly transformed the quiet of the early summer day into a profusion of colors, sounds, and smoke. The barn vaporized into a rising brown cloud of splinters against the deep blue sky. Three men lay face down in the weed-ridden grass, arms protecting their heads, as a rain of fragments poured around them. Ross raced the helicopter away from the airborne debris at maximum speed, chiding himself for his recklessness. Moments later, a rescue helicopter searched for a safe area to land as numberless sirens wailed in the distance.

* * *

"Just a little cut," Penny commented as she inspected her small patch job on Ross' right arm biceps. "I cleaned it, but keep an eye on it for a few days." Glancing up at him, she hesitated, and then added, "You know, you shouldn't have taken the chance you did to bring our Robinson back. It's insured. Not really something to risk your life over."

He looked thoughtfully at her brown eyes while he tried to gather the right words to explain his impulsiveness. "That happens to me occasionally. I am thinking of doing one thing and suddenly I discover I'm doing something else entirely. Don't know how else to explain it. Like in this case, I was thinking of running for cover along with your father and the others, and next I knew, I was opening the door to your helicopter. I know it sounds wacky, but that's happened to me more than a few times. Do you think I have a mental disorder?"

Penny looked past him to the front window. "Dad's back from his talk with the aviation officials."

With her fingertips lingering on his skin, Ross grew uncomfortable and said, "I'll go out and see him." Slowly pulling his arm from her care, he managed a half-smile.

Standing outside the office door with Ross, Ernie removed the Cincinnati Reds baseball cap and ran his fingers through his hair. "I owe you Professor. Real guts getting our pilot and his student out of that mess. My chopper would have been scrap metal, too, if you hadn't been foolhardy enough to get it away from that explosion. The way I figure it, I owe you a few free lessons when you get back from your field trip."

"Research," Ross corrected with a smile.

"Yeah right, research trip. I see Penny gave you medical attention." Ernie grinned.

"Amazing how much blood came out of a little nick.
"I'm sure she enjoyed helping you out," he observed
with a wink. "You do fly like you sold your soul to the
devil." Ernie put his cap back on and adjusted the brim. "I
see why Penny likes you. Real backbone."

"Thanks for the compliments, I didn't even think to
thank Penny. I'm not very good with women," Ross replied.
"Can't recall if I've ever had more than a couple of dates
with the same one. I eventually get turned down with an
excuse like, 'Sorry, not tonight, I need to baby sit my fish.'"

A black and white cat wandered to the men, and moved
directly to Ross, rubbing against his leg. Ross bent down and
stroked between the cat's ears. It purred loudly in appreciation. "Hey there fella," he said softly to the feline. "This
yours?" he asked Ernie.

"Naw, just a stray that hangs around. Probably 'cause
Penny is always putting food out for it. She has a soft spot
for cats. You like cats, Professor?"

"Yes, but I also seem to have this weakness for any stray.
As a kid, I was always picking up wandering cats, dogs,
injured rabbits. My mother finally put an end to it. But I still
do it. Don't know why, just compelled to help out homeless,
injured or lost animals."

Chapter 2

"Ross, you're going to have to get out more and mingle. It's no good to lock yourself up in your house and vegetate."

"You make it sound like I'm some kind of cave dweller, Mom. I see hundreds of students and other faculty members every day . . . and I've been taking flying lessons."

"That's your father's fault, bless his soul. Too dangerous. Hear about those things crashing into mountains and trees daily. Usually everyone dies."

"I jog, go to the gym, and I've been doing gymnastics at the school," he continued in his defense. "I'm active, healthy and in good shape."

"But you're thirty-five and don't even have a steady girl."

Now we're getting to her reason for the phone call, Ross thought, wondering why any conversation with his mother eventually wandered into this subject.

"When's the last time you had a date?" she parried.

"Let's see . . . about four months ago."

"And have you seen or talked to that girl since?" she questioned, moving in for the kill.

"No. We didn't have much in common."

"Ross, it's always the same. You haven't dated the same girl twice in years," she scored. "You should be married by now."

"Ease up, Mom, I'm happy with my life. I've never found a woman who I'd want to spend my life with. Listen," he said, cutting her off, "Look, I have an early class tomorrow and need to get some sleep. I have to say goodbye now. And don't forget, you won't be able to reach me after Friday."

"Oh that's right, you'll be going on your field trip."

"Mom, it's not a field trip, it's my *research* field work on the effects of atmospheric pollutants on plant life."

"Well, whatever you call it, I don't understand why you have to travel all the way to Vermont. We have plenty of trees right here in Michigan or down there by you in Indiana."

Ross knew that further debate on the rationale for his botanical studies would be pointless, so he decided to end the conversation once more by saying, "Goodnight Mom. I'll give you a call when I get back on August twenty-fifth."

"Three weeks? Why so long?" she asked, unwilling to end their exchange. "Oh, before you hang up, I've been meaning to tell you about that weird stuff going on up there."

Ross let out an audible sigh. "Weird stuff?"

"Yeah, I saw it on that news channel, 568 I think. Strange things in the sky at night and reports of an explosion. They claim it's something to do with missile testing; but I don't buy it. I don't think it's safe. You should go on your field trip somewhere else."

Recalling his flight instructor's mention of "strange shit" in Vermont, Ross asked against his better judgment, "What else did the news report have about it?"

"That it's a government cover-up for an alien landing," she whispered as if government officials bugged her apartment.

"Wait a second, is that 'news station' the one you had on covering the Dogman of Michigan last time I visited?"

His mother paused, then answered tentatively, "Yeah, so?"

"Christ, Ma, that's not a news station. That's the program that covers crackpot legends."

"Ross, do not use the Lord's name in vain," she chastised.

"Mom, that's ridiculous," Ross said, and then laughed. "I assure you, there are no alien landings in Vermont. UFOs are not real. And for the third time, it's a *research* trip."

"Just 'cause you're a professor doesn't make you an expert on everything," she chided.

"Goodnight Mom!" Ross emphasized. "Love you."

"Goodnight Ross. Please be careful. And see if you can be less picky and find some nice girl to settle down with."

"I'll try," he answered, rolling his eyes at his mother's persistence and ending the call.

* * *

The two men in white lab coats lifted the last of the gold colored cylinders from the handcart.

"Glad this is the last of them," one uttered between grunts as they lowered it slowly, placing it alongside the other fourteen on the storage room floor.

A bearded man, identically attired, stared out through the open double doors at the darkening sky above. "I hope the truck gets here soon. Those clouds moving in look nasty."

Placing his hands at his sore back as he stood erect, one of the men asked, "Why is headquarters providing the transportation instead of one of our Portsmouth trucks? Just seems stupid since they're going to the Portsmouth facility anyway. Headquarters has to send a truck all the way from Boston. Seems a waste of time and money."

The bearded leader turned from the doorway to face his employee but merely glared.

The sound of rain on the metal roof filled the room.

"Truck's coming," the bearded leader announced.

The dim silhouette of the approaching vehicle instantly lit up under a flash of lightning. A clap of thunder reverberated off the walls. Hard rain streaked to the ground.

The three crowded the open doorway, watching the driver maneuver the vehicle in the narrow drive until it stopped at least one hundred feet away.

"Can't he get any closer than that?" a tech asked his bearded leader. "We're going to get soaked in this stuff. We should wait until the storm passes."

"Portsmouth wants them now."

Pulling back from the doorway to avoid the splashing cascade of water outside, the three watched the driver run from his truck towards them.

"Hi, I'm Mike," the new arrival said once inside, his thick black hair dripping streams of water down his neck. Not waiting for a response, he continued, "They want me at Portsmouth ASAP, so I need you guys to help me get the back of the truck ready. Should only take about fifteen minutes, then we can load them in and I'll be on my way. Sorry I couldn't pull in any closer. Too tight a space for this size truck. Whoever designed this place wasn't thinking ahead."

The bearded man in charge nodded.

Cold sweeps of gusting rain drenched the four as they attacked the rear of the truck to open its doors and extend the loading ramp. As they charged up the ramp to ready the cargo area, an ear-splitting crack of lightning exploded close by, rendering them momentarily deaf.

Startled heads swiveled to examine the trees and building for evidence of a lightning strike.

Another deafening gunshot-like noise and blinding light assaulted them, drawing their attention to the sound of a breaking tree. All eight eyes locked onto a tall white pine between them and the building. The upper part of the tree cocked at an angle to the lower half. A splintered break smoldered.

Instinct sparked all four to run from the danger. They scattered into the woods beyond the front of the truck, putting distance between themselves and the critically wounded pine. They heard the unmistakable crashing sound of the severed trunk striking the earth, causing the ground to quake under their feet.

Thunder rumbled in the distance.

But within minutes, a soft, gentle rain replaced the forceful hissing downpour.

Stillness settled over the scene.

The four men wandered slowly back to the loading ramp, their eyes irresistibly drawn to the broken half-tree still standing and the jumble of white pine branches and needles laying on the ground.

"Well, that was something," one lab tech declared as if providing profound information that escaped the attention of the other three.

The bearded man moved to the severed treetop spread across his path. In the diminished twilight he lingered a few minutes to inspect the heaps of needles and branches before walking to the open building doorway. Reaching inside, he flipped the light switch.

His eyes widened.

"The cylinders. They're all gone!" he screamed.

* * *

Since final exams took place during the prior session, Ross used the last class for a brief review of the key points he wanted his students to remember. Although he fielded a few general questions, the majority of students were anxious to get out to summer activities and away from their school-books, and so he dismissed the class twenty minutes shy of the allotted time. While most of the students scrambled to the doorway, a small number lined up in front of Ross, each waiting their turn to thank him, compliment his teaching methods, or just say goodbye.

After talking to the last student in line, Ross turned to gather his notes. His eyes caught movement at one of the desks, startling him. A woman, whose name he recalled as Marsha, remained seated in the empty classroom.

Responding to Ross' gaze, she pivoted in her seat, swinging her legs into the aisle, forcing her slit skirt to separate to reveal a goodly portion of her upper thigh. She smiled, aware of Ross' interest in her exposed skin.

Ross felt a warmth flood his face at being caught.

Instead of rounding the desk and exiting as the other students had, she walked directly to his desk, locking her sky-blue eyes onto his.

"Hello, Professor Barton. Could I talk to you a few minutes?"

It was an accident I looked at your legs, he thought. "Sure," he answered.

"I was wondering . . . have you worked out the grades yet? If you have, would it be possible for me to find out how I did?"

Oh good, nothing to do with your legs, he thought. "A," he answered.

She smiled broadly, and asked, "Do you always remember your students' grades? I thought you'd have to look it up."

Stop playing with me. I don't know what to say next, he thought. "Yes, I do," he answered.

She paused as if waiting for him to elaborate.

I need a coffee, he thought.

Finally she broke the dreadful silence. "I found your class very interesting, particularly the studies about computer simulation of evolution. That sounds fascinating and something I'd like to follow up on."

Oh good, you want to talk about my work, he thought. "Yes. It's an interesting field. I'm developing some new approaches," he said.

"Would it be an imposition if I asked you to share some of your opinions on it with me sometime?"

You and me alone? he thought. "Anytime," he answered.

"How about tonight?" she asked, her voice betraying excitement.

I'm busy would be a good answer, he thought. "I'm free," he calmly answered.

"How about the Front Door? I'll buy dinner."

"We could meet here or in the library if you prefer."

"Come on, we both have to eat. So, I'll meet you there at seven."

I'm not sure this is a good idea, he thought. "Fine, see you at seven," he answered.

"Thanks," she bubbled, then hurried to the door.

Ross watched her move, fully understanding why she had drawn the interest of every male in his class at one time or another.

* * *

Although the Front Door was in an area of Indianapolis unfamiliar to him, Ross found it easily. That alleviated at least a small part of the apprehension associated with actually having a rendezvous with a female student off campus. A woman. An attractive woman.

Turning his Escape into the circular driveway of the restaurant, Ross realized he should have researched the appropriate attire for dinner at the Front Door. He looked down at his clothes and summarized his feelings. *Idiot.*

He released care of his Escape to the valet with reluctance because he always felt insecure about someone else using or watching over anything that belonged to him. Glancing at his watch, he saw he was twenty minutes early. "Idiot," he mumbled again in disgust. Once inside, his discomfort increased measurably. The opulence of the place was even greater than that hinted by the exterior.

"May I help you, sir?" asked the stylishly attired, pinched-faced, elderly hostess as she looked over his Topsiders, casual jeans, and polo shirt. Her inflections and highbred tones used in spitting the question suggested she had rather said, "Get lost scum."

"Yes. You have a reservation for a Ms. Cooper at seven. I know I'm a little early but I . . ."

"This way, sir," Miss Congeniality stated sharply, obviously not interested in anything he had to say.

As she led Ross across the plush carpet, through tables of elegantly dressed patrons, he surmised it might be best if he wrote the whole evening off as a bad experience and go home. But his plans for retreat abruptly vanished when he saw Marsha already seated at the table ahead. Her white knit dress hugged each wondrous curve and her sun-like hair cascaded luxuriously to her shoulders. Against the backdrop of the soft, dark green velvet expanse of the high back booth, Marsha became his vision of a royal princess awaiting an audience. Prince Charming he was not, but nothing short of a rampaging rogue elephant would keep him from getting closer to her.

"Hi Professor Barton, I guess we're both early," she welcomed him with a cheery smile.

"Hello Ms. Cooper," he returned as he sat across from her.

"Call me Marsha. Thanks for meeting me to discuss your research."

"Ross is my first name. I see I'm a bit underdressed. I didn't know this place was so upscale. I should have asked."

"I thought you knew when you didn't ask. Don't worry, you look fine."

Marsha understood Ross' reluctance to be meeting a student off campus and worked to ease uncomfortable silences with short bouts of filler conversation about the restaurant's celebrated chef, the next day's weather forecast, and the condition of the roads in the state. She maintained the awkward discourse until the waiter took their order for drinks, which opened to a short discussion about their favorite wines.

Ross studied Marsha, fully aware he was not holding his own and that their meeting had degenerated to the hallmark reason his other dates always failed and his single status. He fully expected a yawn, or folded arms against him—but instead of the anticipated boredom, he saw nervousness. She was different from the others.

I think I came up with a brilliant question, Ross thought, his face brightening. "So why did you take my class?" he asked. "What's your major?"

"Oh, I was thinking about applying for a job at a florist and thought a class in botany would look impressive on my resume."

Ross was silent as his mind grappled with her answer. The drinks arrived and she again attempted to get a conversation off the ground, and again he failed to sustain one. He fidgeted with the stem of his glass for several minutes then abruptly emptied its contents down his throat. She reacted with a questioning look, but said nothing.

Small talk going nowhere, Marsha asked, "Could we talk about your research for a few minutes?"

I think your hair looks like the color of a daffodil on an early summer morning, he thought. "Sure," he said aloud.

"You just hinted about it in class. Could you tell me more? It sounded so interesting."

Your skin looks as soft as butter to the touch. "Okay," he answered, his voice an octave higher than normal.

"Go ahead," she encouraged, anxious to explore any avenue to meaningful dialogue.

He leaned forward, placing his arms alongside his place setting, and took a deep breath and paused. As he was about to speak, he raised his arm and in the process, seemingly in slow motion, swiped the half-full bottle of Zinfandel and watched it fall to the table and roll until the mouth teetered over Marsha's lap. The contents gurgled out, pouring onto the knit fabric that bridged her upper thighs. The ice-cold liquid seeped through to assault her warm, delicate skin. He helplessly watched her eyes transform into two large circles.

Reflexively, he threw his napkin to her and said, "Sorry."

Her face broke into a grin as she worked at sopping up the mess. "It's okay," she gallantly reassured him, "it won't stain."

Ross considered hiding in the men's room until closing, but instead chose to acquire more napkins from the waiter. In the act of sliding his chair out from the table, it bumped into an obstruction behind him. Before he could turn to uncover the nature of the difficulty, his eyes caught a glimpse of a strange, unidentified substance hurtling over his head through space. Hearing a thump and swearing from the floor behind him, Ross thought, *I think I located the waiter.*

The dark brown, airborne mass, he then recognized as chocolate mousse, found a landing place to its liking in the alcoholic lake between Marsha's legs. Ross watched as a series of ugly contortions cycle through Marsha's face before a half-smile returned to her lips.

"Let's have dinner at my place," she said, looking at the ugly gelatinous sludge smearing her once pristine white dress.

Thinking any level of apology to be insufficient, he responded, "No. I think it would be best if we just leave. I'll pay for the drinks and walk you to your car. Just send me the bill for a new dress. Let's go, Marsha."

She grabbed his wrist before he had a chance to stand. "No Ross. It was an accident. I want to hear whatever it was you were going to tell me about your research before I was deluged with wine and attacked by the mousse."

"That is kind of you Marsha, but before I do you more-bodily harm, I think it best we see each other some other time."

"No, tonight. I'll give you my address. I'll go home, shower and change, while you pick up a pizza. Please?"

"Okay, I'll give you another chance. But try not to be so clumsy."

She giggled as she deposited the wayward mousse onto a dish. He marveled how, like a gazelle, she stood with poise, and delicately stepped over the waiter who remained sprawled on the floor. With head held erect, she strode to the ladies room.

Miss Congeniality now arrived to investigate the source of the commotion, glared an I-knew-it-would-be-you look at Ross, and then stooped to assist the groaning man he had knocked to the floor.

Chapter 3

Two men in white lab coats nervously paced around the extended, rectangular table in the small conference room. Both stared at their feet as they moved lost in thought, occasionally brushing shoulders. The bearded man, similarly dressed in white, sat at the table head, resting his chin in his hands, and gazed glumly, without focus.

The door to the room swung open, bouncing off the rubber floor stop with such force that it quivered. The startled faces of the three men turned in unison to see two soldiers rush in and take positions on either side of the open doorway, rifles poised across their chests. A stubby, unlit cigar protruding from the lips of a hefty soldier entered the room; he had the shape of a man given to excess. Placing his hands on his hips, he studied each of the three lab coats through squinted eyes. "So what the hell happened here?" he shouted, tobacco mixing with spit dribbling from his lips.

The bearded man rose to attention and said, "Welcome Major." He cleared his throat, and continued, "We were expecting you, sir. We're at your disposal for anything you or your men need. Can I get you water?"

Clenching the cigar between his bared teeth, the major grimaced. "What's with you guys? This is no company picnic." The major's chest expanded and he continued, "National security is at stake here and you're talking about refreshments. I'm in charge now." He paused for effect; his eyes under furrowed brows lingered one by one on each of the three faces. "Tell me how this happened and what you know about where they went. My men are scouring the area as we speak, but it would help if you gents could give us some clues. Just make things go faster. Let's have a seat, shall we? And could someone get me a coffee? Black."

All three men promptly sat at stiff attention, poised for a complete humiliation. The major swaggered to the opposite head of the table, and lowered himself slowly into the seat. His untrusting eyes never left the three, as if they might produce a hand grenade.

Satisfied they harbored no threat to his person, his posture softened and he leaned back in the chair, sighed, and for the first time removed the cigar from his mouth. He examined it, and then set it down on the fake mahogany surface. Putting his hands behind his head, he rocked the chair back, staring at the ceiling. "So what happened here?"

All three spoke at once, but stopped simultaneously when the bearded man frowned at his coworkers—obviously the ranking member of the three. "Our work here was finished and we were going to transfer them to our facility in Portsmouth. We were moving them to the truck when a thunderstorm came up. A nearby tree was struck by lightning and we took cover. Then they were gone. All of them. We searched, but couldn't find a trace."

The major removed his hands from behind his head and planted them with angry force on the table. His eyes bored into the speaker. "This is a joke, right? They got away because of a little bad weather? Can't believe something this big was in the hands of civilians." As he lifted his right hand he saw the flattened cigar pasted to his palm. Shaking his hand until the soggy, squashed tobacco stub flew across the room to the opposite wall, he stated, "We'll straighten out your screw up and get them back." Abruptly standing, he wiped his hand on his pants and started to the door.

* * *

Juggling a pepperoni pizza in his left hand, a Caesar salad and bottle of wine in his right, Ross rapped the door with his elbow. The door swung open with such speed that he tottered into Marsha's arms, thankfully avoiding another food catastrophe.

"The pizza goes on the table, not me."

The near disaster was forgotten as his eyes swept over her body. She wore nothing underneath her white, silk robe ornately embroidered with oriental figures. Both confused and optimistic, he asked himself *What am I in for?* Averting her eyes, he assured, "I'll do my best."

Setting the pizza on a stylish, glass coffee table he turned to take in the rest of the room. He did not like it, but lied and said, "Nice apartment." Everything in sight was sterile white, light grey, or chrome, which added to his discomfort.

She ferried silverware, dishes, and two wine bottles to the table while he continued to study her tidy "space." It registered that even the abstract artwork on the walls was austere and lacked color. He studied the white on white print of a calla lily, pretty, but common. He wondered if the surroundings reflected her personality. Was she pretty on the outside but common and cold on the inside?

When they sat down to eat he said, "You were so gracious at the restaurant. I must have embarrassed you. And I do want to pay for your dress."

Taking the glass of wine from her lips, she said forgivingly, "Forget it. At least I'll always remember our first date."

As they ate, she chatted about her friends. He noted she drank quite heavily, one of the bottles already more than half-empty. He wondered if she normally consumed alcohol that way or if his reserved manner bored her. Suspecting it the latter, he thought, *I should bring up my research again.* But mesmerized by her smile, his mouth asked instead, "Would you like to go like to go out to a movie together tomorrow night?"

She placed her elbows on the table and propped her chin in her hands. "Yes."

She lifted her head from her hands and finished her fourth glass of wine. "I'll clear the table, then we can discuss the simulation work. Go sit on the sofa and make yourself comfortable. Would you like to put on some music?"

There had been no discernible hesitation to his offer. None. She seemingly accepted going out together without a flinch. Or was she smashed and too numb to care? Four glasses of wine in that short a time would have him crawling on the floor.

"Where do you keep it?" he asked.

"CDs are under the receiver," she shouted from the kitchen. "I have more music on my iPod, but I'd have to find it."

Pulling out the drawers, he discovered she owned about fifty or so CDs, mostly country. Frowning, he found the remainder of the collection dance music you would use at parties. Inferring they did not have much in common regarding music, he slid the drawers in and closed the glass cabinet doors, then retreated to one corner of the white-leather, three-person sofa.

"Change your mind about the music?"

"Couldn't find anything I like," he answered, hoping he did not offend her.

"Let me see," she said thoughtfully as she seated herself at the opposite corner of the sofa. "A college professor . . . classical, right? I do have a few. Tchaikovsky, Rossini, and Borodin, I think."

Ross grinned, pleasantly amazed at the confidence he felt in her company. His asking her out on a real date with a positive result dissipated all his tension. He was almost comfortable with a woman for the very first time in his life.

"No, not quite. I enjoy rock."

"My, my, you're just full of surprises, aren't you?"

Ross thought it wise to change the subject so he awkwardly jumped into the reason for their get together. "Okay Ms. Cooper, you invited me here to discuss botany, not music or dating. So let's get on with it.

"As you know, evolution is the process of gradual change in species' characteristics which permits improved adaptation to their environmental condition."

Marsha leaned forward, causing the lower portion of her robe to separate and reveal half of her well-tanned, shapely thighs. "Aren't these adaptations initiated by the environmental changes?" she asked, noting that Ross' eyes had found the inadvertent rearrangement of her robe.

"No, the genetic mutations are random and continue at the same rate regardless of the current state of success or failure of the species. The number of these mutations are related to the environment. For example, a species such as the shark that has existed in its current form for millions of years still produces genetic mutations, but since the species is already in harmony with its environment those mutations are inferior to their parentage and therefore less suited for survival. No need for evolution. Now, for argument's sake, if the oceans in which the sharks live were to change appreciably, thereby placing the sharks in a less advantageous position in the food chain, some of the random mutants could possibly be more in tune with the environmental changes. The result, they would have an enhanced probability of survival and would transfer their revised genetic makeup to their offspring. This is evolution."

"I see," she commented, shifting her position. The silk material slid off another section of left thigh.

Although trying desperately not to be obvious, his eyes caught the movement of fabric and darted to a newly exposed section of leg. His mind searched for his last thoughts as he wrestled it away from the distraction. "In theory, it should be feasible to mimic this process with a mathematical model. The potential genetic mutations must be defined along with prevalent environmental conditions. The model for an advance life form such as a human would be impossibly complex, but early prehistoric plant life should be simple enough to accurately define. Programs have now been developed at Cornell University that can simulate the evolution of several primitive plant species."

"The subject is interesting, but what useful function can a simulation like that perform?" Marsha inquired, leaning further forward and uncovering another inch or two of skin.

He struggled to maintain his focus by locking his eyes on her face. "Plenty. The simulation could fill in the gaps in fossil records. It could confirm or disprove evolutionary theories, for instance whether or not a particular discovery belongs in one classification or another. Those types of debates happen frequently among scientists. And even more importantly, the simulation could predict evolutionary changes resulting from environmental changes. It could predict the future."

Marsha leaned back against the sofa, interlacing her fingers behind her head, and summarized his presentation, "Cool."

Ross looked up to see her latest position had succeeded in opening her robe even further. His concentration on the topic of evolution slipped away. "And that's what I've been working on. I hope to demonstrate a predictive simulation on certain species of trees. I'm going to spend three weeks in Vermont to gather missing factors relating to the effects of acid rain."

"When are you going?" she asked, obviously enjoying the effects of her feminine display on his composure.

"Next Friday," he answered unsteadily, seeing an odd glint in her eyes.

The striptease performance abruptly ended when she announced, "I'll be right back," and rushed into the interior hallway. Within minutes, she called out for his assistance.

Had he heard seduction in her voice? *Hardly*, he thought and slowly walked down the hall. He checked into the first open doorway and found her lying on the bed wearing only a sultry smile.

* * *

When Ross opened his eyes in the bright morning sunlight and saw Marsha sleeping on the bed aside him, his fears that the night's events had only been a wonderful dream vanished. Studying her face, a new concern crept into his mind. What if she had made love to him as a consequence of the amount of wine she consumed and not because she liked him? That concern also vaporized when her eyelids fluttered open, and a warm smile set into her lips.

"Hi lover," she cooed.

"Morning Marsha," he responded and ran his finger lightly over her lips.

Her reaction to his tender touch soon led to relaxed exploratory petting, and eventually to another vigorous round of lovemaking.

They spent the remainder of that Saturday together, then Sunday, Monday, Tuesday, and Wednesday. Some nights they slept at his home and sometimes hers, the choice dependent only on which locale happened to be the most convenient on that particular evening. Wednesday night's convenience was Marsha's bed. After finishing more than an hour of lustful play, Ross stared thoughtfully at the ceiling above the bed and stated, "I've decided to cancel my trip to Vermont on Friday."

"But why?" she asked, surprise evident in her tone.

"I want to spend my time with you."

"But the research is so important to you."

"I'd rather research you."

"I'm flattered that you want to be with me, but we'll have as much time as we want when you get back. This field trip will have to be put off for a year if you don't go this summer. I want you to go. I'd feel guilty if you didn't."

"It is not a field trip, it's research."

"Okay, okay, research trip. But you should go."

"Would you come with me?"

"Oh Ross, I'd love to, but I'm not the outdoorsy type. I'd never be able to spend three whole days in the woods, never mind three weeks." She reached over and kissed his lips softly. "You do understand, don't you?"

"Of course." He stretched over and turned off the table light. "We'll talk about it in the morning."

* * *

When he awoke on Thursday morning, Ross sensed Marsha's absence from bed even before his eyes opened. He sniffed at the air, anticipating trace aromas of bacon cooking or eggs frying. Nothing but her sweet scent on the sheets registered. Deciding to join her in the kitchen, he slipped into his jeans, hoping she at least had coffee brewing. He stopped after a few paces when the sound of Marsha's whispers reached his ears. Curious, he moved his bare feet silently on the plush carpet until he almost reached the doorway to the living room, and again stopped.

"He's a professor at the University," he overheard her say clearly.

After a moment of silence, Marsha continued, "No, he taught my botany class." The lapse between her sentences indicated a conversation to a friend on a phone. Hearing his name mentioned, he smiled, looking forward to overhearing compliments.

"Handsome, great body, extremely intelligent, great in bed, considerate, and single," she again answered the invisible companion.

Ross' smile broadened into a grin.

"Yes."

Ross inched closer.

"I know he's falling for me."

Ross considered sneaking behind her, giving her a loving tickle.

"No."

He decided to wait and listen longer.

"I don't know. Too dull, maybe. No spark."

His smile faded.

"Yes, I'm sure I can get him to tell me he loves me sooner or later. I'm working at it."

A half-smile reappeared on his face.

"Don't lecture me, Jane. I am not terrible. You're married. You don't know what it's like to come home to an empty apartment day after day. I'm already twenty-nine, and statistics show that my prospects of finding someone are pretty bleak. I've lived alone two years now and I'm fed up."

Humiliation tightened Ross' chest.

"I know there are plenty of other more interesting men but they just want to get into my pants. They don't want commitment, just fun and no ring. Believe me, I know. I've tried enough of them. Ross is different. He'd give me anything I ask for."

After quite a long silence, Marsha answered angrily, "No, I don't feel like a whore. I can give him everything he wants in a wife. Hell, he told me I am his fantasy dream girl." She laughed now. "Look Jane, I can give him friendship, something to look at, good sex and someone to spend his money on." She laughed again.

Unable to tolerate anymore, Ross slid back to the bedroom and slouched on the side of the bed. He stared blankly out the window and questioned his feelings about what he'd overheard, bleakly admitting he was being played. Finally he showered, shaved, and dressed before joining Marsha in the kitchen, frying eggs at the cook-top. She threw him a kiss as he sat at the table. She soon brought over their meals and kissed his cheek. "Sleep well?" she asked pleasantly.

"I've decided to go to Vermont," he declared, staring out the window.

"Good," she said encouragingly.

You can't wait to be rid of me for a while, can you? he thought. "I'll leave in a few minutes because I have a lot of equipment to pack," he said.

"Anything wrong?"

"No, what could possibly be wrong?"

She picked up the chill in his voice, but chose not to pursue the subject and instead said, "I'll stop over later and we can spend the night together."

"Marsha, I'm tired and have a busy day ahead. I'll call you when I get back."

"Can I at least see you off tomorrow? What time is your flight?"

"As you said before, we will have all the time in the world when I get back. Don't worry about it. Thanks for a great week. It really was one of the best I've ever had."

She returned a befuddled, weak smile as he left.

* * *

When finished packing for the trip Ross picked up his phone and called his mother. After an exchange of warm hellos he said, "Mom, I'm leaving tomorrow morning for Vermont, so I wanted to say goodbye again. I'll call when I get back."

"Oh, already?" she answered. "The field trip, right?"

Tired of correcting her, he agreed, "Yeah, the field trip."

"Please be careful son and promise me you'll stay away from those weird lights. I tell you they could be real aliens."

"I promise Mom, I'll stay away from the aliens," he answered and lightly laughed at her persistence.

"And don't pick up any wild animals. You're always too good-natured. Most of them can be mean."

"Got it, no strays," he sighed. "Mom, gotta go. Got a text coming in. May be a message about the trip."

"Make sure you call when you get back. Love you son."

He said goodbye, then read the message on the screen: "Found out from war buddy. Military has section of forest restricted. He said you should check when you get there. Said strange shit getting stranger. Have a good field trip. Penny says hi. Ernie"

* * *

A knock on the door abruptly brought him back into focus. Glancing down at his watch, he swore. It was nearly 10:00 p.m. He had been pacing the rooms of his apartment in misery for nearly three hours—turning the TV on, then off, folding and unfolding the clothes in his suitcase, sorting through old magazines, doing anything to shift his thoughts away from his disappointment in Marsha, but mostly himself. He called out, "It's open."

Marsha poked her head between the door and the frame. "Hi," she said brightly. Her wet trench coat gave him a clue that the weatherman's stated sixty percent change of rain a good bet. "I was working out at the gym and thought that since I was in the neighborhood I'd see if you needed anything."

"No, I'm all packed."

"Can I stay awhile?"

He wanted to say no but could only conceive of doing so if he was willing to confront her with what he overheard. Too emotionally drained to deal with such a scenario, he answered, "Sure, come in."

She thanked him, closed the door and unbuttoned her coat. With a deliberately seductive movement, she opened it.

He watched it drop to the floor. When he saw her outfit, he groaned.

"Like it?" she asked as she spun slowly on her toes.

Her black, two-piece exercise suit with a Lycra halter-top and matching ankle-length pants that clung tightly to each and every curve and bump on her body caused him to shutter. "My God," he murmured to himself, certain she could not possibly wear the outfit publicly without risk of arrest for indecent exposure.

Reading the surrender in his eyes, she strutted over, threw her arms around his neck and kissed him hungrily. Despising his own weakness, Ross returned the kiss and held her closer. *I can hate her some other time*, he thought, feeling her soft flesh against him.

Chapter 4

Classifying his motel room as a disappointment would have been an upgrade; it was a pigsty. Water-stained, faded wallpaper curled in large sheets exposing the crumbling, rough plaster in patches. To bring light into the room, he opened the dust-filled curtains to clusters of dead flies lining the windowsill. Ross threw his suitcase onto the tattered blanket covering the bed, forcing him to cough when a cloud of dust plumed into the room. He walked to the bathroom and abruptly halted at the threshold. Looking down he could only shake his head and laugh out loud at the exposed floor joists and the long rectangular gaps filled with insulation. "Thank heavens it's only one night," he said walking back to the foot of the bed. He sat on the edge of the creaky mattress and dropped his head into his hands. The flight, combined with the previous night's acrobatics with Marsha had sapped all his energy. Thoughts of Marsha brought his head up to face the filmy, cracked mirror above the dresser to confront the reflection of a tired, bloodshot-eyed loser. "Well, here we are again, alone as usual. She was so loving. I can't believe the bitch was just using me," he argued. "Okay, I'm a jerk."

Ross glanced at the tilted painting to the right of the mirror. Dogs playing poker on a velvet canvas layered with dust.

"I could beat her at her own game. I could live with her, have my fun, and then dump her." A fleeting smile cracked his face for the first time since eavesdropping on her phone conversation. "Who am I kidding? I could never do that to her. After all, I didn't even have the courage to ask her to leave last night.

"Well, I have three long weeks to get her out of my system," he summarized, knowing time would give him a more logical perspective. Even if he never saw her again, he had to admit that their brief relationship, although deceitful on her part, was the most pleasurable week of his life. During his time with her, he had felt a new confidence relating to a woman and it felt good. Addressing the mirror, he said, "Thanks for listening. I knew you'd understand."

Ross turned to his more immediate needs. He placed all his camping and research paraphernalia on the bed and began running through a final check. Halfway through his checklist he muttered, "Shit," in frustration. The humiliation he suffered after leaving Marsha's apartment had caused careless packing, and he now discovered he forgot the camp stove, cooking kit, and prepackaged food supplies.

* * *

He found a radio station reporting the weather forecast just as his Ford Focus rental nosed past the Smithfield town line. The announcer's voice that carried all the inflections of a heavy New England accent informed his listeners that the unusual heat wave and high humidity levels would continue for at least the next five days, the possibility of widely scattered showers predicted on each. When the radio station reported ninety-two for the current temperature, he turned it off, wondering what he had done to merit such a wave of bad luck: the Front Door restaurant catastrophe, Marsha's deceitful motives, this "falling to pieces" motel room, then his absent-minded packing that called for a trip to purchase the missing supplies thereby forcing a second unplanned night at the palace. And now a forecast of sweltering heat that was sure to make his days in the forest uncomfortable.

The heavily wooded borders of the wide, two-lane roadway gradually transformed into suburbia and soon into a small downtown area. Ross spotted the sporting goods store the motel clerk had described on the right-hand side of the street, pulled to the curb and parked behind a rickety old Jeep. Reluctant to leave the cool environment of the Ford Focus, he checked the side mirror, opened the door and stepped out into the oppressive heat.

Chilled air welcomed him into the supply store. After a few steps he became aware of a funny creaking sound rising from the floor in unison with the shifting of his weight. Looking down, he discovered the floor was built of narrow wood boards, old and heavily worn. He began walking with a bounce to his step, curiously testing the surprising springiness of the construction. Glancing up, he spotted more supplies located a few aisles ahead. As he moved forward, he remained intrigued by the interesting antique floor and the way it deflected visibly under his feet. So distracted by his floor experimentation, his shoulder collided with a body in his path. He heard the sound of objects crashing to the floor and reached out to brace himself against a display shelf.

Quickly turning to the source of the racket, he saw a woman partially buried in a disarrayed heap of various hiking and camping equipment. She glared at him, wearing a very ugly sneer on her face.

If looks could kill I'd best pick out a tombstone. "Oh, I'm sorry," he said aloud then moved toward her and added, "Let me help you."

"Stay away!" she growled.

"It was an accident," he explained as he came to a complete stop.

Slowly pulling herself to her feet, she glared at Ross before bending down to gather up the scattered items ranging from hiking clothes to a frame pack.

"Can I help you pick up your stuff?"

"You have done enough. Go away."

Ross heard her request well enough, but stood captivated watching this unique, imposing figure of a woman collect her equipment. Tall, he guessed nearly six feet, and neither fat nor thin. Although she wore a loose-fitting plaid, cotton shirt and knee-length shorts that looked two sizes too large, her form hinted at a full bust, slim waist, and slender thighs. The parts of her body free of the shapeless garments were robustly muscled, yet sleek, imparting an overall impression of her being an unusual cross between a girl-next-door and a female body builder.

Looking up, she brushed back her loosely curled, glossy black hair. "Why are you staring at me?" she challenged. "I said, go away."

I think she wants me to go, he thought. "I'm soooo sorry," came out his mouth. "You sure I can't help you?"

The woman's magnetic violet-blue eyes fixed on his. She squinted.

"Okay, then . . . I'll leave you alone." Turning to the camping display to gather the remainder of his supplies, he added, "Have a nice day."

Eager to place the experience behind him, he hastily acquired the items he needed then hurried to the register at the front of the store. As he approached, he came within earshot of what sounded like an argument. After a few more steps, he could see a shiny black mass of tousled hair above the display shelves in an area he guessed to be the register. When his mind connected the voice and the hair with his "crash encounter," he considered turning around to do more shopping, but his legs carried him to the checkout before his brain could implement the change of direction.

"Pick out something to return and we'll be all set," the clerk said politely.

The amazon hesitated thoughtfully then stated flatly, "No, I need everything here."

"But you're four-ninety-five over. Something will have to go back."

"No, you will have to accept the money. It is all I have," she answered matter-of-factly.

"Lady, we don't do business that way. I'm sorry."

"I gave you over five hundred dollars, and the amount you want is relatively insignificant. I am not going to discuss this any longer. I must be going." And with that final statement, she began lifting her packages from the counter.

Disbelief enlarged the clerk's eyes. He lunged, grabbing her wrist. "Now wait a minute. You're not about to . . ." His words choked off when the woman reached over the counter and gripped his shirt collar, causing a button to fly off and land at Ross' feet.

Ross rushed to her side while a group of curious shoppers gathered to watch the spectacle. He put his hand on the clerk's and said, "Let the lady alone; I'll pay the difference."

Seizing the opportunity for the peaceful settlement Ross' offer provided, the clerk released her and mumbled, "You call her a lady?"

She glanced at Ross, bewildered by his intervention, then turned a menacing face to the clerk and cautiously released her hold on the shirt.

The clerk stretched his neck and began tallying Ross' purchase, his eyes avoiding the woman as if she no longer existed. "Your items plus the four-ninety-five for the lady, comes to eighty-one-forty-three."

Ross handed over his credit card, noticing the woman's massive stack of boxes and bags on the counter.

"You will help me carry these to my vehicle," she demanded, addressing the clerk.

"We don't provide that service to our customers. Do it yourself." He handed Ross his card.

Ross suppressed a laugh, waiting for a violent response.

Instead, she calmly moved her eyes to him. "You. Help me carry these."

"Yes, sir," he saluted then gathered an armful of the boxes. He made one trip, putting his supplies in the Focus and three more for hers. When finished, he stood next to the open Jeep's passenger side anticipating a "thank you" while she slid behind the wheel. It soon became apparent she had no intention of thanking him, so he asked, "Are you planning on doing some camping?"

"Yes, is there something wrong with that?"

"Why no. I am sorry about knocking you over."

"You are repeating yourself."

He shrugged off her rebuff and said, "My name's Ross Barton."

She started the engine.

"What's yours?" he pushed.

"My name is not required," she responded.

"But a fair trade for the money I paid for you," he tested.

She looked at him, thinking over his statement. "Jay," she stated and turned away.

"Nice to meet you Jay."

She looked ahead at the bumper of a pickup, then twisted and checked the distance to his car.

Ross, seeing only a foot clearance at either end of the Jeep, became alarmed when she placed the shift lever in gear and began racing the engine. "Wait!" he screamed. "Let me move my car." Assuming she would just as soon ram his car and create her own space as wait for him to move, he sprinted to the Focus and crept rearward until he allowed her several feet of room. He watched as she backed the Jeep then swept out into the road, continuing in an arc until she had completed a full U-turn and was driving down the opposite side of the road. He shook his head in amazement as other cars blew their horns and swerved to avoid the daredevil driver.

Jay's haunting image lingered in her wake as he started the engine, then pulled out into traffic.

* * *

He turned the Focus into the lot, parking under the sign appropriately reading "Restaurant." He whistled an old Beatles' tune as he walked across the crumbling asphalt, soft from the morning heat. His spirits were rising now that his preparations were complete and he could look forward to beginning his research the next day. The sight of the old Jeep illegally parked directly in front of the entrance door ended the tune on the twelfth note. "Can't be," he told the vehicle and patted its rust-spotted fender. Pushing open the restaurant door, he held his breath and scanned the faces of the five patrons. Finding all unfamiliar, he released the air held in his lungs and continued forward more confidently. As the door swung closed, he saw a portion of the room previously hidden. There she sat. Assuming he could not ignore her presence, he went to her table. "Hi Jay," he said with as much composure as he could rally, then added, "Mind if I join you?"

"Join me for what?"

"Dinner?"

"Are you trying to . . . what is it called . . . yes, that is it . . . pick me up?"

"Absolutely not. I thought that in light of knocking you over I could be a little friendly, buy you dinner."

"Go away. I do not like you."

He stared at her quizzically for a moment then retreated to a table on the far side of the room, placing as much distance as possible between them. He ordered, and while he waited for his food, he replayed his interactions with Jay. She did not intimidate him; but something about her made him uneasy. It was not her abrasiveness. She just was so extremely peculiar in both behavior and appearance.

After his meal arrived, he tried to block Jay the Terrible from his thoughts but found himself sneaking glances at her. And each time he did, he saw her looking at him as if expecting an assault. Near the end of his meal he heard a chair scrape across the floor. Raising his eyes, he watched her stand and walk coolly to the door.

"Hey you," a woman server called out. She reminded Ross of a red-haired clown, with a bulbous, red nose, cheeks to match, and a body of a puffer fish. "What the hell are you trying to get away with?"

Jay stopped and turned. "Me?"

"Don't be cute sweetie. How about paying up?"

"I do not have any money," Jay stated as if describing the weather.

Ross grinned, shaking his head as the puffer fish in white pressed her chin close to Jay's chest, wagged her finger at the towering woman, and shouted, "Pay up or I call the police."

Jay's eyes narrowed, alerting him to the impending physical action. He could visualize her lifting her adversary off the floor and tossing her across the room. "I'm paying for her meal," Ross heard himself call out, not understanding what demon had crawled into his brain to give the command to speak those words.

Hesitantly, the waitress turned her head, looked at Ross, and said, "You're not going to bail her out. She pays."

"You don't understand, she's with me."

She stepped away from Jay, put her hands on her hips and challenged, "Oh yeah, then why you two sittin' at different tables?"

"You know how it is. We had a little fight and she's just being stubborn. Typical of women."

The waitress' body posture softened. As her mouth relaxed into a motherly grin, she placed a hand tenderly on Jay's shoulder. "Men, they're all the same. I'm sorry, Dear. Run along and I'll make sure he pays up." Then, standing on tiptoes, she whispered in Jay's ear, "Don't give an inch. He'll come begging. Trust me, I know."

Jay nodded in agreement and left while the waitress threw Ross a reprimanding look before exiting into the kitchen. He sipped his coffee, heard the sound of the Jeep's engine, and contemplated that, if nothing else, the strange woman had provided him with entertaining interludes that justified the few dollars he spent on her behalf.

When he paid their bills fifteen minutes later, he was advised to be more considerate of his pretty, young girl-friend and to bring her a gift as a peace offering. He promised to mend his ill ways, then departed, barely succeeding in restraining the laughter threatening to burst out.

* * *

Just as he turned into the parking lot in front of his motel room, his grip tightened on the steering wheel. "Why me?" he complained to the old Jeep parked in the next space. "Christ, I'll probably end up paying her motel bill," he fumed, slamming the Focus door closed. "I've never met anyone with so much nerve," he said to the empty room as he shoved the door closed.

He sat at the edge of the bed, puzzled why her staying at the same rundown motel bothered him. When he could think of no valid reason for being emotional about her choice of motels, he turned his attention to the preparations necessary for his trip.

He checked his GPS topographical maps, botanical notes, and supply checklist until ten, and then took a shower. The cool, stinging jets of water refreshed his body and cleared his mind, allowing his thoughts to drift to another unsettling subject: Marsha. Ross acknowledged that he missed the fantasy week of companionship with her. Although hating what she had done to him, he still had a lingering urge to see her again. Reconciling that the pain of deceit would be with him for a long time to come, he shelved the thoughts.

After shutting off the flow of water, he stepped out onto the floor joists with a towel loosely wrapped at his waist and made his way out the bathroom. The first step onto the hard, carpeted floor caused a sharp pain at the ball of his right foot.

Guessing he had likely picked up a splinter from one of the unfinished beams, he toweled dry then limped over to the bed. The offending shard of wood was impossible to detect in the dim light, so he hopped off the bed and hobbled to a lamp sitting on a table by the door connecting the adjoining room. He braced his back against the door and pulled up his right foot while he balanced on the left. The bright light enabled him to see the sliver. After pinching the projecting shard of the wood between his fingernails, he gave a quick yank.

A "clack" registered in his left ear.

He realized the door was swinging out behind him.

Abruptly, he felt himself falling.

His head crashed onto the unforgiving floor in the adjoining room causing a field of sparkling light to pepper his vision. Dazed, he raised his head to see he lie in a rectangle of light projected through the doorway from his room. The remainder of the room was black. He was on a magic carpet of light floating in the dark void of space.

A spinning sensation forced Ross to lay his head back on the floor. As he peered into the darkness he saw a pair of ghostly, iridescent purple eyes suspended in the inky blackness. And they were watching him.

The creaking sounds of mattress springs, quickly followed by sliding noises, prompted him to scramble to his feet, but before he could move a limb, two legs straddled his hips. The shapely nude extremities that disappeared up into the darkness at mid-thigh level were undoubtedly the property of the female gender. About to identify himself, a metallic click sounded in the quiet room, and the muzzle of a gun appeared only inches from the bridge of his nose. Examining the bore diameter and the wall thickness of the barrel, he surmised that the threatening weapon was a .357 Magnum. Not wishing to frighten or alarm its owner in any way, he said nothing, moved nothing, and waited for her next move.

"Why are you following me?" said a voice from somewhere above the beautiful legs.

"Is that you, Jay?"

"Why are you following me?" she repeated.

"I just thought I'd drop in."

"I do not understand your answer."

"Just a joke. Forget it. I'm not following you. It was an accident. I didn't know you were in this room."

"Why do you always plan accidents with me?"

"Put the gun away and we'll talk."

The gun remained steady at his head. "Tell me what you want."

"I fell through the door. Why do you think I'm laying here?"

"Are you trying to touch my female parts?"

"What the hell do you take me for? Have you ever heard of a man trying to cop a feel on a woman by falling on her floor and waiting while she gets a gun? And besides, if I ever did have the disgusting desire to assault anyone, you'd be my last choice."

"Why did you pay for my supplies at the store and my food at the restaurant?"

"Because you didn't have any money, and I felt I owed you after knocking you down. Look, after my shower I got a splinter in my foot walking across the under-construction floor in my bathroom. I leaned against your door, which is next to the lamp in my room, so I could see the splinter. The door gave, and here I am."

She did not respond, but lowered the gun to her side. He heard the releasing click of the hammer.

When she did not move or speak for a few moments, he said, "What now? Can I get up?"

The legs disappeared into the darkness, and he slowly got to his feet, an activity he found surprisingly difficult. When he saw her dimly lit silhouette he said, "Thanks Jay, I won't bother you again. None of my business, but something smells kind of gamy in here."

"Gamy?"

He sniffed at the air and soon realized she was the source. "Since I don't think you could like me any less, let me give you a tip. An attractive woman like you should shower more often."

"I smell bad?"

"Very bad." He walked back into his room, closed the door, and prayed he would never set eyes on that lunatic again.

A smile crept onto his face when, as he lay in the darkness, the sound of a running shower came through the wall.

Chapter 5

Ross awoke for the third time at six a.m., determined to get an early start. He dressed, packed the Focus, and went to the office to pay his bill. The individual behind the counter matched the decorum of the motel rooms perfectly. New England-lost-in-time-rough. He greeted Ross with a "don't bother me, can't you see I'm resting" look.

"I'm checking out," Ross informed him.

"Okay, unit six . . . two nights . . . comes to a hundred and four."

Ross handed him his card as he asked, "Did the lady in five checkout yet? I noticed her Jeep is gone."

He peeked through the window behind Ross then ran out the door. When he returned minutes later, gasping for breath, he wheezed out, "That bitch skipped out on me. I'll get the state police on her ass."

Here we go again, Ross thought. "What's she owe?" his mouth asked, seemingly disconnected from his mind.

"Fifty-two. Can you believe the nerve of that tramp?"

"Yes I can, I'll cover her," he answered, dreading what his mother would say if she found out he was helping another stray. "Just add it to my card."

The greaseball's disposition improved as he ran Ross' card through a worn slide machine that sounded like it doubled as a shredder. "Oh, I see. Gave you a good time, hey? She is quite a looker. Big in more ways than one. Know what I mean?" He inserted a grotesque cackle, then continued, "Bet she was a good lay."

"Don't know. Didn't touch her. Unfriendly type."

"Yeah, some of those bitches are a real tease," he sympathized knowingly.

"What name did she register under?"

"Not suppose to give out that info, but since you paid her tab . . ." He took out a worn leather register and opened it on the countertop in front of Ross.

Ross grinned and read, "Jay Jay?"

"I don't ask questions. Just follow the rules. Wait a minute; if she didn't do you any favors, and you don't even know her name, then why the hell did you pay her bill?"

"I don't really know, but it's getting to be a bad habit of mine," he answered honestly. "I guess I just like her style and don't want to see her end up in trouble."

"Well if she keeps pulling this shit, she'll get trouble."

Ross nodded as he collected his Visa, surprised it survived the chamber of horrors credit card machine in a single piece. Glad to have the motel experience behind him, he strolled out into the invigorating morning chill to his car. Driving out onto the northbound side of the roadway, he relaxed, pushed a CD into the radio, but did not listen to the music as his mind wandered to comparisons of the two most recent women in his life. Marsha matched the image of a desirable woman, at least in appearance. Although she presented him with one little problem in that she did not care for him very much. By contrast, Jay was the weirdest woman he had ever run across. But weird didn't explain her properly. Bizarre, strange, peculiar also applied. She would no doubt be appealing to some men, but not him. Yet, there was some attraction. Physically, she was eye-catching, but not his type. And her personality was not exactly endearing, so why did he feel some draw for her? Her actions toward him and her verbal hostility during their encounters should have invoked anger, but on the contrary, he repeatedly felt the need to help her. "Christ, she almost blew my head off!" he complained to the windshield. Whatever it was about her that interested him no longer mattered since the odds of seeing her again were astronomical.

His mind sought refuge in his thoughts of Marsha. Those pleasant recollections of his days and nights with her were his companion for the next twenty minutes until the impossible happened. Driving on one of the few straight downgrades, he noticed a vehicle ahead on the right shoulder. A person standing in the road faced the rear of their vehicle. As he slowed his car, getting closer to the person, the words, "This is ridiculous," slipped between his lips.

He glanced to his right as he passed and quickly noticed that the Jeep's left rear tire was flat. Jay stood there, her back to his car, just staring at the crippled wheel. Fully intending to continue on his way, Ross was surprised when his foot hit the brake pedal. Angry at his own weakness for this woman, he came to a complete stop on the shoulder, and sat looking into the rearview mirror. Jay was still gawking at the tire as if it would re-inflate by itself.

He opened the door and stomped off toward her, thinking how refreshing it would be if she greeted him with a smiling, "Oh, hi Ross. Thanks for stopping. It's so nice to see you again." However, he knew he walked toward a very different type of reception. Helping her was like taunting a frightened skunk; his frustration increased with each step.

When he was within a few paces, she turned her head toward him, and before she had the opportunity to open her mouth, he shouted, "I'm not following you! I'm not going to touch your female parts. And I'm not interested in the fact that you don't like me." He walked past her, around the rear of the Jeep, and put his hands on the spare tire.

"You are angry," she observed.

"Damn right!"

"Why?" she questioned as she cocked her head.

"Because only a fool would stop to help you."

"Then you consider yourself a fool?"

"Yes, and that makes me angry."

"Why do you always help me?"

He looked into her probing eyes. The tone of his voice softened, "God help me, I have no idea." Holding back the anger threatening to resurface, he said, "Jay, your spare tire is useless. There's a cut in the sidewall and it's deflated." He stood back, pondering the new circumstances.

Unexpectedly, Jay moved directly in front of him then inched closer until her chest touched his. Her purpose unclear, she simply stayed there, peering into his eyes.

The oddity of her action disturbed him. "What are you doing?"

"Do I smell . . . gamy?"

He smiled, "No you don't Jay, you smell fine." The directness of her question identified the trait he liked in this woman. Although seemingly intelligent and very mature physically, she had an inkling of innocence, almost child-like. To Ross, it felt like jumping into an ice-cold pool on a sweltering summer day, shock at first followed by refreshing relief.

Her proximity made him uneasy, so he stepped back. He walked around her, and pulled her only visible luggage from the Jeep: a fully outfitted backpack. As he reached to extract the key from the ignition, she warned, "Put those back."

"The way I see it you only have two choices: one, come with me and I'll drop you off at the nearest town so you can find help; or two, I can drive away alone, and we can forget we ever saw each other again."

"I'm not going anywhere with you. I do not . . ."

"I know, I know, you don't like me. Fine. Goodbye and good luck." He tossed the pack back in the Jeep, inserted the key into the ignition, brushed his hands together, and said, "There, everything is the way I found it."

"Wait. I have changed my mind. I will ride with you. Carry my pack." She walked around to the passenger side and lifted out a box from under the dashboard.

"And what in hell makes you think I'll help you now?" Ross screamed.

"You are a strange man. You stopped to help me, so you will help me now that I am willing to accept it."

Furious with her irrefutable logic and his own irrational behavior, he jerked up her backpack and yanked the keys out of the ignition. "What's in the box?"

"A pet," she answered, peeping into one of the small holes in its side.

"A cat?"

"Aaaa . . . yes, a cat."

"I like cats. Can I see it?"

"No," she responded sharply, and then strode toward the Focus.

Ross followed her to the car, opened the trunk, and placed her pack on the floor. She continued past him to sit in the passenger seat. Positioning the box on her lap, she moved her hands to the top edges, holding it tightly in place.

Once on their way, Ross resolved he would remain quiet, waiting for her to initiate conversation. Fifteen speechless minutes later, he said, "So Jay, where you from?"

"It is not important."

Just as I thought, talking to you is a complete waste of my time. "What are you doing in this area?" he asked.

"It is personal."

The chances of getting a straight answer from you is about as likely as a chipmunk making a hit song, so I will not say another word, he thought. "Last name?"

"Must you always talk?"

He laughed. "You're the only woman ever to accuse me of talking too much. Usually I'm considered a bore."

"I do not understand. A boar is either an animal, or the process of creating a hole. It seems you use the word out of place."

He laughed again. "Where in the world have you been all your life? 'Bore' is the name used to describe a person who is boring. You know, dull, not interesting." Pursuing the subject, "Did you grow up in this country? I don't detect an accent."

"Yes, and I do not wish to answer any more of your pointless inquiries."

"Okay, no more questions. I'll talk, you listen." He checked for a reaction, but she continued to stare through the windshield.

"I'm a thirty-five-year-old botany professor, and live in Indiana. I'm going to spend roughly three weeks in the National Forest doing research. How old are you? Right, sorry, no questions. Well, I'd guess you're about . . . twenty-four, twenty-five."

"Am I pretty?"

"In your own unique fashion, yes, you're very pretty."

"What is that noise?"

"What noise? I don't hear . . ." A rapid, thumping rattle vibrated through the car. Its intensity grew steadily, the sounds resonating like a series of short interval and muffled thunder claps. He lowered his *window*, and identified "Helicopters," just as a group of four cleared the treetops, completely drowning out the sound of his voice. They passed over the roadway only a hundred yards ahead then quickly disappeared above the trees. "Military. I wonder what they're up to out here?" Glancing to his right, he noticed that Jay continued to stare disinterestedly through the windshield at the road.

A few minutes passed and Jay startled him by blurting out: "Stop the car."

Ross reflexively placed his foot on the brake pedal. "What for?" he asked, slowly accelerating again.

"I said stop the car!" she shouted.

"Why?"

"I am getting out here."

"Why? There's nothing but forest ahead."

"Please do not ask questions. Just do what I ask."

He brought the car to a stop, killed the engine and looked at her quizzically.

"I am going to start my hike here," she explained.

"But there's no trail here, what are you going to do with your cat, and what about the Jeep?"

She answered by opening the door and stepping outside.

Swearing, he followed her out.

"I do not want to discuss it," she declared as she lifted her pack from the trunk floor, thus preempting any further dialogue.

He thought, *Girl, you're one hell of a scatterbrain. You need a shrink.* "Here, let me help you put on your pack." Taking it from her, he hefted it up while she slipped into the harness. "This weighs a ton. What the devil do you have in this thing, rocks?"

True to form, she did not respond as she fastened the buckles without a word. With the straps secured, she moved to the car to lift out her boxed cat. "Thank you for your assistance. You may leave now."

"One minute," Ross said, withdrawing a wallet from his back pocket. After sorting through the contents, he inserted folded twenties and a card into a side pouch in her backpack. "Some money. You may need it."

"I am not going to accept anything else from you."

"It's not a gift. The business card has my name and address on it. Reimburse me when you get home. Keep it or else I'll follow you."

"You are an odd person."

"Me? Odd? Lady if there was ever a . . ." He cut off his sentence and cinched the strap at her waist tighter. "It'll bounce on your back unless you keep that snug." He added, "You do smell nice. Maybe we'll see each other again someday."

"I do not think that is probable," she responded coolly.

He nodded with a smile, leaned against the car, watching while she and her cat box trekked out of his life once again, disappearing into the trees. He stayed, listening to the diminishing sounds of her footfalls until there were only the lazy summer noises of chirping birds and buzzing insects.

* * *

The service station where Ross had arranged to store the Focus was easy to locate since it was the only one in town. Complying with the prearranged instructions, he parked the car in waist high weeds in a small field behind the station then waded back to the decades-old, white service station/grocery store/post office. Brushing off small brown and green souvenirs from the field that clung to the hair on his legs and heavy cotton socks, he considered calling Marsha. By the time he rid himself of the tenacious seeds, he decided, yes, he would call her, let her know they were through as a couple, let her get on with her quest for that lifelong companionship.

Finding the best signal strength by the post office window, he tried her cell. After several rings, he ended the call, glad she had not answered. What kind of man ended a relationship by phone, text, or e-mail? He would tell her face to face. Tucking the phone in his pocket, it signaled and Marsha's name flashed on the screen. He swore and connected the call.

A sleepy, seductive voice said, "Hello, Ross?"

"Marsha?" he answered, not sure what to say.

"Did you just call? Are you okay?"

"Ah, yeah," he answered as his mind struggled to invent a reason for calling. "Just wanted to tell you I made it all right and am about to go into the forest."

"I'm wearing something you like," she purred.

"What's that?"

"Absolutely nothing. I miss you already. Three weeks without you is going to be unbearable. Where are you calling from? Shouldn't you be out in the woods by now with the raccoons and squirrels?"

Ross gave her a brief synopsis of his series of setbacks, including a recap of his run-ins with Jay.

When he completed his story Marsha reacted by saying, "What a bitch. Why did you give money to that horrible woman? You should have had her arrested."

"Guilt I guess. I don't know."

"She could have killed you."

"I don't think so. She just doesn't strike me as the killing type." Pausing, he added, "But I'm not always good at judging the character of women." He thought, maybe hoped, Marsha would react to his indirect comment. Instead, she let it ride.

"Since she had a gun and did point it at your head, I wouldn't exactly call her Mother Goose. Enough of her. She's gone and will become someone else's problem. Do you miss me?"

"I've thought about you a lot," he answered, realizing what a sap he was for evading the intended topic. He abruptly announced, "I have to go Marsha. See you when I get back and we can talk."

"I'll be waiting."

"Bye," he answered curtly, cutting the conversation short.

"Bye, and don't pick up any more strays."

He sighed, and began searching for someone to talk to about his car. The proprietor of the multipurpose establishment was finally unearthed in the garage, busily probing wrenches into the grease-laden engine compartment of an early eighties, vintage Chevy pickup.

After Ross identified himself and the reason for his visit, the mechanic/gas attendant/stock boy/grocery clerk/postman/owner suspended the automotive surgery, introduced himself as "Bob Here." The terms for the car's storage described by Bob Here were "fifty-in-advanced-cash." Once Ross produced the exact cash, he watched the oil and grease-stained fist shove it into the pocket of his grungy jeans.

Bob Here said, "Thank yah," then placed his head back into the open jaws of the faded blue relic, resuming his operation. Understanding the long-winded conversation with Bob Here had ended, Ross headed for the front door.

* * *

The regional branch of the U.S. Forest Service was not difficult to find as it was situated on the opposite side of the road, only a few hundred feet north of the service station. The most notable features evident on the property were signs. One, of enormous proportions at the entrance to the parking lot read "Parking," of all things. This sturdy, rustic cabin stood as a snapshot of the American journey. Nearby Long Trail was the oldest long-distance trail in the United

States, being constructed between the years 1910 and 1930. It ran 272 miles through the state between the Massachusetts and Canadian borders.

He approached the front door to find a handwritten note: Back in 15 minutes. Ross laid his pack down and sat on the edge of the porch. He admired the craftsmanship of the regulations carved into a six-by-ten-foot wooden sign:

DAY USE HOURS 6 AM – 10 PM
NO FIGHTING OR BOISTEROUS BEHAVIOR
DO NOT CARVE, CHOP, OR DAMAGE LIVING TREES
FIREWORKS AND EXPLOSIVES ARE PROHIBITED
ALL STATE FISHING REGULATIONS ENFORCED
KEEP PETS ON A LEASH AT ALL TIMES
PETS ARE PROHIBITED IN WATER
PICK UP AND REMOVE EXCREMENT

He watched a family of four white-tailed deer graze on the fallen fruit under an apple tree, unaware of the man on the porch steps enjoying them feast in this natural environment. To his left, a small cascading waterfall poured into a twisting brook. His eyes followed the mini ripples carry leaves down the winding stream, its movement and soothing sounds sending him to a light sleep.

An hour and twenty minutes later, he was still sitting there, frustration blending with anger, hoping this was not a precursor of what was to come and the success of his research.

"Hi there," called a cheerful voice from behind. Ross turned and saw a ranger standing in the open doorway. "If you're wait'n for a bus, you'll have a loooong wait 'cause there ain't any."

Standing, Ross answered, "No, I was waiting for you."

The ranger shook his head and pulled the sign from the door. "I got to remember to take this damn thing down when I get back. The Mrs. is always tell'n me I'm too forgetful.

Maybe she's got a point. Come in young fella and we'll see if we can help you."

Once inside the one-room, air-conditioned office, Ross explained his profession, plans, and how he just wanted to inform the Forest Service of his presence on the trail.

"Considerate of ya' to notify us like this, 'specially you being alone. Too often I've had to calm hysterical women whose husbands are overdue, and we don't have one iota of where to start look'n. Considering that you're not going to be sightsee'n, you can save yourself almost a day's walk'n by tak'n an unmarked trail that branches off to the left about a half-mile into the woods. The marked trail that hooks up with Long Trail has lots of ups and downs that eat up time and energy. The other trail crosses Long further north and stays in the valleys. Saves lots of time and sweat.

"Almost forgot. Military boys got a section restricted. Said somethin' 'bout maneuvers." The ranger leaned towards Ross then whispered as if government agents were posted around back, "But rumor 'round here is that they are look'n for some damn top-secret missile they accidentally dropped from a plane further north. Seems kinda reckless to me. Lost. Imagine that. Those boys could get kinda touchy if you got too close, so keep an eye out."

Chapter 6

By the time Ross reached Long Trail it was sunset; he was exhausted. He admonished himself for neglecting his workout routine in preparation for the trip; he should have done more to increase his stamina than just reading fitness blogs on the internet. His back tired from the weight of the forty-five pound pack, his feet ached, and he lacked the stamina to go much further. Dropping his equipment on the first patch of ground he could find that appeared spacious enough to pitch a tent, he began setting up his temporary home. Once Ross erected the tent, he paused to look up over the trees at the brilliant red clouds that streaked the darkening sky. Reflecting on nature's serene masterpiece of hues and colors, he recalled a Vermont version of a legendary weather verse read in some past issue of the Farmer's Almanac:

> Evening red and morning gray,
> Sends the traveler on his way.
> Evening gray and morning red,
> Stays the traveler home in bed.

Gratified by the foretelling of a clear day of travel ahead, he knelt down and began unlacing his shoes. The simple task turned out to be a messy one because the moist clay coated most of his shoes in addition to the laces. The ranger had not mentioned the valley trail would be a quagmire of thick, slippery, soft clay, causing Ross to regret the assumption the shortcut would be easygoing. Once free of the crusty footgear, he slipped into the tent and collapsed atop his foam sleeping-pad. Every muscle in his body relaxed. After nearly twenty minutes of thoughtless unwinding, Ross sat up, forced his body out of neutral, and began unrolling the sleeping bag.

When he finally switched off the lantern, and wrapped comfortably in his bag, he stared up into the darkness. The solitude and peacefulness permitted clear, undaunted concentration, and his mind returned to the subject of Marsha. Logic told him that being with her would be a mistake. His heart told him he needed someone to share life's experiences. And what was so wrong if that someone came wrapped in a very sexy package?

Inexplicably, Jay came to mind. He imagined her somewhere out in the same forest, lying in thought in her own tent. He wondered if she, too, was lonely, and then felt a nagging pang of sympathy for her. Positive he had detected fear beneath her hard exterior, he wondered about the underlying reasons for her behaving so secretively. One would think she was on the run. Was she a fugitive from justice, a runaway wife, a loner . . . or just a mental case? He sensed he was not yet free of her complications.

* * *

The pit-pattering sounds of rain reached Ross' ears as he emerged from a restless sleep. His eyes opened slowly to the dimly lit tent, reinforcing his initial impression of it being a dismal day. Although he would have enjoyed the recuperative aspects of a day spent lounging lazily in the dry nylon shelter, such a waste of time was not consistent with his goals. A fine mist speckled his face when he poked his head into the early morning air. "So much for cute Vermont weather verses," he grunted.

After dressing, he ate, repacked his equipment, slipped on a poncho, and started north on Long Trail. At first, the fine drizzle reinforced the dreariness he felt since waking; but after an hour or so traipsing through the rugged terrain, he forgot how physically uncomfortable he felt trapped in the dampness under the poncho, and began to appreciate the qualities this area afforded. The beauty of the trees and lush vegetation against the back drop of the nebulous curtain of haze warmed his heart, creating a permanent smile on his face. The mist emphasized the glory of the white birch trunks, with the bark nearly glowing whiteness in the subdued lighting. His eyes and mind, captivated by the rapture of nature, were unaware of both the passage of time and the steady climb until rays of sunshine punched through the treetops. He squinted, and lifting his wrist to shield his eyes from the glare, guessed it was close to noon.

With the morning behind him, he now faced the broiling effects of the blazing sun and rising temperatures. The air was heavy with humidity. Oppressive. Unwilling to continue to endure the sauna-like conditions imposed by the poncho, he stopped for a lunch break.

Snacking on a dried apricot, he pulled the GPS from his pocket and laid it on the ground to determine his current location. Following the apricot, he brought out dessert and began gnawing at a chunk of freeze-dried ice cream as he turned on the device.

A shadowy silhouette momentarily darkened the screen. Then vanished. Startled, he looked up quickly, seeing nothing above him but trees and patches of light blue sky. He scanned the surrounding forest, pivoting slowly around, hoping to catch the elusive form. But finding no detectable movement among the trees, he returned his attention to the GPS, only to be distracted by a streaking, reddish-brown blur just to the right and above him. Immediately flicking his eyes in the direction he instinctively guessed the object was flying, he saw it burst through a small shaft of sunlight and disappear. Instantly his mind recorded the image like a snapshot, but it resembled nothing in his memory bank. The only characteristic he recognized was that it flew. Ross concluded the phantom must have been a medium- or small-sized bird.

Returning his attention to his map, he soon established his approximate location, and noted the trail ahead doubled back for a distance on the other side of the hill behind him. It then resumed a northward direction. Curious about the local plant life, he decided to traverse the hill to pick up the trail on the other side.

The deviation in his journey did not reveal any unusual botanical information, but the perspective from a section of barren rock at the top did afford a breathtaking view. Halfway down the other side, Ross paused for a breather and squinted to see an object up ahead shining through the branches of a large bush. Always in pursuit of the unusual find, he moved to the bush with the furtiveness of a hunter stalking a wild boar. Truth being, he enjoyed this kind of quest so much he had the habit of prolonging the process so the act of discovery could be savored as a fine wine, or likened to the manner in which children eat their potatoes, vegetables, and meat first in order to preserve the best part of the meal, the dessert, for the last.

As he approached the bush, he assessed the object to be possibly as big as a small refrigerator. How anyone could have dumped anything that large up in the hills puzzled him, thereby amplifying his excitement and curiosity. Circling the bush, he maintained his eyes on a sliver of a metallic surface visible through the dense foliage. Upon closer inspection, he saw it was not a discarded bike nor a rusty refrigerator nor anything familiar. "What is it?" he said aloud, fascinated.

Hurriedly, he unpacked his Nikon camera. The object in the viewfinder was a dull gold, bullet-shaped container lying on its side in a bed of brown oak leaves. Roughly the size of a home hot water heater, it was approximately five feet long and two feet in diameter. Midway between its base and its hemispherical nose was a perimeter of transparent circular ports, each being three or four inches in diameter. Booms or struts of some type stuck out from the flat circular base into the air. He snapped off a picture, moved, and then snapped another. He took about eight photos in all from various positions before he placed the camera strap around his neck and moved closer.

The odd apparatus at the bottom of the device was the first to draw his closer examination. After getting down on all fours and placing his head in the center of the four bottom appendages, he gained an important insight into their purpose. They were obviously articulated legs designed for locomotion. Although inconceivable to him, their construction could serve no other purpose. He pulled himself alongside to the ports and, peering into one of them, saw only darkness. Running his hand along the satin-textured metal, he crawled to the nose, abruptly halting when his fingers felt a crevice in the surface. Studying the surface more carefully, he could see a very small seam between the cylindrical body and the hemispherical nose.

He pushed with both hands against the nose, and to his delight, it slowly opened on hinges, apparently located on the opposite side. A foul stench similar to that of decaying fish assaulted his nostrils, forcing him to move away. He found a long maple branch on the ground and used it to open the top further while maintaining a respectful distance. Once he had created a substantial opening, he dropped the stick and peered into the cavity. Some of his excitement faded when he found there was nothing to see; it was hollow.

He gazed thoughtfully at it, trying to comprehend the purpose of a self-propelled, all-terrain container. Conceding his inability to decipher its intended function, he dug out his flashlight and moved closer while holding his breath. He probed deep into the interior with the beam only to find the inside empty, except for an unidentifiable substance of some kind on the lowest side. Stepping back, he released his breath, inhaled and exhaled deeply a few times to capture fresh air in his lungs, and returned to his study. On closer inspection, he saw that the substance appeared as some kind of residue. He withdrew again, retrieved the stick, and prodded the material. Its texture and consistency reminded him of a beached jellyfish he had toyed with as a child on a family vacation to Cape Cod.

Baffled, he ended his investigation by taking a series of close-up photos of the interior and the outer legs. He took pictures of the surrounding area intent on identification the location for later use. The bed of overturned leaves and broken twigs suggested it had been placed there recently, but no evidence of having been dragged along the ground. He took out his notebook and pen to check the GPS and record the coordinates. He wanted to carry the thing with him, but knew it would be folly to consider such an undertaking. The only explanation regarding the origin of the object that seemed halfway plausible to Ross was it being part of a government experiment. Was this the object of the search the ranger had heard rumors about? As he walked away, he decided to report his discovery to the ranger upon his return. The magnificent view from the top, the time saved, and now this find certainly combined to have made his detour a worthwhile endeavor.

Fortunately, Ross had judged accurately and his descent led him to Long Trail exactly where he expected it to be. After traveling a distance of a half-mile that brought him to a northern bearing again, a faint swooshing sound startled him. He froze and allowed his eyes to sweep across the white pine stand on the trail ahead, but he heard nothing more, and so he continued forward, careful that his footfalls on the bed of pine needles produced no sound. But the noise, much louder now, suddenly repeated in his right ear, and he stooped down automatically to escape the phantom airborne intruder. Once again, he saw a streaking, reddish-brown blur disappear into the trees, but this time he had seen enough to identify the intruder as a bird; he had definitely seen wings.

He stood erect, certain it had been the same form that buzzed him during lunch. If so, what attracted the crazy bird to him in particular? Perhaps he was too close to its nest. Placing the minor curiosity aside, Ross resumed his journey through the pines and intense heat.

One hundred yards later, he picked out another hiker on the trail ahead. The individual, seemingly traveling in the same direction since his back was toward Ross, did not appear to be moving, however. When Ross moved in closer to the stranger, he saw that the hiker, indeed, simply stood there. "Hello there," Ross called out through cupped hands. "You okay?" Still no response. The guy stood so immobile, he could have been a stuffed decoy. But when he was within a hundred feet of the motionless hiker, he could see at the bare legs visible below the large pack—much too shapely to be the property of a man. At a distance of fifty feet, he recognized the legs. Ross thought it peculiar he felt happy.

He was poised to call her name when she spun and faced him. Under most circumstances, the gun she pointed at his chest would draw his attention, but other particulars captured his sight. She was dressed in a sheer yellow nylon bra and matching bikini pants. Both garments saturated with sweat, they masked little of her feminine outlines. He astutely noted that those curves were far more picturesque than he had previously imagined. Prying his eyes away from her body and looking into her eyes, he said, "So we meet again Jay."

"Turn around and go back. And do not try to follow me again or I will kill you."

Not disturbed in the least by her threat, he unstrapped his pack, letting it drop to the ground. Resting on a fallen pine log, Ross wiped the sweat from his brow as he looked up at her. He groaned. "Jay, we've been through this before and it's wearing a little thin. Put the gun away," he said. "One, I'm here for research on the environmental effect on plant evolution, not you. I'm headed for an area about thirty miles north of here. Two, I'm not following you. Three, I'm not planning to touch you, although your current outfit doesn't help in the matter. Four, you and I both know that you're not going to kill me so put that stupid gun away before you drop it on your toes. Five, I'm not about to change my plans just because I frighten you."

"Why are you confident I would not shoot this weapon at you?"

Ignoring the question, he asked, "Why on Earth are you dressed like that?"

She lowered the gun and approached him. "What is wrong with my clothing?"

"There's so little of it. Showing yourself off like that may give someone the wrong idea."

"It is practical," she answered confidently, and added, "I was overheating."

"Practical? Turn around."

"Why?"

"Quit playing games. I'm not going to attack you, just do as I ask."

She turned her body slowly while maintaining a distrustful watch on Ross.

"Unfasten your pack."

This time she complied without hesitation, allowing him to lift it off her back.

"Just as I thought, the pack is beginning to cut into your skin. Doesn't it hurt?"

"Yes, I feel pain," she responded in her routine monotone.

He retrieved a first aid kit from his pack, rummaged through it for a few seconds until he found the tube of cortisone ointment. Smearing the grease tenderly on the abrasions covering her shoulder blades, he felt glad to be with her again. As he continued to coat the damaged skin, he asked, "Where's your cat?"

"Cat? Yes, my cat. It is lost."

"Sorry to hear that," he said sympathetically while not believing there ever was a cat, and wondering what had actually been inside her cat box. Aware of the rising pleasure he was getting by his sense of touch on her soft skin, he quickly withdrew his hands. "Get some clothes on now, and keep them on before I contemplate doing something I'd regret."

"You said you would not harm me."

"Just kidding Jay. I was being facetious."

"I see, a joke."

"Yes, a joke. Talking to you is strange."

"Then do not converse," she retorted while she buttoned her shirt.

Watching her wiggle into her shorts with more enjoyment that he would care to admit, he asked, "What are you doing out here in the middle of nowhere? And don't tell me this is a pleasure hike."

"I cannot tell you. Do not ask again."

"Are you running from someone? Maybe I can help?"

"I am not running. And I do not need your assistance. I will leave now. Help me with my pack."

"I thought you didn't need assistance?" he teased.

"Another joke?"

"Best I can do," he said with a grin. "Why don't we stay together? The sun is already setting. We could camp here tonight, and then tomorrow we could walk together. We seem to be going in the same direction. And we get along so famously."

"No, I will travel alone."

"But it's getting dark. You could hurt yourself walking the trail with so little light. At least spend the night here."

She fastened the straps and defiantly turned away from him. "Goodbye Ross Barton," she said.

Ross watched her strut off into the dusk.

Chapter 7

After a restless night, Ross attacked the trail at sunrise, anxious to cover a lot of ground before evening. Jay nagged his subconscious thoughts. Whatever his interest in her, he feared it was growing like an unwanted weed in a meticulously manicured lawn. When he sighted another hiker descending a distant hill directly ahead, he grew cheerful. The mood faded with the emergence of a second hiker behind the first. That change, from the high he felt at the first sighting, to the emptiness that followed upon seeing the pair, only highlighted his intruding fascination with Jay and the hope she would return to take him up on his offer to travel as a twosome.

When he later encountered the two travelers, he discovered they were two boys in their late teens. The leader, a pimply-faced redhead with freckles, carried the weight of a kid living on a diet of greasy burgers and French fries. The brown-haired, dark complexioned one seemed malnourished, his companion having eaten all his meals. Given the camaraderie usually characteristic between hikers, they all exchanged warm and friendly hellos. Ross was about to ask them if they had passed a tall girl with black hair but was preempted when the skinny fellow blurted, "You may want to consider turning around. Some fuck'n giant chic pulled a cannon on us and told us to get lost. No shit, she must have been six-five."

Freckles nodded emphatically in agreement.

The skinny one continued, "Hell, I would have gotten out of the bitch's way even if she didn't have a gun. Mean look'n."

Ross held in a laugh, and asked, "What color was her hair?" As if he needed to ask.

"Black as fuck'n coal," the skinny with brown hair kid described. "Why?"

"I want to know what she looks like so I can stay away from her."

"I still think you'd be better off turning around."

"Can't. I have to reach a place north of here. You were just walking on the trail and this girl pulled a gun on you?"

"Well, not exactly," Freckles spoke for the first time.

His friend took his cue and elaborated, "There's an old shelter off the trail on the other side of this hill. We thought we'd stop there and have our breakfast. The girl was sleeping inside. She woke up when she heard us at the doorway and I said, 'Hi.' She didn't say a word. She just whipped out the gun and told us to clear out. She stood at the door with the gun pointed at us until we were out of sight."

"Sure sounds like some kind of nut," Ross agreed. "Thanks for the warning. I'll make sure I don't run into her. I'd better get going. Nice meeting you."

"Yeah, good luck," Freckles responded.

The skinny one nodded.

Spurred by the report on Jay, Ross' walking speed increased to a maximum sustainable rate. When he later became hungry, he consumed lunch without missing a step. He reached the old shelter by late afternoon. Built of logs, it had a short front porch supported by stacks of flat stones. A narrow, open doorway and the weathered, plastic-covered window, afforded no view to the interior. Knowing Jay would have departed much earlier in the day, he considered passing the site and not wasting time. Although avoidance of the decrepit old structure aligned with his desire to move as quickly as possible, something about the place seemed to beckon him, so he hesitated. He contemplated the building a few seconds before walking toward it, reasoning she might have forgotten something that would help him understand her purpose for being alone in the forest. That is what he reasoned. Insatiable drive for exploration is what in fact drew him.

Approaching the ancient shelter, he heard a voice and halted. Determining the voice was that of a man, he turned to get back on the trail, but then swiveled his head back to the shelter when he overheard, "Damn it! One of you two help me get this beast off my back!" Ross pivoted, and crept noiselessly toward the commotion, pausing a few feet outside the entrance to listen.

The sounds reaching his ears baffled him completely: men cursing, a woman grunting as if struggling, and a beating sound, much like a bird's flapping wings. Judging by the heavy breathing associated with intense physical exertion, he determined there were more than two people in a scuffle. Ross dropped to a crouch and moved to the shelter's lone window.

Inside, Jay was pinned on a wire mesh bunk by two men, while a third man wearing a blue plaid shirt bent over her, attempting to tear off her clothing with his left hand. He held her gun in his right. Gun or no gun, they were not having an easy time of it. Jay twisted, turned, and arched feverishly in her desperation to free herself.

A reddish-brown bird with outstretched claws dove at the plaid shirt man with the gun. The bird, clearly identifiable as a medium-sized owl, latched into his hair, and drove punching thrusts with its beak into the offender's skull. Ross watched the man try, unsuccessfully, to strike down his airborne adversary with his gun. Buttons from Jay's shirt bounced across the rough wood floor. The owl circled out of Ross' sight momentarily then repeated the tactic.

Ross pulled away from the window and leaned his back against the log wall. In an instant, questions crisscrossed his thoughts: Why was she still here? Why was the owl fighting off her attackers? Was the owl the same bird who had twice before buzzed him? And most importantly, what the hell was he going to do to help her? Setting aside his questions for a later time, he prepared himself to act. And fast. But how?

Ross hesitated. That trio of men in the act of attempting rape were dangerous. If he took the wrong action, he might be responsible for her death. Whenever confronting danger in the past, he placed his own life at risk. Another life was a stake here. Jay's life.

Lacking any weapons, real or having the appearance of being real, his only chance of rescuing Jay and preserving his life in the process, would involve using the element of surprise. He needed to get his hands on Jay's gun before they could react to a single-handed assault. Since the two men holding her were facing the only entrance, sneaking inside undetected was hopeless. He pictured himself running through the door like a bullet train and overpowering Jay's attacker before the other two got to him. However, there was a pathway of large boulders and bushes leading up to the porch that would force him to run straight at the door for a distance before reaching it, thereby giving them time to see him and react prior to his execution of swashbuckling heroics.

The turmoil inside the shelter grew suddenly louder, forcing Ross to return to the window. The owl lay motionless on the floor and Mr. Plaid Shirt, gun still in his right hand, was struggling with Jay's shorts. Ross saw a bright red welt on her left cheek. The situation plainly suggested the time for hypothetical planning well past. He gave the interior of the shelter one last quick glance, then pulled back from the window and stepped away from the sidewall. Desperate, he scrutinized the building, and glanced at a large oak tree to his side. A new plan sprung in his mind, which he impulsively adopted. Hesitation vanished like a stone dropped in a well.

He moved quickly to the base of the tree, and began climbing up its large trunk. After a few feet of ascent, he reached up, grasped the lowest branch, and then pulled himself up to it. Sure-footedly, he climbed on nature's ladder of limbs until he mounted the one he selected from the ground. Without delay, he stepped out along its length, carefully maintaining his balance by imagining being on a balance beam in the gym. He stopped at a point on the branch closest to the roof of the shelter and studied its construction. Looking through the window earlier, he noted many shafts of light illuminating patches on the floor, likely from gaps in the roof. A single look at the rotting, wood boards exposed through the torn sections of the tarpaper covering, verified his estimate of its condition.

He paused only seconds to assemble his courage, then launched himself gracefully across the four-foot gulf to the center of the roof. The structure stopped his fall for only a fraction of a second before it gave, allowing his body to resume its calling to gravity. Thanks to a lucky trajectory, the first substantial resistance his feet met, moved upon contact, and he soon saw that the obstacle was none other than the fellow in a plaid shirt hovering over Jay with the gun. Ross prepared himself for a violent meeting with the hard floor but instead fell from Mr. Plaid Shirt's back onto Jay's body. Ross' head fortunately landed beside hers. He heard her grunt, and saw the gun skitter across the floor. Then someone screamed, "Get'um asshole!"

Ross decided he had lingered long enough. Quickly, he lifted his face, smiled at her and said, "Hi there," while scrambling off her body, bringing another series of short grunts to escape her clenched teeth.

Mr. Plaid Shirt lay face down on the floor, moaning. Beyond him in the corner was the gun. Just as Ross lunged for the weapon, a hand grabbed his ankle from behind, causing his forward momentum to drop him to the floor with a hard, jarring thud. Ross raised his head in time to see another man in a red T-shirt dashing past Jay's side, apparently interested in recovering the same toy as he. As Mr. Red T-shirt passed her, she brought back her knees then thrust both feet at his posterior. The strike drove her target forward, his head smashing into the wall with such a force that dust and wood shavings fluttered from the roof. Two down.

The recoil of Jay's action jarred her off the cot to the floor.

Ross kicked with his free foot at what he hoped would be the man's face holding his ankle. After feeling a jolting impact against his heel, the man's grip released. Ross sat upright, surveying the status through a haze of fine airborne debris.

The man he kicked sat on the floor, his back propped against the wall, his eyes closed. Blood trickled between the fingers of the hand covering his mouth, dripping to spot his white T-shirt with red dots.

Mr. Red T-shirt, Jay's human projectile, lay curled on the floor in the corner. He looked unconscious.

Mr. Plaid Shirt, who once held Jay's gun and provided the cushion for Ross' grand entrance, remained on the floor in the center of the room, gasping for breath.

He could see Jay through the space below the bunk, lying face down. She groaned.

The brazen owl appeared dead.

Ross shook his head to clear it before getting to his feet. He staggered over to the gun, then picked it up uncontested. He walked to Jay and gently rolled her over. Her eyes fluttered open. Ross smiled and whispered, "Not bad, huh?"

She sat up, looked over the room, and then answered, "I did not need your help."

Finding Jay relatively unharmed, he knelt to her. Moving a hand to her face, Ross softly touched her cheek and gently brushed strands of her black hair away from her eyes.

Confused by his actions, she asked coldly, "Why did you do that?"

Ignoring the question, Ross checked her over. Bright red splotches were evident on her cheek and forehead; otherwise, she appeared undamaged. "This is yours," he said, handing the gun to her before moving to the other side of the room. He knelt down and ran his fingertips over the soft feathers of the fallen bird. "It tried to help you. Damndest thing I ever saw. I think they might have gotten what they wanted from you if this owl hadn't given them such a hard time. Wonder why it did that?" He slid his fingers under the bird and lifted it cautiously while rubbing its breast with his thumbs.

Abruptly, Jay was at his side. "Is she dead?" she asked, anguish in her voice.

Once the initial surprise at her first display of emotion had passed, he shook his head. "I feel a heartbeat." As if answering, the owl's wings moved, and soon after its eyes opened. It swiveled its head, looking at Jay, then back to Ross, seemingly unafraid. Ross was again amazed when he saw a faint smile creep into Jay's lips.

"Oswald likes you," she said, her face reverting to deadpan.

"Oswald?"

"My pet."

"This is the cat?"

"Yes."

"Why the hell did you . . . never mind, it's not important. Screech owl, isn't it?"

"Otus asio."

"Yes, that's what I said, screech owl. You called it a she. Oswald is a male's name."

"That does not alter the fact that she is female," she countered.

He lowered the bird to the floor, allowing it to stand on its own feet. It wavered for a moment, steadied itself, then flew into the air, circled the room once, its flight terminating on Jay's shoulder. Its large, light green-yellow eyes locked onto Ross. Unable to resist the appeal of the beautiful bird, he moved closer and stroked the feathers on Oswald's head. One of the men stirred, interrupting his admiration of Jay's owl.

Within fifteen minutes, all three depraved men were conscious and standing against the wall at the muzzle of Jay's gun.

"Jay, let's pack up your stuff and get these creeps to the law," Ross said.

"No."

"What do you mean, no?" Ross questioned, not believing her answer.

"We let them go."

"You can't be serious! Jay, they were attacking you. We can't just let them go. They might try again on you or someone else."

"I do not care." She poked the apparent leader of the desperados, Mr. Plaid Shirt, in the middle of his spine with the barrel. "Go away and do not come back. Understand?" His head bobbed rapidly in agreement, and then all three hustled through the doorway at once, briefly wedging against one another in their haste to escape.

"Why did you do that?" Ross asked after watching them run through the trees to the trail. When she did not answer, but instead began picking up her things, he accused, "You are in trouble with the police."

"I am not. You do not understand."

"Then tell me . . . I'll listen."

"No."

Deciding that pressing this issue, or any other for that matter, to be fruitless, he helped her put together her pack. She was about to mount it when he said, "Wait a minute. I know you have this fetish about taking off your clothes when I'm around, but you're not going to go strolling off in your underwear again."

"Humor again. My clothing was torn. This is all I have."

He laughed, and said, "Wait here. I'll get my pack and get you something to wear." Oswald followed, flying and circling above Ross as he retrieved his pack, then returned to Jay. He dug out a T-shirt with his university logo across the front and handed it to Jay. Oswald flew off her shoulder when she began to raise her arms, choosing Ross' shoulder for her next landing. Ross spoke lovingly to the owl in warm tones while Jay pulled his shirt over her head. Looking away from the bird momentarily, he saw that his shirt would never be the same, for although roomy at her shoulders and waist, its material was strained at the middle of her chest. He searched through the pack for shorts. Oswald watched with interest as Ross rummaged through the contents. Finally, he extracted his spare shorts and threw them to her. He and Oswald watched while Jay pulled, tugged, and wiggled the shorts to her waist. "Looks good, doesn't it Oswald," he commented, thoroughly enjoying the fashion show. The shorts fit similarly to the shirt, loose at the waist, but nicely snug at her hips. "You're welcome," Ross said.

"I do not have a reason to thank you," she responded.

He shrugged, then began re-stuffing his pack while she lifted hers by the shoulder strap and walked outside. Oswald followed.

When Ross joined her, she announced, "Oswald thinks we should travel together. Although I do not like it, she does point out some valid advantages."

Ross smiled at the bird, rubbed her breast feathers with the back of his finger, and commented, "Oh she does, does she? What if I don't want to come with you?"

"Oswald says you will agree."

Smile fading, his eyes darted from Oswald to Jay. *You are one very irritating woman,* he thought. Disconnected from his reason, Ross' mouth answered, "I wouldn't want to disappoint your bird."

As she fastened the pack straps, she added aloofly, "Oswald says you look at me a lot. She thinks you want to mate with me."

Ross' face flushed slightly. "I'd rather mate with a wooly mammoth."

"They are extinct," Jay informed him, then started forward.

Chapter 8

They traveled for the remainder of the afternoon, finally stopping at a more modern, Adirondack type, three-sided, log shelter. Considering the acquisition of a trail companion to be a special event, Ross heated freeze-dried spaghetti and meatballs for their dinner. The invitation to accompany her aside, her inclination for friendly conversation had not improved. Not only had it not improved, it did not exist.

After finishing his meal, he decided he would attempt to extract some verbiage from her by example. Searching for some interesting topic, he gazed around the camp until a sugar maple tree caught his eye. "Did you know it takes forty to fifty gallons of sap from a maple tree to get just one single gallon of maple syrup?"

"No," she responded with disinterest.

He felt a quick chill, either a result of the falling temperature or Jay's icy response. Stubbornly, he tried again. "There's an old Vermont saying that states: 'A Vermont year is nine months winter and three months poor sleddin'.'"

She glanced at him blankly, obviously immune to his sense of humor.

"That's supposed to be funny," he explained.

"I see."

While she stared down at the ground, seemingly preoccupied in deep internal thought, Ross studied her. He wondered why, despite her aloofness, he enjoyed being near her. True, he appreciated her physical attractiveness more than he did initially, but he could not identify much in her character to like, yet he did. Moreover, how had she sensed he watched her more often than he cared to admit? The probable explanation was a clairvoyant ability that many women were said to have when it came to men. That belief originated from secondhand accounts by other men and from reading material since Ross' infrequent experiences with women had not exposed him to the talent. It made him feel as if his soul was naked in her presence.

Her eyes moved up to his, causing him to look away. A porcupine waddled into view, its body rocking side to side with each step. He picked up a small stone and tossed it several feet in front of the animal. The quills rose, revealing the underlying brown, white tipped hair and pinkish skin. It swiveled with little hops of its hind feet and brought its tail in front of its belly. "Porcupines have approximately 30,000 quills. Did you know they're a member of the rodent family?"

"Erethizon dorsatum, yes."

"Are you a zoologist or something like that? Are you doing research?"

Her violet-blue eyes looked through his, communicating her unwillingness to answer.

"You know, you could at least treat me as if I was human."

"I am," she countered then retreated to her sleeping bag.

* * *

Jay's gregariousness did not improve the next day. She set a blistering pace, walking in long strides and maintaining a distance varying between fifteen to twenty-five feet in front of her male companion. Each time Ross made an effort to close the gap, she conveniently picked up her pace, so he resigned himself to his lagging position and thereby prevented Jay from escalating her gait to a full run. Oswald spent increasing durations on Ross' shoulder. He welcomed the owl's company, talking incessantly to the bird, which appeared to be almost as interested in the conversation as Ross, sometimes returning sounds that were like a plaintive whinny. He easily understood how Jay could imagine hearing the pet talk, since he began to consider the feathered passenger as an intelligent friend. The occasions Oswald was not on Ross' shoulder, she was flying ahead along the trail or sometimes off to the sides, disappearing into the forest for fifteen to twenty minutes at a stretch.

Once, when they approached three oncoming hikers, Jay slowed to walk by Ross' side while Oswald departed for the security of the treetops. Jay remained silently at his side as Ross exchanged pleasantries with the strangers, then when the three were out of sight she increased the length of her strides until she was again fifteen feet ahead.

During their stop for lunch at a lush green meadow bordered by birch, maple, and a small mountain lake, Jay treated Ross to another curious behavior. She withdrew a black plastic, one-inch wide band from her supplies and positioned it on her forehead so that it wrapped around her head. When he asked about the purpose of the headband, thinking cheap jewelry to be out of character, she only stared into his eyes, indicating she was not about to enlighten him.

After eating her meal, she rose and strolled down to the lake's edge, some five hundred feet away. Ross shared his trail bar with Oswald while he watched Jay disrobe completely save the headband, and wade into the water. "She is beautiful," he murmured to Oswald. "I wish I could help her solve her problem, whatever it is. You know, dear bird, I know why she agreed to have me tag along. It's obvious by the way she behaved when we came across those other hikers this morning. She's using me. I'm just here for appearances so she won't run into any more men harboring evil thoughts for a lone female. Funny, I don't care."

Oswald warbled a few notes.

"I know there's a warm, caring person hidden beneath that hard shell, otherwise she wouldn't have you for a friend, would she?"

Oswald gave a haunting, short, trebling call, bringing a smile to Ross' face.

"It doesn't make sense, does it? I don't know anything about her yet she is important to me. Marsha is going to be very upset when she finds out I've been off in the woods alone with another woman. She'll suspect me of some torrid love affair, but she'll forgive me. But I really don't give a damn what Marsha thinks. She also wants to use me, although for different reasons."

Oswald emitted a piercing noise.

"Be quiet. She'll think I'm hurting you."

Oswald blew him a soothing, musical note.

"I didn't know talking about Marsha would upset you. I won't mention her again. God what a touchy bird."

Ross' attention went back to Jay's body, glistening in the bright sunlight as she emerged from the water. "You don't think I'm falling for her, do you?"

Oswald flew at his head.

"Hey, don't worry, I won't touch her," he said, laughing. "She's too young. I like blonds. And besides, she hates me."

Once Jay dressed and started across the meadow, Oswald flew off to greet her. Feeling dirty and sweaty, Ross decided to follow Jay's example, and walked past her just as she reached their camp. Upon arriving at the shore, he looked back. He could see Jay busily putting away cooking utensils. Glad she was not looking his way, he stripped facing the lake. Being far more modest than his companion, he avoided turning his body even slightly toward the camp as he stepped into the lake. Each inch of skin touched by the icy, clear water stung as he slowly entered. When the water reached thigh level, he decided to forgo the slow torture and dove in. The frigid liquid instantly shocked his body. That sensation soon dissipated, replaced by a refreshing escape from the day's heat. Again, a reminder of Jay's personality poked into his head.

He repeatedly swam under the surface, thoroughly enjoying the invigorating elixir the lake provided. As numbness spread into his extremities, he stood in chest high water and turned toward shore, surprised to see Jay sitting on the grass at the water's edge, his clothes in her lap and Oswald on her shoulder. Since she had been in various stages of nakedness in his company before, and had not even hinted that he should look away, Ross reluctantly walked center stage out of the water. He felt on display as he sauntered up the short distance to where she sat; and she certainly did not help matters when he saw her eyes appraising his body, without a glimmer of approval.

She casually handed him his clothes and asked, "Ready to leave?"

"A-a-sh-sh-ure," he shivered the words and with unusual speed began pulling on his clothes.

* * *

Jay again set a swift tempo during the afternoon, Ross occasionally losing sight of her on the twisting sections of trail that were becoming more common. Frequently, he would break into a jog in order to close the gap. He called out to her on a few occasions to slow down. As was typical, she never acknowledged his pleas. It was as though he did not exist. Oswald disappeared into the forest ahead for periods of time, always returning to Ross' shoulder for more one-way conversation.

They entered a white birch stand an hour before sunset. He marveled at how a faint orange hue painted the white bark with the changing light. Ross, his concentration on the beautiful colors, bumped into Jay's back, causing her to stumble forward.

"You are not a careful person," Jay declared.

"You stopped in the middle of the trail," Ross defended. He looked passed her and saw the wide, fast moving river ahead. "The trail goes to the right, following the bank," he told her.

Oswald jumped into the air, flapped her wings, and disappeared into the forest on the far side of the water. She returned in minutes, landing on her master's shoulder.

"The trail continues on the other side," Jay stated.

Ross stared at the two, shook his head, and then took out his GPS. Studying the map, he reported, "The trail crosses the river about two miles downstream, then back up along the other bank to a point across from here. How did you know that?"

"It is only logical."

"If you say so, but it doesn't matter," Ross commented, wondering if Oswald's flight across the river related to her logic. "We can cover a little more ground and set up camp."

"We cross here," said Jay.

Watching branches of various sizes race by in the rain-swollen water, he said, "I think it's too dangerous. And we don't know how deep it is."

"I think it is no higher than my waist. It will save a minimum of two hours."

Oswald sounded a short trill, as if signaling agreement.

Ross looked again. The river was only about three car lengths across, but he could see no visible evidence of depth. "Trust me Jay, it's a bad idea."

"I will cross here," she declared. "I no longer need your company."

Looking at her face and hair, both highlighted by the reds of the setting sun, his shoulders slumped. "Lead the way, fair maiden."

"What is a 'fair maiden'?" she asked.

"Really not important. Let's do this."

Her eyes took on a humorless squint, a look he had witnessed before with the store clerk and waitress in town. "Did you call me a bad name?"

Oswald flapped her wings, glaring intently at him.

"I swear that bird understands English. No Jay, it's actually a phrase that expresses fondness."

"I see," she said, her expression relaxing. She turned and stepped into the water.

Shrugging his shoulders, Ross moved the items in his pockets into a compartment high on his pack, and followed.

"Hey, try to keep your gun dry," he shouted.

"That is of no concern," she answered.

"No, really it's not . . ."

Cutting him off, she stated, "I do not have ammunition for it."

"Son of a bitch. All this time it was unloaded?"

"I did not wish to harm anyone," she said.

The water near the bank was calm, but the force of the current became very evident within several steps. The river bottom was slick, being comprised of stones of varying sizes covered by a layer of silt. As the level rose higher and higher on his legs, he found the temperature cold, but his skin adjusting quickly.

Reaching midway, the current increased, but they managed it with careful foot placement. They both evaded floating forest deadfall successfully, easily avoiding the potential menaces by constantly surveying upstream. Jay, only a couple feet ahead, never checked for his presence. *Not exactly the model hiking buddy,* he thought. "How's it going up there?" he called.

She did not respond, but Oswald, still perched on Jay's shoulder, swiveled her head toward him, blowing a soft, haunting note.

The water rose to a level just below his waist just as Jay predicted. A smile formed on his lips.

Something below the surface caught Ross' right hip. The murky image of huge grey mass stretched above him. He was underwater. He held his breath and pawed at the log compressing his chest, working in desperation to push free. His heels slid atop the slippery stones on the bottom as the current carried him downstream, preventing his feet from digging in to grip anything for leverage. His mind raced for a solution. Pressing up on the partially sunken log that pinned him, he attempted to gain clearance underneath to allow it to pass over. He could only manage an inch or two of additional space. Feeling the pressure of an obstacle against his side, he knew he was wedged between the log and a large limb on it. Ross tried a twisting motion, hoping to break free, but again his movements were constrained.

Desperation was beginning to morph into panic, his lungs crying out for air. When a hazy likeness of Jay's face manifested in front of him in the water, he knew his grip on consciousness was taking leave. The world became black.

* * *

Ross gazed up at the canopy of birch, their leaves and limbs aglow with the beauty only sunset can provide. His sight jumped to the movement over his body. Jay's face came into focus. Her mass of lustrous black hair was drenched and hanging limply in lazy waves alongside her cheeks. She breathed heavily. "You look like a drowned rat," he said.

"Was that also a show of affection?" she asked before an exhale.

"Just an observation. Thanks for saving me."

"I did what was necessary. You were slowing my progress."

Ross sat up, his eyes drawn to a small cut on her outer thigh. "Let me clean and bandage that and we can be on our way."

Jay looked down to her leg injury. "You wish to touch me again?"

Ross laughed.

* * *

Sipping his hot chocolate, he watched Jay over the rim of his cup through the rising steam. Hands tucked behind her head, she lay gazing up at the jeweled night sky while moonlight bathed her face with glowing white. She looked stunning.

"The stars are pretty," she spoke softly.

Ross hesitated, not believing she had actually said something to him that conveyed sentiment, atypical of her usual flat statement. Anxious to seize the opportunity, he answered somewhat hurriedly, "Yes they are."

"I have never had the chance to enjoy them prior to this night."

Ross looked up at the moon. "That is unfortunate. Nature has so much to offer. It kind of puts things in perspective. You begin to realize how insignificant the human race, this planet, and our solar system are in relation to the rest of the universe. Jay, just imagine how many other races are out there at this very second, their eyes looking at the very same stars as you and I."

Her eyes remaining affixed to the sky, she asked, "Why are you so kind to me?"

"I don't know. Look! A meteor. Did you see it?"

"What does love mean?"

"I don't know," he answered truthfully, knowing he never truly experienced the emotion. He looked at her face in the moonlight.

"I am confused."

"Why," he asked, finding pleasure in the sight of her eyes twinkling with the celestial lights.

"You say you do not know what love means, yet you plan to be with this woman, Marsha, and you are falling in love with me. It makes no sense."

Ross tried to recall mentioning Marsha to her, but could only remember bringing her up with Oswald earlier at the lake. "How did you get the ridiculous idea I was falling in love with you of all people. And, not that it's any of your business, but I have no plans to continue a relationship with Marsha."

"Is it not true?"

He swallowed the remaining quarter cup of chocolate, stretched, and announced, "I'm tired. I'm going to bed now. Goodnight Jay."

"Seems we share something in common. We both hide secrets inside."

Glancing at her as he stood, he thought he saw the side of her lips upturned in a contented smile, but concluded the apparition was due to illusions created by the poor lighting or wishful thinking.

Sleep settled over Ross only because of his physical tiredness and not as a result of any restful state of mind. Jay's question bothered him. What was the correct description of his attraction to her?

One nightmarish dream after another plagued his sleep, all including Jay in various roles, and most involving ugly injuries to her. Those horrors of his subconscious mind brought him to the brink of waking numerous times, so when daybreak did arrive, he found himself fatigued rather than rested.

By midday, Ross was about ripe for surrender and considered stopping to take a nap, reasoning he could always recover the lost time later. As if reading his mind, Oswald reappeared from the forest then swooped by only inches from his shoulder. "All right, all right, Oswald. I'll keep moving, but it's her fault I didn't have a good sleep. I dreamt that some awful things were going to happen to her."

Oswald screeched, his bill clapped, *click-click-click,* intermittently.

"Don't worry, I'll stick close to her beautiful tail. They are just dreams. I'm sure she'll be fine. Don't go worrying your feathers about her; let me do that. I wonder how the hell she got the idea I was beginning to fall for her? Go keep her company. Go on."

Oswald jumped and flew straight to her shoulder.

"I'll be damned," Ross muttered.

A few minutes later, the sound of helicopters shattered the serene forest silence. Ross jogged up to Jay and commented, "The ranger must have been wrong. The military was supposed to be searching far north of here, but maybe they found what they were looking for and are returning."

Jay froze in her tracks and stared at Ross. "What did he say they sought?"

Puzzled by the frightened expression on her face, he answered, "Rumors were some new top secret missile, or something like that. I think. Official story was that they are conducting maneuvers."

Two helicopters came into view through the red pine above them. Their paths indicated they were not returning to the south but were moving in a large circular pattern.

Ross relayed his opinion of that to Jay.

She instantly turned to the trail and started forward at an even greater rate than before.

"What's the hurry?" Ross called out to deaf ears. As he followed, a thought struck home for the first time; she had to be mixed up in the military operation, otherwise, why had she reacted to the sight of the helicopters in both instances with a sense of urgency? And she had displayed emotion. Only two events seemed to elicit emotion of any significance. Once concerning Oswald, and now the alarm she had plainly shown toward the aircraft. Putting his emotional attachment to her aside, he knew he should not trust her. The whole mysterious cloud that shrouded her supported his logical deduction that she could not be trusted, at least not without further explanations about who she was, and what she was doing out here.

Unexpectedly, she slowed, thereby allowing him to join her. Oswald flew off into the trees. As they walked a distance of a few feet together, he saw the reason for her abrupt permissiveness. A soldier wearing a Green Mountain Boys National Guard patch stood imposingly in the center of the trail, an M16 held diagonally across his chest.

When near enough, Ross called, "Hello."

The man waited until they reached him, and then responded, "Hello. Sorry, but no one is permitted beyond this point. Military maneuvers."

"I'm a botany professor and was planning to do some important research just north of here. A ranger told me you fellows were operating much further north."

"Sorry, no exceptions."

"All this for nothing. Incidentally, the ranger said there were rumors about you looking for some kind of missile."

"Sorry for the inconvenience, sir," was the canned reply.

"I understand. You're not free to discuss it. If you're interested, I found this weird canister back along the trail."

In unison, both Jay and the man looked at him, surprise registering in their wide eyes, indicating that both happened to be very interested in his find. The man stepped away and spoke into his walkie-talkie. He chatted with the receiver only a short time before turning his eyes directly on the pair of hikers. When he returned, he requested information from the two, specifically about the canister. Ross gave his name, address, university, and outline of his research trip, a description of the object he found and its location.

The soldier wrote furiously while Ross talked, then nodded to Jay. "What about you?"

Ross smiled inwardly and thought, *This ought to be good.*

"Jay Jay. I am a student. I am at the same address as the professor."

The soldier grinned widely, jotted a few words down on paper, and then said, "I understand. Just a little research, hey professor?" Satisfied, he stepped away again and read from his pad into the radio.

"Why did you not inform me of the object you found?" Jay asked in a whisper.

"You didn't seem interested in anything concerning me. Why would I think you would be interested in that? Why are you interested? And, why did you lie about who you are? What are you hiding?"

She gazed off into the trees.

The soldier returned smiling. "HQ said we should give you two a ride to the other side of the off-limits area. Follow me."

"Great!" Ross rejoiced, believing his luck was changing.

"A lift is unnecessary," Jay objected.

"What's with her?" the soldier asked Ross, trying to get a fix on this unconventional woman.

Ross took her aside out of earshot of the soldier. "Jay, they won't give you a choice," he explained in a low voice.

"I will follow," she said.

* * *

They came upon a small clearing concurrent with the arrival of the helicopter. "What about Oswald?" Ross nearly shouted in Jay's ear above the roar of the engine as they climbed into the fuselage.

"She will find me," Jay assured him.

Their ride was disappointing to Ross because they could see nothing other than the stark interior of their transportation. Only minutes after ascending, they felt the aircraft descend. Ross thanked the pilot and stepped down into a marshy field. The helicopter vanished above the trees and Oswald flew into view minutes later.

"I think we should camp here tonight," Jay suggested.

"But we have a good three hours of daylight left. I thought you wanted to move fast."

"I am tired. You are tired. It would be best if we rested."

Although her concern for their rest struck him as being peculiar, he agreed. He erected his tent on a high section of dry ground, and she hers. While she stretched out in her tent, resting, Ross played with Oswald until darkness, and then crawled into his tent. He shed his outer clothing and lay in his sleeping bag, leaving the zipper partially open to admit cool night air into the over-efficient, insulated cocoon. Confident in a better night's sleep than the prior evening, he closed his eyes, and relaxed to the nocturnal chorus of owls and crickets and cicadas until he heard a zipper sliding from the direction of Jay's tent. As he strained to pick out additional sounds, he nearly jumped out of his bag when the zipper of his own tent slid all the way open.

His eyes registered only blackness, but his ears heard a disembodied, "Ross?"

Wondering how she had managed to move so easily in the darkness, he asked, "What is it Jay?"

He heard something that sounded like material sliding on the tent floor, and then felt a puff of air as a sleeping bag was placed beside his. "It is me," she stated as if eliminating twenty other possible candidates who might have snuck in his accommodation.

"What are you doing?" he inquired, while she slipped into her bag. He heard her zip it closed.

"I do not have adequate space," she complained, ignoring the query. "Move please."

"Jay, what are you doing here?" he repeated.

"I have decided to sleep with you," she stated matter-of-factly. "Please provide more space."

Ross wriggled in his bag toward the nylon wall, creating at least a foot of additional room. Jay squirmed in her bag, closing the gap between them until he could feel the length of her body lightly against his through the shells of both sleeping bags. "Are you comfortable now?" he asked a little sarcastically.

"Yes, I am content," she answered, her face only inches from his.

"Good. Now why are you here in my tent, not in yours, laying next to me?"

"Because I decided to . . ."

"'. . . sleep with you'," he finished her sentence. "But why did you decide to sleep with me? You have been keeping your distance until now. What changed?"

"Oswald thinks it is best."

"I see," Ross said, almost laughing aloud. "So, what now?"

"I do not understand your inquiry," she said, obviously confused.

"Do you want to talk about something, or did you want . . ."

"I do not wish to converse with you," she interrupted. She was silent for a few moments, and then added as if reaching a revelation, "I will not tolerate your touching me in a sexual manner. I am not here for mating."

"I see," Ross commented, struggling to maintain composure.

"I wish only to be near you," she finally confessed.

Emotionally touched by her simple declaration, he whispered, "Goodnight, Jay."

She did not reply and closed her eyes.

Ross fell asleep to the sound of Jay's gentle, restful breathing, and the sensation of the warm, moist air from her nose.

Chapter 9

The brilliance of the sun shining through the tent walls made opening his eyes a difficult task. Reaching to his side, he discovered Jay's bag empty. He struggled to keep his eyelids open enough to squint at his wristwatch. Alarmed to find it already late morning, he scrambled from the sleeping bag and quickly dressed.

His eyes scoured the surrounding field, and upon not finding her, assumed she had returned to her tent. Appreciative of her company the night before, he thought he would surprise her with a warm, hearty breakfast.

The coffee hot, and one pancake ready, he called her name. When she did not answer, he walked to her tent and peeked through the mesh. Disappointment set in at the sight of bare fabric floor. Thinking she might be out for a morning walk, his mind eased until he noticed her backpack missing.

He began circling the tent at a distance that put him in the soggy, marshy field. He stepped very slowly, searching the ground for any impressions made by her rugged hiking shoes. Soon he found what he was looking for and after further tracking, determined she had departed in a south-eastern direction. The choice of that direction meant she had planned to intercept Long Trail for southern travel, a direction leading back to the military quarantined area.

This latest turn of events only confirmed what he already expected. Jay must be a foreign agent whose objective involved finding whatever the government sought before they did. Her unwillingness to reveal her identity, her interest in the helicopters, her disregard for the value of her personal possessions, her distrust of others, her desire to be alone, her odd usage of the English language, and her gun, all of which taken together, did not spell Mary Poppins. Although he anticipated something like this sooner or later, he felt cheated it was not later.

He broke camp, his mood to travel to the area specified for his research gone. Sitting in the shade of an oak tree, he stared out over the area, reprimanding himself for allowing the woman get to him. He stayed in that state for hours, feeling worse than he had overhearing Marsha brag about using him to her friend.

"Well, my mother warned me about picking up strays," he said bitterly to the Monarch butterfly fluttering in the sunlight on a weed a short distance away. A shadow raced over the butterfly, causing it to flee. Looking up for the source of the shadow, Ross saw Oswald soaring above. He leaped to his feet, rushed out into the field, waving his arms and shouting the bird's name.

Oswald banked, and then glided toward Ross. Expecting his friend to land on his shoulder in the traditional manner, he stopped and waited, but the owl did not follow the script. Instead, she hung midair to his right, flapping her wings furiously to maintain her position in space. Slowly, Ross interpreted her request and extended his right arm. Oswald perched instantly. "What's this all about my lady? Where is Jay?"

The bird's large eyes trained on his.

"Just drop by to say farewell?"

Oswald gave a short call.

"You know how I feel about her don't you?"

Without provocation, she gripped his wrist tightly with her claws, breaking the skin lightly and, flapping her wings, pulled his arm forward.

Confused, Ross only stared at Oswald.

She stopped flapping, then folded her wings and again called.

"You're behaving strangely."

She repeated the same routine.

"What are you up to?"

Again, she tugged on his arm.

"Do you want me to follow?"

She gave a chilly descending whinny.

"Lead the way."

As if answering, Oswald flew across the field, and landed on the trail. Knowing owls were not in the habit of landing on the ground where they were most vulnerable to enemies, he ran. Oswald remained standing on the dirt footpath until he arrived, then flew and hovered to his right. Ross extended his arm immediately this time. Oswald tugged south. "Are you bringing me to Jay?"

She screeched.

"My God, is she hurt?"

Oswald's answer echoed through the trees. She jumped from his arm and shot into the air. Ross ran in pursuit of the fast-moving bird, but soon lost sight of her. Although now separated from his feathered guide, he continued to move with all the speed he could muster. Trees streaked by as he kept his eyes glued to the trail ahead. His legs and lungs pumped rhythmically for twenty minutes while the fears of having already passed Jay threatened to undermine his obsession to run faster.

His eyes picked up something ahead on the trail, causing him to slow, and then halt. Breathing heavily, he bent over, put his hands on his knees and read the large sign suspended above the center of the trail by florescent orange, nylon cords tied to a red pine on one side, and a white birch on the other.

LONG TRAIL CLOSED TEMPORARILY
U.S. GOVERNMENT TEST AREA
TRESPASSERS WILL BE SUBJECT TO ARREST
OR PERSONAL INJURY

Oswald glided onto the sign, causing it to swing back and forth. But before Ross could catch his breath well enough to speak, she returned to the air and again disappeared down the trail behind the sign, confirming that Jay had violated the quarantined area. He grasped the risk a trespasser, like Jay, takes for crossing into a restricted section. The consequences could be severe and, although unwilling to think about it, possibly lethal. He ducked under the sign to enter the off-limits zone.

He walked a short distance before meeting the soldier on duty guarding that section of trail.

"Can't you read?" welcomed the soldier.

"I'm looking for a woman," Ross offered in explanation.

"Aren't we all," he wisecracked with a sneer. "Now turn around like a good little man and get the hell out of here before I lock you up."

"No, you don't understand, I'm looking for a friend. Her name is Jay. I think she may have wandered into your restricted area. Has anyone seen her?"

"Hold on . . ." he said impatiently, raising his walkie-talkie. "This is Macroy on north trail entrance. I got a guy here that says he's looking for some girl. Says she's lost. Name's Jay." The man tapped his toe on the dirt; his eyes remained fixed on Ross. After an interminable wait, he snapped to attention and began nodding, repeating, "Yes, sir . . . yes, sir . . ." After his final, "Yes, sir," he lunged out and grabbed Ross' arm roughly. "You're coming with me."

"Did they find her?"

"Just come along quietly so I don't have to get physical."

As Ross walked in front of his escort, he caught occasional glimpses of his guardian angel flying overhead at treetop level. His attempts to extract information regarding Jay were met with, "Shut up and keep moving," so he eventually stopped trying.

They trudged a lengthy distance along a narrow path until they stepped into a clearing. The fallen, freshly cut trees scattered around the area indicated it had been cleared only days ago. Ross winced at the needless devastation to a good size piece of forest. The reason for the destruction became apparent when he saw three small helicopters, and one large, twin rotor, cargo helicopter sitting on the cleared ground. Incredibly, a fairly large, one-story, white prefabricated building sat amongst the low-cut tree stumps at the far end of the clearing. "So this is the government's idea of camping in the woods?"

The soldier nudged him toward the building. Just outside the front entrance the guard told Ross to stay put, then opened the flimsy aluminum door and shouted, "He's here, Major." After closing it, he stood at attention aside Ross. The door swung open moments later, and a square jawed, fiftyish looking face appeared.

"Barton?"

Ross nodded.

"Thought you'd come after her. Come in."

Knowing Jay was there nearly brought lightness to his step, and he smiled inwardly. The coolness of the air-conditioned building struck him as the military officer led him down a short hall, then into an eight-by-ten office. The major sat behind a portable table, then motioned him to a folding chair. Ross sat gawking at the three computer display screens arranged in a partial circle facing the major. A jungle of electrical cords flowed from the table, across the floor, and into a hole at the base of an interior wall.

"You've seen Jay?" Ross asked, partially dazzled by all he had seen in the last ten minutes.

"How are you mixed up in this?"

Ross' forehead wrinkled. "In what?"

"Don't play games Barton."

"Major, I'm confused. I just want to know what happened to Jay."

"Why?"

"She's my friend."

"Okay, let's start at the beginning." He stood to gaze through the small plastic windowpane. "How long have you known her?"

"A few days."

"She said she lives with you."

"A little lie."

"Why did she lie?" the major asked, turning to face Ross.

"I don't know."

"Why didn't you tell the guard that she was lying?"

"I didn't think it was important."

"What's her last name?"

"I don't know," Ross answered, embarrassed by how foolish his responses must sound to someone in the major's position. Attempting to recover his dignity, he described the sequence of events that brought him here, from his initial incident with her, to her disappearance. He omitted Oswald.

The major shook his head disbelievingly, then yelled, "And you didn't think her actions were just a little suspect?" holding his thumb and forefinger a little apart in front of Ross' nose as emphasis.

"Yes I did, but I guess I didn't want to believe she was mixed up in something illegal until she headed back here."

"My God, you are gullible!"

"You're right Major. I don't know what to say. Could I ask some questions now?"

"I buy your whole ridiculous story, particularly because you seemed to be trying to help by telling us about the thing you found, but we'll need to check you out before you leave."

"Understandable."

"Okay, Barton, shoot. What're your questions?"

"Is she here?"

Before answering, the major sat, produced a cigar, and began the ritual of lighting it: smell, lick, light, lift and puff. "Yeah, she's here," he said, nonchalantly placing his hands behind his head.

"What is she mixed up in? Is she a foreign agent?"

"Oh, we know what she wants. Same thing we're looking for. Don't really know how anyone outside our government found out about it, but there are always leaks. Bastards. Who she's working for, we don't know. Won't say a word."

"What are you looking for?"

"Classified," he answered, then leaned back leisurely to study the billowing ring of smoke from his last puff.

Something about the major's casual attitude struck Ross as arrogant.

"The object I reported finding to your guard . . . is that connected to all of this?"

"Classified," the major again answered and duplicated his previous smoke performance.

"What will you do with her?"

"Depends. Classified."

"Could I see her?"

The major brought his eyes slowly from the rising smoke, placed the cigar in an ashtray, and then leaned on his elbows. "Do you have a thing for this girl?"

"I just want to say goodbye."

"Jesus, Barton, being a professor and in your thirties, you ought to know better than get hooked on a young thing like her. Face it. She used you."

"I know. Can I see her?"

"That can't be allowed," the major answered, his face beginning to show traces of sympathy.

Ross thinking to play on this man's self-importance, pleaded, "Come on Major, I can't hurt anything by just seeing her." He looked around the room, and added, "You are in command here and have this place under your complete control. You can't possibly fear anything from me, can you?"

"Shit, you're pathetic." Picking his cigar up again, he shoved it into his mouth, leaned back and grinned like he was the reigning king over a realm of ignorant peasants. "As soon as we clear your story, I'll let you see the bitch."

* * *

Ross sat in a barren, windowless eight-by-eight holding room for nearly two hours before the major returned.

"You're everything you say you are Professor. You're free to go."

"Jay?"

"Oh yeah, you wanted to see her before you go. Really not worth the trip, but if it'll ease your mind . . . follow me."

They walked the full length of the central hallway, halting in front of a closed door on the left. The officer rapped his knuckles on the door, and shouted, "It's the major, Doc. The girl has a visitor."

Ross asked, "Is she hurt?" The door opened, answering his question. He stepped into the room behind the major and went into semi-shock when he saw the swollen and split lower lip, the bandaged right calf spotted with blood, the intravenous tube in her left forearm, and the glossy blank stare in her open eyes.

"Aaaaaa, she had a little accident," the major responded to his unspoken question. She wouldn't stop when one of my men spotted her. He shot her in the leg to slow her down. Just a graze. Lost a little blood, but she'll be all right. Aaaah, the lip. When they got to her, she fought them off like a wildcat. Had to subdue her. Doesn't look pretty, but it'll heal."

"Why is she staring at the ceiling like that?"

"Drugged," Doc informed him.

"Yeah," the major continued. "I told you that she won't say a word. We need to find out who she's working for and what she knows. You understand. National security."

Ross moved slowly to the stainless steel table she lay upon and looked into her eyes. "Hi, it's me."

Her eyes rolled to meet his. She blinked. He ran his eyes over the clothes she wore. His clothes. She blinked again, continuing to stare directly into his eyes. He wanted desperately to hold her. "Yes, I understand," he finally muttered, then added, "I've had enough. I'd like to leave now."

* * *

Sitting by his pack, he looked thoughtfully at the glowing red clouds that seemed to touch the summits of the distant mountains. The sun had sunk below the hills minutes ago but its light reached up to color the cloud undersides. They looked like thousands of small, fluffy cotton balls, blended together to form an expansive blanket covering the Earth. It was spectacular. His eyes moved to the field where his tent had been, and where Jay's remained. Recalling the completeness he felt with just the simple act of sleeping next to Jay, tears welled in his lower lids. He felt old, tired, and beaten. "How can people inflict such suffering on one another, always hiding behind a cause for an excuse?" he questioned. Did it make it justified in a country of individual freedom to hold a person against their will on the chance of wrongdoing? What happened to innocent until proven guilty? He thought these were basic principles of the United States pushed aside in the name of national security.

The stars flickered visibly in the darkening sky, which reminded him of the pleasure Jay showed when she momentarily stepped off her private treadmill and took the time to observe nature. Whatever her role in life, she certainly did not deserve what they had done, and were planning to do to her. One lone individual could not affect all the human suffering in the world, but he could try to do something about her particular case. He laughed at himself for his illogical compassion for this odd woman. Convinced she was innocent of any malice, his mind focused on her rescue. He had no idea why he was so certain about her integrity as a person, but doubt about her vanished like a mist with the rising sun.

Guessing the use of Long Trail would quickly terminate his crusade to right one wrong, he chose a point approximately one hundred yards from the trail and moved into the trees, heading south. It did not take long before he learned that hiking shoes equated to undesirable noise, and so he removed them, tied the laces together and slung them over his shoulder. Once his eyes adjusted to the darkness he was surprised by the amount of lighting the moon provided for picking his way through the trees. Although the moon made his travel through the woods easier than anticipated, he knew its light would increase the risk of his being spotted when he reached the government's base of operation. Because of the necessity for silent travel, Ross moved with caution, frequently checking his GPS to prevent straying in the wrong direction.

He felt great relief when he located lights in the distance through the pines. Automatically, he assumed a crouching position and crept forward. When he reached the edge of the tree line, his concern about the moonlight became unnecessary since the white building and surrounding area were bathed in brilliant artificial light. Glancing at his wristwatch, he saw it was nearly midnight; therefore, most of the soldiers should be asleep.

Remaining in the cover of the woods, Ross moved to a position closest to the corner of the building he thought housed Jay. The location of the two windows on the walls of the corner room seemed to be in the same area he remembered from the inside. He knew that if wrong, he would end up under lock and key in minutes, but since that likelihood was high anyway, he whispered, "What the hell," and concentrated on one of those windows as his target. He wondered whether he should run across the 150 feet of cleared, lighted ground or crawl. He opted for the run, wanting to get it over with.

He took one last look at the area, saw no one, and launched himself into the clearing. A third of the way to the building his peripheral vision caught a movement to his right and he dove to the ground. After a few minutes of tense waiting for the moment of discovery he was sure was imminent, he carefully raised his head. A soldier sat on a stump near the front of the building. Ross would be in line of sight until only a few feet from the window. He dropped his face back down to the fresh, aromatic earth and began slithering forward. The floodlights offered no opportunity for cover; he was completely exposed to anyone who happened to gaze in his direction. But perhaps, from the perspective of the sitting soldier, he had some camouflage if he continued to hug the rough ground and made no sound. If the soldier chose to stand, however, all bets were off. Perspiration dotted his face as he inched forward. His arms and legs began to tremble, anticipating discovery.

Miraculously, he made the wall undetected. He paused in brief celebration, and then stood. The window was higher than he had estimated; he could just about touch the bottom of the plastic pane with his fingertips. Thanking the gods for small favors, he reminded himself that at least there were no interior lights on. The height of the window, without aid, became another obstacle. He wondered if they would loan him a stepladder.

He slumped down to the ground, his back supported by the wall beneath the window. Self-pity and defeat, not easy emotions for him to accept, took over. That is, until he sensed movement at his back connected to his breathing. With each repeated deep breath, he felt the wall shift. He twisted around and pushed with both hands. It became clear that in order to keep the transportation weight of their head-quarters to a minimum, the unit had been constructed utilizing paper-thin sheets of aluminum. Ross turned, kneeling toward the wall, and drew a large camp knife from the sheath attached to the back of his belt. He placed the point in contact with the wall, pushed, then grinned as the blade sank through. He rocked the razor sharp cutting edge of the knife while applying pressure down on it. Amazingly, the ultra thin metal sheet parted under the blade. The crude hole he managed to cut in the wall was not exactly a work of art, but Ross looked at it pridefully. Cautiously, he poked his head into the opening, relieved to find the room completely dark as hoped. The absence of lighting in the room hinted he probably chose the correct one. Either that or someone inside was waiting in ambush for him to consummate the trespass.

Slowly, he crawled through the small opening and onto the floor, then moved away from the area lit by the hole in the violated wall. He sat, straining his vision to see something beyond the lighted patch of floor. Unable to discern anything, he stood on his bare feet and moved to the nearly inaudible sound of faint breathing. A horizontal, smooth metal edge contacted the front of his thighs causing him to halt abruptly.

He reached his hand forward with a series of start and stop movements, almost fearing what his sense of touch might reveal. Ross froze when he contacted something that felt like cloth. Pushing aside his nervousness, he flattened his slightly trembling hand against the object, beads of sweat dropping into his eyes, stinging them. His tongue dried. He allowed a brief smile to form on his lips when he felt the small, firm bump pressing the center of his palm. Definitely female.

He groped until he found her head, then lowered his mouth to her ear. "Jay," he whispered directly into it.

She moaned loudly.

Ross instantly placed his fingers over her mouth. "Shhh. It's Ross. Be quiet."

Her head rolled toward him and he lowered his ear to her mouth. "Did you come to mate with me?" she whispered with slurred speech as her hot, moist breath tickled his ear.

"No Jay, not now," he told her, dismayed that she remained under the influence of drugs. "I came to get you out of here. You're going to have to walk. Please try."

Her mind seemed to clear a little and she rolled her head to him again and said, "I will try. Ross, get my equipment, I will need it."

"Let's just get you out of here and I'll buy you a new backpack."

"Ross, please. There are some important items."

"Okay, okay, be right back." Taking a penlight from his pocket, he began a search of the room. He returned within minutes, not surprised they had seized her backpack, leaving only her headband behind. "It's all I could find."

"We must find the rest of my things."

"Jay, we'll be lucky to get us out of here. They must have your pack in another room."

"But you do not understand . . ."

He silenced her by putting a finger over her lips. "Sorry, we'll see what we can do later. Right now let's get you out of here."

Accepting Ross' conditions, she sat up and slid her legs from the table. She paused for a moment before standing, then wavered, and collapsed onto the floor.

"You're not making this easy," Ross complained. Kneeling, he put his arm under her armpit and hoisted her up. He could see her legs teetering uncontrollably and knew she would be of little help. Supporting as much of her weight as he could, he brought her to the wall hole, sat her on the floor, and then backed through the opening. Once outside, he reached in, gripped her ankles, and pulled her out by her legs. He removed her shoes, laced them together, and tiptoed away from the building. When he saw the soldier no longer sitting on the stump or anywhere in sight, he darted back to Jay. He put both pairs of shoes over his shoulder, put his arm around her and said, "Time to go."

She nodded with exaggerated motions, and then slurred, "I am ready." They moved into the cleared area, Jay trying desperately to walk, but soon Ross was practically dragging her feet across the ground.

Suddenly a "Hey you, stop!" rang out, shattering the night stillness. In a speedy series of maneuvers, Ross wrestled her onto his back. Once he got her legs around his hips, he ran.

"God you're heavy," he said to his bouncing burden as his legs strained to move faster while trying not to buckle under the load nearly equal in mass to his own. They reached the tree line just as a shot reverberated from behind. Fifty feet into the forest, Ross realized capture would come quickly unless he came up with something more ingenious than simply running away. He veered sharply to the right, running in a path parallel to the trees that bordered the government clearing. When they obtained a position on the edge of the clearing across from the wall adjacent to the one he had cut through, he stopped, lowering Jay to the ground.

He watched as three soldiers ran into the woods where he and Jay had first entered. Several men fanned out across the area to their helicopters. Sounds of turbine engines filled the air as the rotors of two of the helicopters began spinning.

Ross looked into Jay's eyes.

She said, "Probability of escape is not high, is it?"

Chapter 10

"Put your shoes on," Ross instructed.

"Got a plan?"

"More or less," he answered, his eyes directed to a rising helicopter. He gently touched her cheek and said, "Wait here. I should be back in a few minutes. If not . . . well . . . good luck."

"What are you going to do?"

"Hijack a helicopter. Since I was a kid, I've always wanted to fly one of those things, so I've been taking lessons. Let's hope I'm good enough to fly this one."

"You never answered my question," Jay said, her voice still showing traces of the drug.

"What question?"

"Are you falling in love with me?" she asked, her head swaying.

Avoiding her eyes, he said, "The drug should be wearing off soon."

"Why are you doing this for me?"

"You haven't hurt anyone. It's wrong for them to treat you as if you were some kind of hunted animal."

"I see."

"Wish me luck."

She closed her eyes and gently kissed him, then asked, "Did I do that properly?"

He touched her damaged lip. "Yes, thank you."

Leaping to his feet, his eyes swept across the clearing. Committing to the plan, Ross launched towards the building. As he rounded its corner at full speed, he saw a pilot climbing into a nearby Black Hawk with its turbines already running. Lowering his head, he pumped his legs and arms faster, fully expecting to trip up and fall forward. But he did not.

He got to the aircraft's open door just as the pilot was positioning his headset. Ross reached in, latched onto the man's arm and yanked him out onto the ground. The shocked pilot, disconnected headset still in place, stared in total disbelief as Ross jumped in, closed the door and twisted the throttle control. A shot zinged up through the floor behind his seat as he flew only a few feet above the building's roof. Once clear of the structure, he quickly descended to a spot near the edge of the clearing, swinging the chopper around so the passenger door faced the woods. He waited, anxiously squeezing the cyclic stick while Jay struggled valiantly to stay on her feet and run to him. She stumbled and fell twice, managing to get to her feet each time, but after the third fall, she lay helplessly on the ground, her arms lacking the strength to lift her torso.

"Oh shit," Ross cried above the boisterous aircraft, then scrambled out the door. He was to her in four long strides. With great effort, he scooped her up, carried her to the awaiting helicopter, and slid her into the passenger seat. He jumped over her to his seat, twisted the throttle, and pulled the collective lever. When he reached treetop level, he moved the stick forward just as another bullet passed in through the side window and out the front bubble.

Once far enough to be protected by the forest below, Jay shouted, "I am sorry. My coordination is poor."

"Not your fault, it's what those bastards put in you," he yelled to be heard above the noise. "I wish I could see better. I'd like to stay just above the trees, but the moon doesn't give enough light and I'll probably run into some stupid sequoia."

Swaying slightly side to side, she corrected, "Sequoias are not native to this region."

Ross shook his head.

Jay sat tall to look through the bubble and said, "Go ahead, fly low. I can guide you."

Ross glanced questioningly at the intent, strange woman to his right. Sensing his apprehension, she explained, "I have extraordinary night vision. Trust me."

"Trust . . . you?" he challenged, although simultaneously thinking that while it was true she had told him some small untruths in the past, she never lied to him about anything important. She usually just refused to answer or ignored him completely.

He swung the helicopter to a due north heading, gradually dropping altitude until Jay called, "Level off." As was typical for her, she did not utter another word until a few moments later when she shouted, "Pull up," then after another lapse of seconds added, "Down," followed by, "Level."

Recognizing he would not have detected most of the tall trees in their path until too late to avoid them, her guidance bewildered him. "Have you always been able to see in the dark like this?"

"Always," she responded, keeping her sight on the speeding carpet of trees below.

Quickly glancing at her, he asked, "Why is that headband you're wearing so important?"

"I did not say it was important," she answered.

"Jay, what are you? Who are you? What am I doing here?"

"The field where we camped is directly ahead. Prepare to descend."

Ross could see Jay's yellow tent glowing dully in the moonlight and brought them down near it. Leaving the turbines running, he jumped out onto the soggy ground, and ran around to lift Jay from her seat. He lowered her as if handling a piece of fragile china. When her feet touched the earth and he was sure she could stand, Ross rushed over to recover the backpack he abandoned in the field. He threw it into the passenger seat and turned to face Jay. "I did what I wanted to do. You have a head start and a fair chance. My advice to you is to put this mess behind you and go home. Who knows, maybe you'll find some young man to mate with."

A surprised appearance came over her face. "Where are you going?"

"I'll get them off your trail, and then I'll turn myself in."

"I want you to come with me."

"No thank you lady, I've had enough of being a sap. I don't know what you and the government are searching for, but somehow I don't think I'd find it worth it. Good luck."

"But it is important," she argued. "I know you, and know you would agree."

"Then tell me, what is it?"

"I cannot tell you. You would not believe me."

"Try me," he shouted impatiently.

"No, trust me."

"Sorry, not this time."

"But you love me."

"Cocky, aren't you?"

"Ross, come with me," she pleaded.

"No."

She pressed her lips to his then said, "I will miss you."

He answered, "No you won't. Goodbye," and ran to the pilot's seat. As the helicopter rose into the air, he saw her standing in the same spot, buffeted by the artificial windstorm induced by the rotors. Angrily, he jerked the stick, thereby getting her comfortably out of sight. He ascended to a normal altitude, and moved southwest. Another helicopter, easily identified by its powerful searchlight underneath its carriage, passed off to his right. He flipped on his own lights, intending to draw the other's attention, but it maintained its flight path back toward the field he had just left.

Disgusted with his own inadequacy at playing decoy, he pushed the stick to the right and swung around in pursuit of the other chopper. When he arrived over the field, he found Jay standing motionless in the circle of light projected on the ground by the other helicopter. "She didn't move a God damn inch," he yelled at the dash. With knowing that instantaneous action was required in order to extract her from certain capture, he put the helicopter into a controlled free-fall. The application of full power near the ground did little to cushion the impact and the helicopter hit the ground with enough force to bend the landing struts, only the marshy soil preventing greater damage.

Ross launched himself through the door, hitting the ground already at a dead run. Jay snapped out of her daze and ran toward him. He latched onto her hand and then towed her to the whirling, idling machine. The other pilot, seeing all this, positioned his bird directly above them. Ross swore, pulled his pack from the helicopter, and dragged Jay into the forest. "What the hell's the matter with you?" he scolded as he pulled her along. "Why didn't you run? You just stood there."

"I do not know. I felt ill."

"Why the great recovery?"

"I do not understand it either," she said, perplexed.

Pausing for a breather, Ross looked behind and saw lights bobbing into the trees, followed by barking. "Dogs," he whispered. "We'd better find water soon or we're finished."

"Water?"

"So the dogs will lose our scent," he explained as they continued to dart among the trees. "Or you could go ahead and I could try to decoy them."

"Your last attempt to play decoy was not very effective. We stay together."

They continued running as Ross thought ahead to the future, wondering what would become of his life after the government got their hands on him. He could see it all: charges of trespassing, breaking and entering, aiding an enemy agent, and stealing a helicopter. A life in prison was a surety. He glanced back to see the lights advancing quickly. Then, between the barking dogs, another familiar sound reached his ears. He veered a little to the left, drawn intuitively to the noise. Soon he connected the sounds with that of running water, spurring him to move faster. Fortunately, the effects of the drug on Jay had almost completely dissipated and although she limped a little, she was able to match his pace. As they ran, the faint "sussshh" grew into a powerful roaring sound that soon drowned out the frenzied barking.

"Large outcrop of rocks ahead," Jay called to him.

He slowed to a jog. They broke out into an area void of trees, enabling Ross to see the rugged line of stone that rose about five feet. Without hesitation, they both reached for rocky edges with their hands and started climbing. Once at the top, they could see moonlight glisten off the churning water rushing through a large stone trough, approximately three feet wide. They scrambled down the irregular embankment to the edge. He marveled at the way the violent stream had cut its path in a saw tooth pattern, weaving back and forth, and changing direction every ten or so feet. He envisioned the centuries of erosion necessary to form such a formation, but the urgency of their circumstances necessitated foregoing any appreciation of the wonders of nature, and so he stepped in. Immediately the turbulent knee-deep water tugged at his legs, making standing difficult at best. As Jay joined him, he looked upstream and saw more of the same, but when he looked downstream, he watched the water disappear about fifty feet away.

"Must be a waterfall," he shouted above the din. "Wait here," he added, then climbed onto the opposite bank and ran into the woods. When he returned, he responded to the perplexed expression on Jay's face, "I wanted to leave my scent on the other side. It may confuse them a little." Lights shining through the tree branches above the rocks grew visible, causing Ross to again study upstream and downstream. Grabbing Jay's arm, he pointed to the downstream direction.

"That is dangerous," she said into his ear. "The other way is a better choice."

"And that's precisely what they'll conclude if my false trail doesn't throw them off."

Nodding comprehension, Jay began stepping carefully downstream. Ross followed, finding the process of walking in the rapidly moving water strange. Each time he lifted a foot from the smooth stone bottom, the force of the water would propel it forward. The only muscular effort required on his part was that he needed to replant his foot on the bottom. They stopped when Jay reached a large "V" notched into a solid, stone wall. Bracing her hand against the upper portion of the "V," Jay leaned forward and looked down. The water ran between and around her legs, funneled through the base of the notch, and then cascaded into air.

"How does it look?" Ross asked anxiously.

"Hazardous," she observed.

"Is it possible?"

"I believe so. It is a small waterfall, running into a large pool. The other side of the pool runs off into a much larger fall. This one is approximately twelve-feet high. The other is difficult to see, but I would estimate about twenty-five feet high at minimum."

"Could we hide in the pool?"

She studied the area below her for a few additional seconds. "Yes. The walls around the pool form a bowl about six-feet high and there does seem to be an area on this side that is undercut into the stone. It should be a good hiding place unless someone knew for certain we were down there."

"Okay, let's go."

"I will go down first since I can see, then I will guide you down."

Ross shook his head, "The moonlight here is bright enough. I'll go first."

"Ross, it is all in shadows. You would be blind."

He considered her argument, then conceded, "Okay, Miss Courageous, but if you get hurt, I want you to remember that I've ruined my life for nothing."

"Humor again?"

"Just shut up and get on with it."

She swung a leg around one side of the rock "V," found a niche in the stone for her right foot, and then brought her other foot around. The power of the water funneling through the tiny notch was greater than she estimated, driving her left foot out behind her. The twisting momentum of her body forced her right foot from its hold and she crashed against the vertical rock wall, her weight supported only by her right hand.

Ross' heart rose in his throat, and he reached around and felt for some grip on her back. His fingers finally found the back of her bra through the material of her jersey. He wiggled his fingers under the back strap and then lifted with all his strength. Recovering from the precarious position with the added boost Ross provided, Jay managed to regain a foothold just as the metal hooks on her bra yielded under the stress. A lightning bolt of panic surged through Ross as he felt the band of nylon fabric separate into two. He then sighed with relief when the woman beneath did not fall.

She gave him a reassuring pat on his arm and said, "I know you want to touch me, but if you wish to remove my clothing just make a request."

"Jay? Can that be you attempting humor?"

"Be silent and keep your mind on our escape."

She began to climb downward. The darkness gobbled her. After several minutes elapsed, Ross began to worry, suddenly realizing he could neither see her nor hear her above the roar of the falls. If she fell, he would never know. A brief flash of light illuminated the rock to his left, suspending concern about her safety. Quickly deducing the likely source, he swung around the notch and gripped onto the same position that Jay had occupied. Knowing what to expect from the force of the water by her previous incident, he attained a more secure footing and waited. Since no flash reappeared on the rocks, he assumed the soldiers had crossed the water and were probably following his false trail. First allowing a few minutes as a precaution, he then swung back to the channel, and not wanting to think about Jay's safety, busied himself by removing his backpack and attaching nylon cord to it.

Upon hearing a faint, "I made it," he maneuvered to the side of the rock "V" and began lowering his backpack, reasoning that if her night vision was as good as she claimed, she would easily notice it. This assessment proved to be correct when he felt the rope go slack, followed by two gentle tugs. He threw his end of the rope out over the falling water and then swung his body through the notch. Although slow, Ross handled the initial six feet of descent with relative ease, but beyond that point, he became immersed in near total blackness.

"There is a small ledge just below you," Jay's voice echoed off the cliff walls.

He reached with the toes of his right foot, found the promised ledge, and then climbed down to it.

"Now jump," the voice instructed.

"Jump?" he shouted down, not trusting what he thought he heard.

"Yes, jump. You will land in deep water. You cannot miss."

Jumping from a ledge into obscurity, hoping to plunge safely into water he could not see was not his idea of a good time, so he yelled, "Are you sure?"

"Trust me," was the anticipated reply.

"Why not," he said to himself. "I've trusted you so far and look what it's done for me." He pushed off into what seemed like a recurring nightmare from his childhood. Feet first, he fell through black space, and before he could adjust to the strange sensation of freefall, he was submerged in churning, chilling, foaming black liquid.

"Over here," greeted him when he surfaced. He shook the water from his hair and swam toward the voice. "See, no problem," she said when he bumped into her in chest high water. She took his hand in hers and led him to a flat, smooth ledge inches above the water level. "This is the only dry spot," she explained. "But unfortunately it is plainly visible if someone looks over the edge."

"Where is the pack?"

"Over there," she answered, pointing.

"Over where? Remember, I can't see anything in this pit."

"Trust me, it is secure."

A dim light on the rocks above caught his eye. "I think we'd better get back in the water."

She led him to a location just behind the cascading shower of falling water, but still close enough to keep them in a fine drizzle. The water depth there was neck high and the temperature, which he had thought invigorating before, now felt frigid. They stood shoulder to shoulder, watching the lights above move across the walls of their bowl. Ross felt numbness begin to penetrate his skin as he wondered how the water could be so cold in the dead of summer. An ellipse of light appeared in the center of the pool and began sweeping toward them. Simultaneously, they both took breaths and crouched below the surface. Looking up, Ross watched a blurred image of the spot of light move across the surface above his head. Two minutes passed, and Ross surfaced for air. Jay followed within seconds. Their hide-away was black again.

After moving to the ledge, they shivered uncontrollably, prompting Ross to suggest they get into the sleeping bag. Jay, welcoming anything that meant heat, retrieved the pack, and then unrolled the bag on the ledge. They opted to shed their wet clothes, agreeing they would warm more quickly if nude, but undressing turned into quite an ordeal as the material had fused to their bodies like a second skin. Finally stripped, they squirmed inside. Jay asked, "What now?"

"We wait until morning."

"Our bodies would produce more heat if we exerted ourselves," she proposed.

"How in the world can we exert ourselves in this . . .?" his words trailed off when he guessed her meaning. He rolled her on top of him, not wanting to subject her lovely backside or her injured calf to the hard stone bed.

He hardly saw her eyes veiled in the darkness, but he could feel them only inches away. He whispered, "Why Jay?"

"I want to mate with you. If you do not choose . . ."

"Yes, I do," he cut her off. "Not exactly a romantic way to put it, but . . ." He wrapped his arms around her, pressing her tightly to his body, and then kissed her. She accepted it, but did not return it. His hand moved down to her perfectly formed bottom and began stroking. Again, she accepted the advance but remained rigid, yielding no apparent willingness for participation.

Stopping, he asked softly, "Jay, do you want to go through with this? Did you change your mind? I'm not going to force you into anything."

"Yes, I want to continue. Tell me what to do."

He paused while he considered the implication of her words, then when the impact of her meaning struck, he pulled away and said, "Christ, don't tell me you're a virgin." His voice became gentler as he added, "Jay, haven't you ever had sex before?"

"No."

"But you're a young, beautiful woman," he argued as if that statement would alter the facts.

"I have not been exposed to men before meeting you. Please do not ask how this came to be, just accept me as I am."

Forgetting his bewilderment, he drew her close. "Put your arms around me."

She complied.

"God, you feel great." He kissed her neck, the aroma of her hot skin filling his nostrils, and began to fondle her dreamily soft breast with one hand while rubbing her taut, velvety bottom with the other.

"What is that?" she asked in reference to his growing excitement.

"Please touch me there."

She followed his instruction, and he again kissed her mouth. This time she responded with a low sound, almost a whimper from her throat.

He moved his hand between her thighs, touching her wetness, bringing a louder, prolonged moan, while her back arched upwards in a spasm.

She broke the kiss. "That is very pleasurable," she whispered, then again hungrily covered his mouth with hers. Her body began to writhe as Ross continued to work his fingers into her. She pulled away again, allowing him the reward of a happy smile on her lips, and then she said, "I think I know what to do now. Thank you." She moved her hips and guided him into her with her hand. She took over then. He laid back and enjoyed her eagerness as she aggressively satisfied desires likely pent up during her years of abstention. The energy and enthusiasm she treated him with, soon brought him to an ecstasy beyond his wildest dreams.

When finished, she lay staring into his eyes, gracing him with a rare smile. "Did I please you?"

He brushed her lips with his, then said, "Jay, you were wonderful."

"I tried my best," she said, with great sincerity.

"It showed."

Finished with him, she worked her way deeper into the bag until her head rested on his chest.

"I am good at mating," she stated proudly.

He smiled, stroked her neck. "Yes you are."

"And you do love me."

"You're getting overly confident in yourself, don't you think?"

"No, I deal only in facts. I did please you."

"True."

"And at this point in time, you believe you are in love with me," she insisted.

"Not true."

"Then you do not know your own heart," she said.

He smiled.

"But your feelings for me will change soon," she added.

"What are you talking about?" he asked.

"I can not explain, but do not feel guilty when this comes to pass. It will not be your fault."

"Jay, you're not going to go on with this spy stuff, are you?"

"I must," she stated sternly. "It is important."

"I don't think so."

"You will agree when you understand the facts."

"I don't want to know the facts," Ross argued.

"Please, just come with me until I find what I seek, then you can act as you see fit."

Suddenly surprised by what he thought her offer to be, he asked, "You mean you would permit me to turn you in if I felt that was the proper thing to do?"

"Yes, but you will not. I trust in your goodness."

"Don't overrate me."

"I do not," she answered confidently.

Changing the subject, he asked, "What happened to Oswald? I miss her."

"She is above in the trees. We will see her tomorrow."

He thought about her unique personality. She was so very different from anyone he had ever met. Then he understood completely. She was right about everything. She had a flair for seeing within him. She knew he would never harm her. She knew he cared about her life. She knew that he would never turn her in. And, she knew, even better than he, that sometime during the past few days she stole his heart.

Chapter 11

A poke to his ribs woke Ross. His eyelids snapped open to a pair of clear violet-blue eyes inches away. Realizing he was still sandwiched between Jay and the rock ledge, he grinned. "Well, what do you have in store for me today dear Jay?"

"Today you discover who I am and for what I search," she said, smiling.

"You wear a smile nicely. You should try it more often."

"You taught me how."

"Are you going to tell me now?" he prodded.

"No, you will see for yourself. Oswald found them."

"How could you possibly know that?" he asked, and then added, "Found what?"

She pressed hard against him, afraid it would be for the last time.

"What's wrong?" he asked tenderly.

"The revelations you witness today will end your feelings for me."

"Do you love me?" he asked.

"I cannot love you."

"Oh, I see."

"No you do not, but you will." She lifted her head and tapped her headband with the tip of her finger. "You asked how I knew what Oswald found."

His forehead creased in confusion.

"This is not a decorative piece of jewelry. It is an amplifier."

"What does it amplify?"

"Signals broadcast by Oswald's brain. I know what she thinks and therefore what she sees. She has one implanted under her skin so she can also read my thoughts. Ross, most brains are capable of transmitting and receiving energy signals. The human brain broadcasts well enough, but is relatively poor at reception. This device amplifies incoming signals to the point where I understand them."

"You know what I'm thinking?" he questioned excitedly, not quite believing what she was saying.

"Yes," she said with a smile. "How else would I know how you feel about me?"

"This is incredible! They're farther ahead of this country than I thought possible."

"Who is?"

"Whatever government you work for. I'm guessing the Russians . . . or maybe the . . ."

Cutting his speculation off, she said, "No, not the Russians. Be patient, you will know soon." She unzipped the bag, and slid off him. He watched while she pulled the shirt over her lightly tanned breasts. She glanced at him, smiled, and said, "I know what you are thinking."

Self-consciously, he blushed and crawled out after her. As she rolled the sleeping bag, he asked, "Can I try it? The headband?"

"No!" her answer echoed off the walls almost instantly.

Concluding debate with the stubborn woman almost useless, Ross discarded the idea and dressed in his damp clothes. After studying the encircling stone, he decided what appeared to be the best line for a climb, then relayed his plan to Jay. Since he did not want to chance further damage to her leg, he proposed climbing out, and then securing the cord from above in order to simplify her ascent. Unable to dispute his rationale, she sat.

Soon after Ross began scaling the rocky face, the benefits of his selected path became apparent. Numerous small outcroppings of stone provided a natural stairway. As a result, he reached the top with relative ease and threw the line to Jay. While waiting for her, Oswald landed on his shoulder. "I missed you girl," he whispered to the bird as he ran his finger softly along the silky feathered tufts resembling ears.

Jay's head soon popped up over the edge and she grunted with exertion. "Quit playing with my bird and give me a hand."

"Oh, good, sarcasm too," he mumbled on his run to assist her.

"I heard that," she complained as she crawled onto level ground.

"Do you always have to wear that thing?" Ross retorted. "You'd make my life simpler if you didn't. Some thoughts aren't meant to be heard."

Both Ross and Jay looked up, hearing the unmistakable "whumpa whumpa whumpa" sounds approaching from somewhere over the forest. They scrambled to retrieve their gear as the noise increased. A Black Hawk, outfitted for search and rescue, flying just above the treetops, burst into the space above them. Oswald streaked into cover of the trees, while the two fugitives sprinted after her. The two threaded their way between tree trunks, anxious to put distance between themselves and the helicopter over the open area they had just vacated. After running for nearly a mile, they stopped to catch their breaths. They could still hear their pursuer somewhere near, apparently able to track their getaway through occasional breaks in the foliage above.

"This is not good," Jay stated.

Ross thought, not about her summary, but about the dilemma in general. Even if they evaded the soldiers above them, they would continue to search in the area, or possibly call for a ground team. Jay would never reach her destination without leading the armed forces to its location. Somehow he needed to create both a diversion and eliminate the threat of the chopper above.

"Jay, we need to take down that helicopter," he finally answered.

Jay stared at Ross.

"Otherwise it will follow us," he added, noting her expression, or lack of.

"I believe you have a bolt unfastened."

Ross put fingertips to his forehead and tilted his head. "What?"

"They are words I read in your mind that are connected to a state of insanity."

Trying to decipher her meaning, Ross was quiet until the clues fell into place. "Oh, that's supposed to be, 'a screw loose.'"

"The exact words are unimportant. We have no weapons and have no means to disable that machine."

Small-arms fire from above into the ground in front of them interrupted the discussion, causing them to bolt ahead. After winding through the trees for another half-mile, they stopped again. Jay leaned her back against one side of a red oak and Ross against another oak, facing her.

"This is very bad," she informed him.

Trying to catch his breath, he put his hands above his knees and bent down. He looked to his right and noticed a small opening in the forest with a ten-foot high sapling. An idea emerged. Not a good idea. Not a bad idea. It was a "screw loose" idea. "Jay, where's Oswald?"

Oswald appeared from the foliage above, landing on Jay's shoulder. She perched, looking attentively at him, her ear tuffs moving rearward.

"Okay, Jay, tell Oswald to find a clearing like that one that has an area with no trees and is open to the sky. It has to be one that has two saplings about that size, not too far apart. I also need to locate some rocks about the size of baseballs." Ross cupped his hands together, demonstrating the dimension.

Oswald leapt into the air, flapped her wings and vanished into the forest. "She understands you," Jay explained.

"Son of a bitch, I knew it. Now Jay, don't get the wrong idea, but if you still have your bra, I need that."

She opened her mouth to speak, but closed it. Instead, reaching into the leg-pouch in her shorts, she retrieved the undergarment and handed it to Ross.

Moments later, Jay reported that Oswald had succeeded in fulfilling the requests, and then began jogging into the forest. Ross followed. As they reached the opening with Oswald perched on a small branch in one of the two hickory saplings, Ross grinned. Hearing the helicopter approaching again, probably in a circular search pattern, he urged Jay to hurry and go with Oswald to gather the stones. Taking out his camp knife and nylon cord, he began his modifications to the saplings.

When Jay and Oswald returned, they gathered at the edge of the clearing, studying Ross' handiwork. The hickory saplings had been transformed into branchless poles, a yellow nylon cord on each, tied to the top and hanging to the ground. He had tied the ends of her bra near the tops of the poles, so it spanned the space between them. She smiled and said, "Oswald says it looks hideous."

Perceiving the helicopter fast approaching, Ross took the stones, piled them on the ground, and instructed Jay to help him bend the saplings by pulling on both cords simultaneously. They tugged in unison until they lowered the bra to chest level. Ross reached down, placed one of the stones in a cup, and then said, "On the count of three, release the cord."

"Oswald is laughing," she reported, as the bird flew to the ground several feet to her right. "Are you starting with the number one?"

"Yes, I am starting with the number one. What else would I start with? Never mind. Tell your bird to behave herself."

"I am ready," she stated.

"Okay, one . . . two . . . three." They released together, watching the stone fly straight into the trunk of a tree at the edge of the clearing. It bounced back nearly with the same velocity, striking the ground a few inches from Oswald. A leaf landed on top of her head.

Oswald swiveled her head toward Ross, pointing her ear tuffs forward.

"Oswald called you many bad names," Jay told him.

Ignoring her information, he explained he just needed to tighten the bra a little so the rock slips out sooner. They pulled the poles down again as Oswald flew up onto a branch of a nearby maple. Ross retied the bra to a shorter length, and then placed another rock in it. He glanced at Jay, and when she nodded, he began his countdown. The two released the cords in perfect coordination, watching the trees whip upwards with a loud swishing noise. The stone projectile launched from the garment much earlier than the last, traveling at a high speed directly vertical. Ross could barely see the rock against bright blue sky as it reached its apex. Soon he realized it was falling directly back to the release point, and them. Instinctively, he pushed Jay to the ground, covering her body with his. Hearing a snapping noise, he lifted his head. Oswald was hopping around on the ground a mere foot from his head yelping unfamiliar short, sharp calls. The branch where she had perched was a splintered stub. He looked down at Jay.

"Ross, I do not believe we have time for . . ."

Pushing off her body and cutting off her words, he sat up in thought.

Jay propped herself up on her elbows, and said, "Oswald is very angry. She claims you are an idiot."

Sounds of the Black Hawk grew in intensity, bringing both Jay and Ross quickly to their feet. "Let's try again, Jay," he called above the deafening noise.

Oswald disappeared into the forest.

As the nose of the helicopter edged into view, the two pulled once more on the cords, as a maelstrom of leaves, dust, and twigs swirled around them. Ross made another frantic adjustment on the homemade catapult, inserted stones in each cup, and then waited for the menacing aircraft to attain a position on the far side of the clearing. A plume of soil created by a bullet striking the ground erupted ahead of Jay's toe, indicating the soldiers above had certainly spotted them. Judging the attackers were in a possible target zone, Ross began counting. Another shot pulverized one of the stones lying on the ground. They released the cords at three, and watched hopefully as the object's trajectory arced to the Black Hawk. One of the turbine engines smoked, spewing flames into the air. The chopper spun while tilting to one side, and then as one of tips of a rotor struck a tree, it plunged to the ground creating a horrific din of crunching metal.

"Need to get out of here before reinforcements show," Ross yelled.

Jay stared at the mangled airframe. "That went better than anticipated."

* * *

They stopped on the side of the steep hill in the early afternoon, resting on a slate shelf that protruded from the ground. Jay sat hugging her knees against her chest, looking thoughtfully at the valley below. A melancholy serenity showed in her face while Ross studied her gentle, beautiful features. He watched admiringly as docile mountain breezes blew her hair onto her high cheekbones. "My search ends in that valley," she announced.

"I thought you would be happy," he commented.

"I am happy, but . . ."

"But what?" he pushed.

She cocked her head and moved her eyes to his. "I will not see you again."

"Does that matter to you?"

"Your feelings for me give me a warm sensation in here," she said pointing to her chest. "I do not look forward to the destruction of your love for me."

"What's so terrible about your big secret that will change the way I feel?"

"Soon you will see."

Ross stood, and extending his open hand to Jay, said, "Come on partner, let's get this over with. We've lingered long enough."

She placed a hand on his, squeezed affectionately, and got to her feet.

Neither of them spoke as they moved down the grade under a crown of birch, maple, and oak foliage. The slope of the hill gradually diminished as they strode until it finally plateaued onto level ground covered with low-lying ferns. Concurrent with Ross noticing a towering cluster of enormous boulders ahead through the trees, Jay stopped, and pointing at it said, "That is it. Behind the boulders. I will go first. Oswald will bring you when I am prepared."

"Jay? Would you prefer if I left you now?"

"Yes, but I will need your help."

"For what?"

She closed her eyes and leaned forward to lightly press her lips against his. As she pulled away he looked on, transfixed by a multitude of vivid, violet rays radiating out from the pupils, into the irises, painting her eyes a unique iridescence. Against all common sense, he felt those eyes take aim to link his mind with hers. He could not break free until she turned. And as she walked briskly away, he knew how impossibly strong the emotion he felt for her could be.

Oswald landed on his shoulder. "She is nothing like the type of woman I thought I would fall for," he told the bird. "She is so pure of heart."

Oswald sounded off.

"Maybe you do understand," he said, and then Oswald tugged at his arm. "I guess that's my cue." He followed the path Jay had taken to the rocks then, one anticipatory step after another, moved around to the other side. When she came fully into view, he froze. Even with all her warnings, confusion took over when he witnessed the scene greeting him.

Jay stood in the center of a circle comprised of about fourteen of those gold canisters he found at the start of his journey. However, these gold canisters did not lay on their sides like the one he had come upon in the woods, but instead stood upright on their mechanical legs. Her face beamed as she went from one to another, peering into the circular windows of each.

Her eyes caught sight of Ross, and the happiness vanished from her face.

As he stepped tentatively toward her, the devices, or whatever they were, suddenly reacted to his presence by crowding around Jay for protection.

She bid him to move forward to look inside. Reluctantly, he bent over to examine the life form within the first container. It was similar in appearance to a grayish squid, but not a squid; its main tubular body mass, approximately three feet, was enclosed in a mantle with small swimming fins attached along the side. At the top, a translucent sac seemingly filled with gas, provided buoyancy in the liquid-filled canister. What distinguished this creature from a squid were the large, unblinking eyes on either side of what appeared to be its head near the bottom of the tank, resting on a mass of coiled arms and tentacles. Those eyes reacted to his presence by increasing in size and pulsating in color from vibrant pink to deep purple, a color he took for wariness or fear or both. He stepped away.

Jay stepped out from the cluster of canisters circling her to stand beside Ross. With a few simple thoughts, she managed to reassure her wards that her companion should not be feared.

He fell back, startled, as the mechanical legs instantly converged around him, crowding his movement in lively animation, at last allowing him to grin. "What are they and where did they come from?" Ross asked.

"We are the dominant intelligent life form on the planet Jupiter," she informed him, pleased that the baffled look on his face expressed curiosity, not revulsion or disapproval.

The "we" in her statement got his attention, and he shot to a full standing position. "We?"

"Yes, Ross. You see that is the problem between us. I am one of them."

Once his shock settled, his face contorted into a question mark. He waited for her to reveal more, disclose the impossible, explain the unexplainable. *Say something.*

She did not.

The only words to reach his lips as his brain grappled to comprehend was, "Funny, where are your tenacles?"

"I will explain," she said.

He nodded drunkenly, his mind struggling to process the implications of her words.

She smiled at the small group of machines, waiting and watching them. "Ross, these are children on a field trip to Earth. They are my responsibility. I hold a position similar to that of a principal in an Earth school system. I am the one who approved their outing to this remote area. They were only to be here for four hours then return home, but someone must have discovered their presence and reported it to your military because just prior to their scheduled departure, they were attacked by soldiers."

He was drawn to her difficult manner of speech and moisture glistening in her eyes; he feared being enticed in too deeply, too quickly.

"Their teacher and one student were killed. They also damaged the spacecraft circling to rescue the children. It crashed into your ocean. Three were killed on that ship. The children were captured and transported to a government installation where one was dissected for biological study." She wiped a tear from her cheek. "They were to be transported somewhere else and somehow managed to escape into the forest. You found one of them whose vehicle malfunctioned. We had no way to find them. If we undertook a major search mission, the risk of discovery would be great. Any action by us would be classified by your government as an invasion by alien monsters.

"My people decided to send a scout to Earth to locate the children so they could be picked up by an orbiting ship. I volunteered. It was my fault! I felt responsible for their trip. I thought they would be safe." She regained composure and continued, "Our scientists manufactured this human body that you see and my life essence was transferred into it. When I return home, I will get my Ruthran body back.

"And Oswald? How does she fit in?"

"Oswald is my pet parrow. She is highly admired on our planet for her intellect. Most important, however, is her loyalty to me. Her natural body looks something like one of your jellyfish."

Ross rose from his rock to examine Oswald, the screech owl perched on a bush in front of him. He willed his eyes to move to the holding containers for the young aliens. Finally his eyes rested on the exceptional looking woman facing him.

Jay probed his face for reaction, understanding that her explanation left many questions unanswered.

Ross took another visual tour of owl-squid-girl in an effort to prepare his brain to assimilate the "too much" information. "As I see it, I am back at the waterfall with you and I'm dreaming," he eventually concluded. "This is wild. Can't wait to tell you about it when we wake up."

"You are not asleep, Ross."

"Are you absolutely sure?" he questioned, believing his logic sound. The alternative was not possible.

"I am sure."

He did the owl-squid-girl round again. "Then you are crazy," he proposed.

"Ross, you see the children."

Turning away from her, he raised his head to the sky. "I knew she wasn't exactly my preconceived notion of the ideal woman, but this is absolutely ridiculous!" he shouted at a small wispy cloud. Facing her, he said, "Wait till my mother hears about what I picked up this time."

Jay stood silent and gazed unblinkingly.

Ross remembered holding her just mere hours ago. That memory compelled the edges of his mouth to curve into a weak smile. "I understand why you must despise all humans, including me. What can I do to help?"

Dropping her head into her lap, she sobbed.

"Although I have a thousand questions, maybe it would be best if I leave now," suggested Ross. "I must look like some hideous monster to you."

"No, no, please no. Do not leave me. Please. I am ashamed."

"Of what?" Ross asked.

"You care about these children, have offered to help me, yet you are concerned that I may find you repulsive. I thought you would find me and the children repulsive." She paused, and asked, "Nothing has changed, has it? You still care for me."

"I don't think you understand. Things have changed radically."

"But . . . but . . . your mind. I read . . . I thought . . ."

"Using that headband again," Ross reprimanded, then clarified, "I just discovered I'm in love with a squid that can float in the atmosphere of Jupiter and you say nothing has changed?"

"Then you do love me?" she asked hesitantly.

"Absurd, isn't it? But yes, I do. Although dating may become a problem when you return to your home and get your old body back."

She laughed sweetly and moved closer, taking his hand.

"Do you find me repulsive?" he asked tentatively.

"The children said you are ugly, but I have learned to tolerate your appearance."

"You do have a way with words." His eyes ran up and down, then he shook his head and said, "You certainly look and feel all woman."

"Oh, I am. When I said I was manufactured, I did not intend to imply I am artificial. I was cloned from the cells of an Earth woman with some minor modification."

Looking her over again more carefully, he questioned, "What modifications?"

"Eyes for night vision. Muscular system for strength. And enhanced senses of hearing, smell, and touch. They could have omitted the increased sensitivity to touch."

"Why?"

"Pain is intolerable, and . . ." she answered, hesitated, then added, "it just has not served any useful purpose."

"You were going to say?" he pursued.

"I was?"

"Yes, 'pain is intolerable, and . . .'" he repeated.

"Not important. I assure you, this body is very authentic female human being."

"I don't like it when people start to say something then don't complete it. Finish your statement," he pleaded.

"What statement?"

"Damn it!" he swore.

"I did not intend to anger you."

"Oh, forget it. At least tell me how did they put you in a human body? Switching brains sounds messy."

"And, you have this effect on me when you touch me."

"I think I've lost the thread of this conversation. Jay! What the hell are we talking about?"

"My intensified senses of course."

"Ohhhh? Tell me about it."

"All right. Every time you touch me I get sexually aroused." Her voice grew faint and she circled her right toe playfully in the leaves.

"You're exaggerating, Jay. I was just holding your hand and . . . and . . ." His voice trailed off as she nodded. Changing the subject, he said, "About your mind . . ."

"All life forms are controlled by individual energy fields that give them the concept of self to varying degrees. The brain of higher forms, such as humans and my race, are merely storage mediums for information, in other words, like very complex computers. The self-energy field controls, operates, and directs the brain, calling upon the life experiences stored in it for decision-making. My self-energy field was transferred into this brain as one would enter data and programs into one of your computers."

His mind mired in a swamp of too many new concepts, he uttered only one word, "Fascinating."

"When I return home my essence will be restored to my body and this one will be deactivated."

"I kind of like that body."

"I know you do," she said with a grin.

"The Ruthra have two sexes? Like our male and female?"

"Yes, I am female."

"That's good. That's very good. Do your people have permanent male-female unions like our marriage?"

"Yes."

"Are you married?" Ross asked.

Her expression plainly telegraphed that she had been insulted. "No! I would not have mated with you if united with another. When Ruthras unite, it is for life. Our ability to learn the true emotions and characteristics of a possible mate is far more accurate than you apparently have between humans since we have direct access to each other's minds. Therefore, the compatibility of married Ruthra is known before the union is undertaken."

"You don't have much privacy, do you? Someone is always aware of your thoughts."

"Not true. We know more of each other than you humans, but the mental communication parallels yours with sound waves. You allow another Ruthra to receive only that information you wish to send."

"Then I don't understand why you say you knew each other's thoughts better than humans."

"The information exchanged is more complete than that which can be achieved by words. You have inflections in your voice, which add different interpretations to your words. You can use the exact same words with different states of mind and convey differing impressions of your feelings. With us not being restricted to sounds, these mental inflections, or color, impart substantially more clues as to the person's true state of mind."

"Have you chosen your future mate?"

"Yes," she answered softly.

"When will you be married?"

"I was to be united ninety Jovian days from now, or about thirty-six Earth days."

"Was?"

"This mission has changed that. I can no longer agree to the planned union. I am already married."

"Jay, you're beginning to lose me again. First you said you are not married, then you said you are planning to, and now you say you are. Which is it?"

"I am. To you."

Ross opened his mouth to speak, but it closed when he found no words to meet the occasion.

She looked into his eyes and clarified, "Our uniting ceremony consists of a mating ritual performed before our relatives and friends. Both male and female are chaste until that first mating."

"But . . . but . . . didn't you need to mention it to me first? I mean . . ." stumbling as he gathered thoughts. He tried again. "But these circumstances . . . You can't be held responsible."

"I did what I was obligated to do by our traditions since I love you. *And* you love me."

"That's what you keep telling me," he said, pulling her into his arms, acquiescing in agreement, and cherishing this new happiness.

Chapter 12

"I don't suppose you could stay here on Earth with me?" Ross asked while watching her head push through the jersey top.

She slowly finished dressing before stating flatly, "It is not permitted. I must return with the children and face the consequences of my action."

"Surely your people must realize what happened here on Earth was the fault of humans, not you."

"I showed poor judgment that cost lives," Jay confessed.

"What is your future?"

"I do not know."

"I will always remember our time together."

Her face softened, and she turned to him and said, "I know."

Pushing down the lump in his throat, he said, "Okay, Jay, how do you get them back home? Do you have a spaceship stashed behind a bush somewhere?"

"The ship is in orbit. I must give them our location so they can pick us up."

"How do you do that?" he asked.

"With the transmitter."

"What transmitter?"

"That is the problem. It is in my backpack. That is the reason I need your help. You will need to get it for us, and it must be soon. The children's life-support systems are dwindling. They are frightened and I must stay here with them."

"I'll get it somehow. What does it look like?"

"A transparent, red-colored glass rod about this long," she said, holding her hands about ten inches apart. She separated her fingers approximately an inch, "And about this thick. It has a thin cloudy zone running its length at the core. You will know it when you see it. Take my headband and Oswald. Ross, if you fail the children will die."

"I understand," he answered, taking the amplifier from her hand.

"Go ahead, put it on," she prodded. "It takes some practice to learn how to use it."

Almost reluctantly, he lowered it onto his head, and then looked at Jay. Suddenly, he felt as if he was in a small room filled with frightened children, all speaking to him simultaneously. Ross was about to remove the amplifier in an effort to escape the free-for-all playing out in his head, when Jay's voice cried out above the others and demanded they leave at once. Gradually, he comprehended that this was not his imagination, but rather Jay's thoughts he was hearing.

The idea that she found gratification by his progress in the use of the amplifier abruptly became clear through her thoughts she transmitted to him. Her encouragement and compassion reinforced his love for her. He wished for the right words, words strong enough to tell her. Then, seemingly by magic, he sensed her love, almost in response to what he was feeling and thinking. It was an impression no form of communication known to him could have ever conveyed. He was actually experiencing the emotion as it felt to her. As pictures say a thousand words, the direct link of thought transported a thousand, three-dimensional motion pictures. He not only saw the thoughts as one would see sophisticated dynamic images, but also lived them. The feeling she held for him was a thing of unselfish beauty. He knew how dearly she wanted to spend her life with him, yet how obligated she was by her loyalty to the Ruthra to return home. Her life's essence was the most glorious gemstone imaginable, each facet shining brilliantly. Comprehension that a true wedding had occurred between them was inescapable, their souls united for eternity.

He made an effort to think thoughts of thanks for the special gift she bestowed on him. The indescribable warm sunshine of her happy response instantly rewarded him.

Beginning to feel more adept at communication by this manner, his thoughts went to the children. Because of Jay's reassurance, they liked him, but were terrified of other humans. They missed their parents. They held no animosity toward Jay, and thought her to be the nice lady who would bring them home. Also, they still thought Ross would look much better if he had tentacles in place of grotesque arms and legs. He transported words of encouragement to them with the promise to get them back with their families.

"I think I have the hang of it now," he said, looking back to Jay, and then reminded by her unadorned head, asked, "How did you know what I was thinking? I have your amplifier?"

She kissed his mind gently. "I guess the human brain has some capability to link minds. I receive you as clearly without the headband as I did with it. I cannot receive Oswald or the children, but you, I do. It appears my feelings for you triggered something within me. Please hurry back. And remember the communication link with Oswald is adequate for a distance of about one mile." She put a finger lovingly on his lip, and turned away.

* * *

By the time Ross and Oswald arrived at the government's forest base, it was well past nightfall. He had hoped that during the journey, he would have developed an inspirational, surefire plan to covertly extract the transmitter from their clutches, but he had not. Wishing for a solution to the challenge produced no magic. Although, Ross did test his newfangled ability to communicate with thoughts by practicing on Oswald. And so, the unlikely team of human and fowl peered out from the trees at the building.

"What do you think?" Ross asked in a silent language.

Sitting on a low branch, she swiveled her head away from the open clearing to him, then turned her body to match the position of her head. "I'm not supposed to think. Remember, I'm just a dumb bird."

"Don't give me that crap Oswald, you're at least as intelligent as the average human."

"I rest my case."

"A comic screech owl is all I need. I just asked your opinion."

"All right, you asked. I think we should wait a few hours until they're all asleep."

"Then what?"

"Hell if I know."

"Birds are not supposed to swear."

"And people aren't supposed to talk to owls," Oswald countered.

Ross sat back against a tree and relaxed, reasoning that if he was going to wait, he might as well be comfortable.

Oswald moved to Ross' right knee and began to stare at his eyes. Ross moved his hand to the bird's head, intending to stroke her feathers, but she disrupted his plans when she struck out and nipped his finger with her beak. Startled, he yanked his hand back and examined it for traces of blood. "Why did you do that?"

"You promised you wouldn't hurt her."

"Hurt Jay? What are you talking about? I'd never hurt her."

"A minute ago you said I was intelligent and now you speak as if I was a dimwit. Christ Ross, I was there!"

"Stop swearing, damn it. You're picking up some very bad habits . . . was where?"

"What did you do to her? She screamed so loud my feathers curled. I don't understand why she didn't try to stop you."

"Can we start over? I don't have the foggiest idea of what you're talking about."

Oswald angrily pecked at Ross' leg, causing him to jump, and then said, "When you mated with her, that's when. She was in agony through the whole affair. She moaned in pain, but you didn't ease up. No, you kept at her until she finally screamed out. She nearly fainted. I thought you were different, but you're not. The only reason she didn't kill you is because she needs you to help get us out of this. Don't think I'll be grateful."

"You are a moron. Oswald, I didn't hurt her. You know Jay better than that. If I had harmed her, do you really think she would let it go without retaliation? Go ahead, read my mind. Tell me you see anything in me that would permit me to hurt her in any way."

Oswald spent a few moments rummaging through the human's brain then flew to his shoulder. "Sorry Ross. You can call me a birdbrain if you like. I never imagined that human mating would be so horrible."

"It is not horrible. I love her dearly."

"I know you do. I guess I just got confused."

"It's okay, you're only concerned about her welfare and I can't fault you for that."

Over the next hours, Ross watched and plotted, eventually narrowing his choice of options to three. First, he could wait until daylight when most personnel would be out scouring the countryside. Second, he could play cat burglar and try to find the transmitter while everyone slept. Or third, he could create a diversion, which would get everyone out of the building, allowing him to ransack the interior undetected. He proposed all three scenarios to Oswald, and after some debate, they reached consensus on the third as being the most feasible. All they needed was an effective diversion.

His eyes swept slowly across the makeshift airfield, then on to the building itself, and finally rested on a junk heap fifty feet to the rear of the structure's back wall. Examining the pile of debris, he noted a composition primarily of logs and brush, presumably the byproduct of the clearing operation, and an assortment of human trash. "That should burn nicely," he mumbled to Oswald, then looked at the bird and added, "Friend, I'm going to give you the opportunity to become a hero."

"Whoooo, me?"

"Very funny but screech owls don't whoot."

"I don't think I'm going to like this."

"Oswald, be serious." Ross dug a small flare from his pack and waved it in front of her face. "This burns. I'll light it, then you hold it in your claws, fly to the dump, drop it in the middle, and fly back here. Simple? And make sure you keep the flame away from your feathers. Jay would never forgive me if I brought you back looking like a miniature Thanksgiving turkey."

Her eyes peered at the small red stick. "Isn't there some Earth regulation against abusing wildlife?"

"You'll be fine if you're careful," Ross encouraged the skeptical bird.

"Are you trying to retaliate for my little harmless nibbles? I don't think . . ."

"Oswald," Ross cut her off. "I'd like to see my bride again before the Earth hits its next ice age. Now, let's see if you can fly with this thing."

Oswald latched onto the cylinder, flapped, soared into the night sky above the floodlights, circled, and landed at Ross' feet.

"Terrific!" he silently applauded then took the flare from her grip. "Ready?"

"No."

"Good, here we go." As soon as he lit the flare, it made hissing noises and sputtered a brilliant red. Fearing it would practically announce their presence to the government camp, he hurriedly shoved the harmless end at Oswald. Unhesitant, she latched onto it, and then burst into the air. Apprehension about discovery eased when the illuminating effect of the ball of light on Ross' location diminished to nothing as Oswald streaked upward. Within seconds, the red burning comet was near the target, arcing down towards impact. The light suddenly extinguished as it hit the pile, and Ross cursed. Oswald returned just as Ross was reaching into his pack for another flare.

"Didn't even singe a feather," boasted the bird.

"You'll have to try again," Ross complained, then looked up and saw Oswald eerily backlit by an orange-red glow. Voices abruptly shattered the night stillness. "It must have fallen between the brush. I thought it had gone out." He peeped out at the ensuing commotion, gratified by the attention their little diversion was drawing. A cooperative breeze blew a shower of sparks rising from the blaze toward two nearby helicopters. That detail apparently upset the soldiers, for they were like a group of unorganized insects scurrying helter-skelter to protect their queen. The turbines on one of the helicopters whined to life, and its rotor began to spin. The rush of air generated by the blades pushed the inferno toward several of the would-be fire fighters thereby causing them to disperse quickly.

Assuming the chaos would never be greater, Ross sprinted out into the clearing, his eyes focused on the front door. He considered glancing to his left to see if anyone had spotted his mad dash, but ignored the urge, assuming if they had, he would confront the bad news soon enough. Not wanting to crash through the door, he reduced his speed as he approached it, then threw it open and boldly entered.

He raced into the first room on his left, came to a skidding halt, and began surveying the room. Not seeing Jay's pack or transmitter, he moved to a file cabinet, roughly opening and closing its drawers. He did the same with the desk, and upon finding nothing but bureaucratic paperwork, shot across the hall to another room. Just as quickly finding nothing resembling Jay's description of the transmitter in that room, he ran back into the hall, then down to the next room on his right. Here he found something that was beginning to become routine: the muzzle of a gun.

The major chomped on his short, cold cigar, pushed the .45 closer to Ross' forehead, and said, "Go ahead, make my day."

"Aaaaa . . . kind of a worn cliché, isn't it Major?"

"Yeah, but I've been wanting to say it for years. Where's your girlfriend?"

"Hiking."

"Look, smart ass, you're in enough trouble already and if you want things to go easy on you, you'll talk." He rolled the cigar to the opposite side of his mouth.

Ross looked away from the major's loathsome eyes; he could not face the arrogance of this man with his closed mind and inability to act in any other way than what was taught to him by the organized military machine. He was trained to obey inflexible regulations with no concern for their specific application. Jay's people were guilty only of naiveté. Although seemingly contradictory, he had fallen in love with her because of her human kindness, harshly contrasting the manifestation of inhuman behavior before him. The major made Ross' choice of allegiance much too easy.

"How are things going?" Oswald's thoughts popped into his head.

"Swimmingly. But don't bother me now, I'm busy," he answered, grateful for the reminder of his hidden talent. Focusing his mind on the major, Ross perceived overconfidence. He quickly raised his right hand in the air to evaluate the major's mental response to an unexpected action, and almost smiled when treated to the major's molasses-like mental reflex. Masking the purpose of the rapid movement, he rubbed his head shakily, in order to paint the image of a cowering, nervous wreck. "I'll cooperate," he announced meekly.

"That's a good boy." The major relaxed, certain he had bent Ross to his will. "Why are you wearing that stupid looking thing on your head? Looks like it belongs on a girl. As a matter of fact, wasn't that the thing the girl had on her head?"

Ross dug deep to bring up a demeanor of fear, one he knew the major would enjoy seeing him wear. "Well, Major-Sir. This girl, Jay. I ran across her on the trail. We talked for a while. Nothing important, just small talk. Then all of a sudden, she began unbuttoning her blouse." He checked and found his listener's mind hanging on every word. "She asked me if I wanted a good time, then began . . ." His words faded as he brought forth the timing and agility of his gymnastic skills into action. Ross kicked his right foot high, knocking the gun from the major's hand. In the same motion, his left hand lunged out, gripped the officer's shirt, and as soon as his foot was on the ground again, he yanked him to the floor. Quickly he retrieved the semiautomatic, then rushed over and pushed the muzzle into the base of the major's skull. The saliva soaked cigar dripped from the bottom lip of the stunned man. It fell onto the floor under his nose.

"You're in big trouble now!" the man threatened half-heartedly.

"I think you've got that backwards. Now, where is the glass rod that was in the girl's backpack?"

"You don't have a chance. My men will kill you. You won't use that thing."

Ross jabbed the gun into the base of the man's head. "Try me, 'make my day.' Where is that rod?"

"So you're in it with her? Should have known the Ruskies would have more than one."

"Ruskies! My God, do you guys see enemies behind every tree? My patience is wearing thin, either tell me where it is or I blow your brains out."

"You wouldn't. My men would hear the shot."

"Doesn't matter. If I don't get that rod, I don't really care."

"You're bluffing," he tried, but Ross could read his mind and knew he believed the threat.

"Fine, if that's the way you want it, I'm running out of time."

"Wait!"

"The rod?"

"We shipped it to Rampfort Air Force Base. Couldn't figure out what it was."

Ross made a mental check, verifying the truth in his answer. "Don't move," he instructed, then stepped back and tore wiring from one of the computer terminals. He wrapped the cord around the major's wrists, binding them together behind his back, then put the gun against his temple and said, "You have a choice, Major. You can come with me, or I can kill you."

"I'll go."

Ross pulled him to his feet and motioned to the door. As he herded the soldier down the hall, he thought, "Oswald."

"At your service," the response formed in his brain.

"Big problem. The transmitter isn't here. It's been shipped out to Rampfort Air Force Base. I've got a hostage. We need to take him or he'll tip them off. We'll take one of their helicopters."

"Shit," was the bird's inspirational response.

Chapter 13

As the helicopter moved over the forest, Ross and Oswald spoke telepathically, "Oswald, I need your eyes up here. We're going to fly low."

"There's a bird in here!" the major yelled.

"Must be a stowaway," Ross chuckled. "No respect for military property."

The major stared in disbelief at the owl peering through the front bubble while Ross' mind fought off the desire to sleep by thinking about Jay. Without her, he felt incomplete. His eyes moved to the south, finding what appeared to be a bright star. "Jupiter," he whispered under his breath. "Home for Jay." He wondered what Marsha would say if he told her. He fantasized sitting at home, reading a scientific journal while comfortably settled in his favorite chair. He sees Marsha lounging on the sofa, engrossed in a dimwitted police show about murder for hire. Looking up from an article on NASA's space program, he says, "Oh that reminds me, we'll have to cancel our wedding next month. While I was in Vermont, I met this woman; you remember. I told you about her on the phone. Jay. Well anyway, to make a long story short, we fell in love and had sex in front of an owl. By her convention that makes us married. Oh, did I mention that she's a squid from the planet Jupiter?"

He imagines Marsha munching on a mouthful of cheese puffs and she mumbles, "That's nice."

"Wake up!" Oswald screamed.

He jumped to face a myriad of glowing instruments; his mind reverted back to the helicopter's instrument panel.

"I'm glad she loves you," Oswald said.

"But I've ruined her life," Ross countered mentally.

"Destiny," Oswald philosophized. "On Jupiter her heart was cold toward adult males. She would have never gone through with the one she was scheduled to marry. I didn't like him. He isn't her type and his tentacles are too short. The warmth you have brought to her heart is a thing of extreme beauty, unmatched in any others I have met."

"Thanks Oswald, you're a little sappy but I do care for her very much."

"Sorry I doubted your intentions. I should have known you could never betray her. Although of different species and separated by the gulf of space, it was meant to be."

"Did you know you are very sentimental for an owl?"

"Stop it, you're choking me up," she parried sarcastically.

"What if we don't get the transmitter? Is there a rendezvous place to meet your ship?"

"No. Jay is either to succeed, or . . ."

"Or what?" Ross question.

"The life support systems for the children will begin failing in forty-eight hours, and if our ship isn't contacted by then . . ."

"They can't just abandon you and Jay," Ross argued as if it could change the facts.

"We have taken Earth forms and can survive. They cannot risk losing another ship. They'd have to leave the children behind."

"You could survive, yes. You eat mice. But Jay. How would they expect her to fit into an alien society? Do you know how many times she came close to being arrested? They'd probably lock her in solitary for the rest of her life."

"She knows the consequences. She volunteered."

"What about you?" Ross pursed.

"I'm a loyal companion. What else could I do?"

Their communication was disrupted when the major, finally getting over the presence of a screech owl in a military helicopter, asked, "What is that glass rod thing anyway?"

Ross ignored him.

"If you two aren't Ruskies, then what country are you from?"

"I'm just what I said I was, a college professor from Indiana. And I'm not working for anyone but myself."

"What about the girl? Don't tell me she's just a sweet young thing from Oklahoma you happened to find strolling through the forest picking wild flowers."

Ross thought, What the hell, then said, "You know those aliens you're searching for?"

"You're not supposed to know about that! It's classified!"

Ross shook his head. "What a jerk. Not only do I know about them, but I also know what you people did to them. God, you guys behave like you're straight out of one of those cheap science fiction movies from the fifties. I'm surprised you didn't drop the 'big one' on them."

"You talk about them like they were people."

"What the hell's the matter with you? They are people. They're more intelligent than me, and certainly more than you. And you imbeciles murdered them. Cut them up like laboratory rats, and destroyed one of their spaceships. And for what? Didn't you think you could learn something from them? Why destroy the ship? Why keep it classified? You missed an important opportunity. Idiots. Some neighborhood welcome wagon."

For a short-lived moment, the major appeared embarrassed, but quickly recovered and shot back, "And how do you know so much? You talk to them?"

"Yes, the woman is one of them."

The major laughed at first, until he recognized Ross' seriousness. Again he challenged, "Get off it. She's human. But those other things, they look like some kind of octopus or something. You want me to believe they're related? What do you take me for?"

"A complete fool."

The major slumped back in his seat sullenly and Ross wondered whether he now knew the error of his ways or if he had decided Ross was loony. Ross checked his thoughts, loony it was. A smile appeared when he considered the major's possible reaction to learning Oswald's true identity.

"You really ought to do something about your temper," Oswald teased Ross.

"I ought to throw him out the door and see if he can fly!" Ross shouted out loud to Oswald, temporarily reverting to normal vocal-cord induced speech.

The major eyed him warily, and shifted as far away as possible from the pilot who he was convinced was insane, almost as if Ross' condition was contagious. When Ross realized what he had done and saw his passenger's reaction, he laughed. The release of tension felt wonderful, so he continued to laugh, and laugh. The major flattened himself against the side of the compartment, praying the lunatic would land before he got the urge to fly into a hill, tree, or the ground.

* * *

As Ross flew, his mind returned to Jay and the seemingly incredulous story he had been told and the one he was now living in. If he had not observed the children with his own eyes, he would have believed her to be deranged. Maybe none of this had actually happened, the major having good reason to be fearful of him.

"That's a pretty light," Oswald said, interrupting Ross' skeptical mental meanderings.

The flashing red indicator drew his eyes to the fuel gauge. "Shit, I should have checked that before," Ross shouted in anger.

"Not too smart for a professor, are you Barton?"

Ignoring the wise crack, Ross began to search for potential landing spots.

"Did I miss something?" Oswald queried.

"Low fuel. Need to land soon and find some."

"Isn't that kind of basic human flying stuff?" the bird complained. "And to think, my chances of getting back home depend on you. Might have better luck flying back to Jupiter with my wings."

Disregarding both judgmental passengers, Ross continued to sweep the terrain ahead. "Oswald, fly out and find a place to get some fuel while I find somewhere to set this down."

Oswald pivoted her head, staring silently at her companion.

Seeing the large green-yellow eyes watching him, Ross prodded, "Oswald, did you hear me?"

"Can we review my job description?" the bird finally questioned. "I don't believe flying from a speeding chopper and searching in the middle of nowhere for aviation fuel was on my list of responsibilities." She turned to the major and added, "Have him do it. He's got nothing to do. About time he started pulling his weight."

"He can't fly," Ross countered.

"He could for a few seconds," Oswald argued.

"Enough playing around. Go!"

As Oswald flew out the open side, she sent Ross her parting thoughts. "Just so you know. I'm filing a grievance with Jay if we make it back."

Ross spotted a small, open field ahead. He was adjusting his flight path to get closer for an examination when Oswald's voice reappeared in his head. "Hey boss. Just occurred to me that I don't know what the hell I'm looking for. What does fuel look like?"

Struggling to recall articles he read on military rotary winged aircraft, he answered, "Just find an airport or a military base."

"You've got to be kidding me? I'm not going to find a fucking airport or base in this wilderness."

"Oswald!" Ross yelled aloud. "Where did you pick up such language?"

The major cowered away, believing his captor was speaking to imaginary companions.

"Okay, you're right," Ross conceded. "See if you can find a farm or someplace with large trucks. I think this thing uses JP8, and not sure . . . but diesel fuel might work all right in it."

"You got it, supreme commander," was the reply.

* * *

Ross knelt in the granite-strewn field, .45 in hand, watching the major reclining against a large red oak. He gazed down to the tall weeds directly in front of him, examining the glistening morning dew on the tall green stems. Oswald had been gone only about twenty minutes, but it seemed like an eternity as he fought off the overwhelming temptation to sleep. His mind again went to Jay, replaying what they had already been through together in such a short time. Smiling, he remembered the night she crawled into his tent just to sleep near him.

A metallic click jolted Ross out of his daze, and when he raised his head, he immediately spotted the source of the noise. The major stood halfway between the oak and Ross, a small semiautomatic pistol in his hand and a grin on his face. "Now put down the gun Barton like a good little man," the major demanded.

Full alertness returning, Ross assessed the situation to be a standoff since his .45 remained leveled at the major. If he simply pulled the trigger the major was dead, bravado or not. Knowing the major banked on him backing down and would not drop his weapon if Ross threatened, he evaluated alternatives.

"Let's end this little game," the major continued, confidence building because of Ross' obvious reluctance to just fire. "Drop the gun and we'll go easy on you."

Ross said, "What the hell," and then fired the .45 semiautomatic. The ground erupted in front of the major's feet, pulverizing his face with dirt, causing him to drop his weapon and cover his eyes. After recovering, the major bolted for the trees.

Shaking his head in disgust and raising his dog-tired body to a standing position, Ross uttered, "Shit, I don't have the energy for this."

"Dad, I'm home," suddenly popped into Ross' head as the reddish brown screech owl appeared over the trees and zoomed onto his landing strip—Ross' shoulder. "Hey, where's our prisoner?"

"Ran that way," Ross explained, pointing in the direction of the escape. "Go find him, then call me."

"You had one little job, and you couldn't handle it?" Oswald complained. "You have me flitting all over the damn countryside flapping my aching wings to find fuel and you lose our major? Unbelievable."

"Quit bitching and just find him."

Oswald launched into the air and bee lined into the trees. Ross jogged across the field to the helicopter in search of nylon cord and a roll of duct tape.

Within minutes, the owl's voice burst into Ross' brain, "Got him. The idiot tripped over a log and banged his head. He looks a little groggy. May need a Band-Aid if you got one. Just a few hundred feet in."

* * *

Once the major was bound, gagged, and seated back in the aircraft, Ross asked, "Well, what did you find?"

"Thought you'd never ask. Didn't find a farm, airport, or any big trucks."

"Why the hell did you come back?" Ross asked, agitation clear in his thoughts.

"Just wanted to get a little suspense," Oswald enlightened. "Found a small town with a gas station only two miles from here. Due north."

"Did it have diesel fuel?" Ross pressed.

"Owls can't read. It had pumps with pretty colored handles."

"Not many choices here," Ross said. "We'll go for it. See any good landing spots?"

"Main road is about it," she reported. "Town is full of big freaking trees."

"This ought to be interesting," Ross muttered aloud as he started the engines.

"So, what's the plan?" Oswald asked as the rotor blades began spinning.

"Mmmuummmbrrrfff," the major sounded through the tape as the helicopter started to rise.

Ross laughed hysterically.

Both the owl and soldier nervously fixed their eyes on the pilot, thinking he had gone mad.

A surge of adrenaline energized Ross; he no longer felt the need to sleep. Guiding the machine skillfully on nearly empty tanks, he saw the small town appear below in minutes. He circled once, verifying Oswald's report, then began a descent to the two-lane highway directly in front of the service station. "Oswald, I have another little job for you," Ross finally thought.

"What the fu ..."

"Oswald!" Ross screamed.

"Sorry, bad habit. What can I do for Sir Lordship?" the screech owl asked, paused, and then added, "Is that better?"

"Christ, what an attitude."

"Didn't your mother tell you not to use the lord's name in vain?" Oswald corrected.

"Enough! I think there's something that looks like a public building a ways south of the gas station. I want you to get inside and set off the fire alarm. There should be something like a red box on a wall with a glass pane. Break it and pull the lever or push the button, however they designed it."

"How the hell am I supposed to get into the building?" Oswald questioned. "I'm just a bird. I can't open doors."

"Owls are supposed to be wise, just figure it out for yourself. Oh, and after you set it off, see if you can find me a cup of coffee."

Ross continued a vertical descent toward street level as Oswald, abandoning the banter, darted out into the sky. He leveled off, giving the owl time for her task.

"In the building," materialized in Ross' head. "Almost got stepped on by some asshole getting through the front door. I see the shiny red box ahead on the wall."

Resuming the drop in altitude on his companion's report, Ross checked the road for traffic as he guided the helicopter lower. Noticing no vehicles approaching his intended landing site, he slowed for a touchdown as he watched leaves blowing from the surrounding trees as if battered by a miniature windstorm. A man ran out of the front door of the station, and halted to gape at the extraordinary spectacle of a military helicopter putting down on the street in front of his establishment. More citizens wandered in the direction of the odd show.

Suddenly people in the street halted and rotated their heads in the direction Ross now identified as a library. Faces turned back and forth between the chopper and the library, as if confused as to which entertainment to seek. "Got it!" popped into Ross' head. "Didn't tell me the glass would be so tough to break. I got a headache. Trying to find a way out of this dump."

A few emergency vehicles arrived at the library, forcing many onlookers to choose *that* circus. Ross jumped out, and walked quickly to the puzzled station attendant. "Hi, there," he began. "My helicopter is out of fuel. Wondering if we could get some diesel for it?"

The tall attendant whose nameplate identified him as Jim had lost his ability to speak. He finally said, "Aaaaaaaaa . . ." followed by, "huh?"

Ross persisted as Oswald landed on his shoulder, "Do you take Visa?"

"Don't forget the painkiller and coffee," Oswald said.

"Pump hose isn't long enough," Jim finally managed to say.

"If you have any stock hose lengths, we could attach it to the nozzle," Ross proposed.

"There's an owl on your shoulder," Jim said, stating the obvious.

"Yeah, a pet," Ross explained, seeing the kid needed management, he added "Don't have much time. I am behind schedule. Important military work."

Jim ran his hand through his matted hair, "I think I have something that might work."

"Then let's get cracking," Oswald said.

"Could we hurry please," Ross pleaded. "My superiors will court marshal me if I don't get the helicopter to base on time."

Jim checked out Ross' hiking clothes and made an inner decision. "Be right back," he said, running in a quick clip back to the office.

"He'd be an idiot to buy your fairytale," Oswald observed.

Within minutes, the attendant returned dragging a long black hose and a roll of duct tape under his arm.

While he worked feverishly attaching the hose to the diesel pump nozzle, Oswald thought, "Well dip me in hog fat. He fell for your tale of crap."

Ross in turn raced back to the aircraft and began readying the fuel access while Oswald circled above. Jim pulled the makeshift fuel supply line to Ross, and once inserted, ran back to the pump.

As Jim started the flow, Oswald said, "Oh shit."

Lifting his head, Ross saw the approaching police car. It stopped in front of the helicopter, and two police officers emerged. The driver asked, "What in the world are you doing with that thing in the middle of the street?"

"Ran out of gas," Ross answered.

"Why don't you come with us," the other one demanded.

"I should move this off the street, don't you think?" Ross offered.

The officer positioned his hands on his hips and took a stand of authority. "Put it in that park across the street, then come back here," he ordered.

"Got it," Ross said. He called to Jim to stop the pump, and withdrew the nozzle from the fuselage. As he stood ready to climb into the cockpit, he looked at the two police officers and pointed to the park, mouthing the word, "There?"

The law enforcement pair nodded in unison and Ross entered, seating himself at the instrument panel to read the amount of gas in the tank. Oswald flew in as Ross, wearing a wide grin, started the engines. He saluted the two-man police force. Adjusting the rotor pitch while increasing throttle resulted in a rapid vertical rise. One of the two awaiting officers astutely ascertained their detainee was not headed for the designated landing spot. "Halt!" he bellowed and withdrew his sidearm.

Ross waved.

The major banged his head against the side in frustration.

Oswald asked, "Did you get your coffee?"

Chapter 14

He landed in an isolated field far into the military's restricted airspace, tied his captive to a tree, and jogged toward the base.

When he reached the ten-foot high, wire-mesh, outer perimeter fence of the air base he fell to his knees. Fatigue and the desire to sleep over-whelmed him once again. His mind worked sluggishly, trying to organize disorganized thoughts into a cohesive plan. He looked up at the barbed wire "V" that topped the fence and eliminated the direct approach of scaling it. While the fence posed no real obstacle to reaching the airfield, he was convinced that in this day and age of terrorist threats, sensitive electronic detection systems lurked beyond.

"Oswald, check it out."

The bird flapped into the air, rapidly swallowed by the night. Images of the base grounds from an aerial perspective materialized in Ross' head, and although now accustomed to the telepathic link, the clarity of the view through the owl's eyes impressed him. It was as if he, himself, glided above the ground.

Ross had cataloged and experienced four distinct modes of the mind's communication system. The first and simplest was direct substitution for audible speech, the English words almost heard in his head. The second mode was an evolution of the first, the words replaced by equivalent, moving, three-dimensional images complete with sound. The third, which he now explored, was direct transmission of perceptual information from another being. He saw, felt, and heard as Oswald did. The forth plateau was the most complete, and he suspected reserved only for exceptionally intimate relationships. That was the one Jay had formed between them. This mode expanded to include the emotional states present in the linked beings. He had felt what Jay felt, understood her fears, bathed in her love, and for precious moments, shared her mind and body.

The words, "Ross, wake up," prodded him to consciousness again. Even before his eyes opened, Ross looked through his companion's eyes onto the perimeter fence line passing below and felt the wind rush though the bird's feathers. The base appeared tranquil with no noticeable activity. He glanced at his watch, and saw it was already three-thirty in the morning. Through Oswald, he found a central office building he designated as his objective. He identified the base's three entrances, one of which was a mere two hundred yards to his right. Satisfied, he began walking toward that entry, filling Oswald in on his plan along the way.

They emerged from the trees at a point on the asphalt road about a half-mile away from the main gate.

Oswald cross-examined, "Are you sure this will work?"

"No. Any other ideas?"

"No, but I'm beginning to get the feeling you don't like me. First, you try to turn me into a Roman candle, and now I could end up resembling a feathered pancake. Jay never had me play such an active role in harebrained schemes."

"Where did you pick up English slang?" Ross questioned.

"From your mind."

"I thought minds communicated only that which the participants wished?"

"True, if you know what you're doing. Until Jay showed you how to use the amplifier your brain was free pickin's."

Ross reached down and brushed the feathered peaks resembling ears on her head.

"I like you too," Oswald purred.

Bird and man sat together for nearly an hour on the deserted road beginning to fear they would need some other method to gain access when lights illuminated the leaves of distant trees. "You're on," Ross said and then hid in a shallow depression at the side of the road.

Oswald walked out to the center of the right lane, folded one wing and extended the other. As the beams of light projected by the oncoming vehicle reached her, she began dancing in a circle while delivering a noisy descending trill. When she surmised the speeding vehicle was not going to stop, she swore, "Oh shit," and scurried toward the near shoulder. Ross lifted his head just as the military Suburban swerved sharply to the left, tires squealing loudly, then back again into the right lane.

"Did you see that?" Oswald cried excitedly. "Bastard missed me by less than an inch. I told you this was an asinine plan."

"Easy, easy," Ross said rushing to the bird. "He didn't hit you. We'll try the center of the road next time."

Oswald's head jerked instantly from the retreating red taillights to Ross. "Try again! That major was right. You are insane. If you think I'm going to stand in the middle of this road and give the next car a better shot at me while you lay safely on the side you're . . ."

"No swearing," Ross cautioned. "Jay is depending on us," he pleaded.

The owl's head swiveled to one direction of the road then the other, and then back to face Ross. "Once more and that's it," she said, each word seeming to carry punctuating emphasis with it.

As if scheduled, the leaves of the trees down the road again burst into light. Ross said, "Make it good," as he dove for cover.

"You're out of my will," Oswald called to him as she repeated her crippled position on the center stripe of the roadway.

Ross heard the oncoming vehicle, the skidding of tires, and then a car door. Lifting his head, he saw a man in uniform rounding the corner of the car, then reach for the pathetic, disabled creature lying six inches in front of the tire. When the do-gooder picked up Oswald and examined her apparently crumpled body with great concern, Ross bolted to the car and eased himself into the rear seat. Hugging the floor, he sent an "All set here," then waited nervously.

Seconds after, Ross heard a flapping of wings, the car rocked as the man's weight hit the front seat. The door closed and Ross released the breath he was holding.

"What now Einstein?" Oswald's telepathic voice assaulted Ross' mind.

"You're finished for now. Just stay close."

"Do you have any idea how close that tire came to me?"

"Quit bitching," Ross retorted.

"Till we meet again, amigo."

"God, what a ham."

Eventually the car slowed, harsh light pouring in through the windows. As it stopped, Ross' heart began thumping so loud he feared the driver would hear it. The window lowered, allowing indistinct words from the outside to drift down to him. He heard the driver state his name, followed by the word "here." Ross presumed he was presenting his identification.

Nearly a too-long minute of silence passed before he heard a clear voice from the open window. "Okay, Lieutenant. You didn't see anything unusual back there, did you?"

"No, nothing but trees and a hurt owl," the driver answered, then inquired, "Why, what's going on?"

"Probably nothing. They picked up a low-level blip earlier. It was so low it couldn't have been a plane. Suddenly it was gone. They got technicians working on the system now. They figure it's just a bug, but thought I'd check."

"Yeah, wonder when they're going to update the junk at this dump?"

"Guess they figure we don't have anything worth protecting."

"Night, Sergeant."

"Night, Sir."

The car moved and it became dark again.

The driver parked, then left. Ross lay motionless for an additional ten minutes to ensure the driver did not return. He carefully opened the door and climbed out with surprising agility, considering his degree of tiredness. Once on his feet, he searched the area and saw the two-story building he had chosen through Oswald's eyes. With an air of nonchalance, he strolled to the glass front doors, and pushed. Amazingly, one opened easily.

A few ceiling florescent cleaning lights dimly lit the inside. Listening carefully for a few moments, he guessed the building likely deserted, and began a systematic search of the offices on the first floor. He found what he was looking for in the ninth one.

"Got it yet?" popped into his head.

"Oswald, be quiet. Trying to focus here."

Ross moved quickly to one of the computer stations and typed in the codes extracted from the reluctant major, pulling up a menu of file names printed out on the gray-green screen. He grimaced at the twenty or so titles on the first page alone. The titles were alphabetized and the bottom one read "Apple Core," indicating the list would be long. The major had not known the code name used for the Ruthran project at the base, which meant it could be any of the hundreds that must be stored in the system. Ross indexed through all the file names, hoping to find a listing of something like "Extraterrestrial."

After fifteen minutes into the search he stared at the last file: Zebra 2. Losing patience, and with his ability to concentrate fading, he imagined himself a person with military backgound. What would he call the project if he were in their shoes? They thought in terms of hostility. He typed in "Invasion" and watched the computer spit out: "File does not exist." How about "alien?" "Martian?" "space beings?" He shot out words in rapid fire, like shooting arrows blind-folded, in the dark, at an invisible target. Every word was a miss. With dawn approaching, an early riser could walk in on him at any moment.

"How about now?" caused Ross to jerk up above the seat.

"Oswald!" he yelled mentally. "Let me work. You scared the crap out of me."

"You know, you're kinda crabby," the bird responded.

"Oswald. Silence. I need to concentrate."

"My beak is sealed."

Ross decided to invest the little time remaining to run through the entire menu once again, praying something would strike him as appropriate on this try. He lifted his finger from the key when the file names beginning with the letter "H" displayed, and stared thoughtfully at one in particular. A light sparked his dulled brain and he moved the cursor to the writer of a famous alien invasion, H G Wells, and hit Enter.

The computer indicated the file as classified and requested the user's security access code. Ross typed in the code he surreptitiously lifted from the major by a mental link, and waited, willing the computer to hurry. Suddenly a chronological log of events displayed on the screen. His fingers trembled as he pressed a key and the daily records scrolled by. His name appeared on many of the entries. Curiosity urged him to stop and read, but he fought off the desire and instead concentrated on those of only the last two days.

The second line above the bottom appeared like a punch in the gut. He glared at the phrase in anger mixed with hopelessness: "Unidentified transparent rod discovered in suspect's backpack transferred to E1530 Boston for scientific investigation."

The remainder of the log did not interest him. He looked out at the new morning gray-blue sky, wondering about Jay's reaction to the news of his failure. Images of the strange alien children floating limply in their gold canisters tumbled into his head. He heard footsteps in the hallway. Turning back to the computer he rapidly pounded in "Directory." He followed the list until he found E1530 Boston, moved the cursor, and hit return.

E1530 Route 128 Boston, Massachusetts
- Classified Scientific Research Laboratory
- Code Required For Additional Information

He cleared the screen, and dashed to the wall alongside the doorway. As luck would have it, footsteps approached the door to that office, and a young woman dressed in a civilian skirt and blouse walked past him into the room. He lunged, clamping his left hand firmly over her mouth and showed her the .45 automatic.

He whispered, "I am not going to harm you. Do not be afraid. Understand?"

She nodded feverishly.

"Good. Do you have a car outside?"

Again, the emphatic nodding.

"Give me your keys."

She fumbled nervously with her purse and handed him the keys with an unsteady hand.

"Good," Ross praised her calmly. "Now listen, this is what we are going to do. You are going to walk with me to your car, then I will get in and drive away. Understand? All I want is your car. I will not hurt you." He focused on her mind and perceived she had no intention of doing anything that might risk injury.

Slowly, he removed his hand from her mouth. The thought of explaining his dilemma and requesting her voluntary assistance crossed his mind but it would take too long, plus she would never believe him, and even if she did, he would be responsible for her becoming an accomplice to his crimes.

He waved the gun toward the door, signaling her to move.

She complied instantly.

They walked awkwardly down the central corridor to the glass doors and stopped while Ross inspected the area out front. "Is that your car?" he asked, pointing to a dark blue Mustang parked to the right of the concrete walkway.

Her nod was a little less vehement this time.

With a firm grip on her arm, he directed her through the doors, and out into the predawn light. Unlocking the car door, he stated, "I hope it's insured."

She did not respond; she was too preoccupied with the fear that he would take her hostage.

"No Mary, I'm not going to force you to come with me," he referenced her unspoken thoughts.

Bewilderment mingled with the fright in her eyes.

"Nasty habit of mine," he commented, then jumped into the front seat and started the engine. "I hope this doesn't spoil your day. And let someone know I left a major tied to a tree outside the base. I wouldn't want him to miss breakfast." Ross managed a smile as he closed the door. The car lurched backward away from the curb and he took one last glance at the frightened owner, still standing transfixed. He knew within moments she would phone for help.

Once he pulled the floor shift handle to the "drive" position, he gently depressed the accelerator until he reached a speed of 30 mph. Not wanting to draw unnecessary attention, he maintained the slow pace all the way to the first intersection then turned right onto the road leading to the main gate.

He stopped. The closed gate stood before him, yet another seemingly impenetrable barrier to his quest. Ross studied it and the armed MPs pacing casually in front of it. His eyes caught a shimmering point of light dancing on the car's highly polished hood, and he looked at the horizon. Venus glowed brightly in the twilight sky. His anger boiled up like the rising magma in a volcano poised for eruption.

"What's taking you so long?" Oswald's thoughts materialized in his head. "Did you doze off again?"

"Not now, I'm in the middle of a big escape."

"A little grouchy without your coffee, aren't you?" the bird retorted.

His hands squeezed the leather-wrapped wheel rim and his foot slammed the accelerator pedal against the carpet. The rear tires pawed for traction on the asphalt with a piercing steady screech. The Mustang launched forward with a throaty roar.

Stunned, the guards only stared uncomprehendingly at the accelerating vehicle. When they realized it was moving toward them and the gate, they knelt in unison, sighting their rifles at the charging metal bull. They waited only seconds for a sign of surrender before they realized none was forthcoming. They opened fire.

When Ross saw orange flashes lash out from the soldiers' weapons, he blinked then ducked his head just as the windshield disintegrated into a webbing of fractures radiating from several holes. Barely able to see through the damaged glass, he steered in a direction he guessed was straight ahead while keeping the accelerator pressed to the floor. Another wave of projectiles struck the vehicle, this time hitting not only parts of the shattered windshield but also sheet metal. A slight jerk in the car's forward motion followed instantly by a shower of reddish-orange sparks passing the side windows told Ross he was through the gate. This fact was confirmed when the rear window glass exploded into small pieces, and some object, either glass or a bullet, zinged past.

"Oswald!" he mentally shouted.

"Here."

"Where are you?"

"Down the road, you will be under me in a minute."

"Find a place in the woods that I can hide this car!"

Ross lowered the side window then leaned his head out so he could pick out the roadway ahead.

"Got it," Oswald called. "Stop. Now."

Ross obliged and pressed down on the brake pedal, bringing the Mustang to a quick but controlled stop and pushed his upper body through the side window. Searching over the roof and ahead on the road, he located Oswald a short distance ahead, perched on a low branch of a red pine in a very owl-like fashion.

"Over here," Oswald beckoned.

Ross followed the bird's thoughts into the forest. The Mustang's doors cleared trees on either side by only fractions of an inch, but the owl had gauged its size properly, enabling Ross to drive almost a quarter-mile into the forest before becoming boxed in by a thick, white pine stand.

Exiting the car, Ross gave the bird the dreaded news, "I didn't get it. It wasn't there. They sent it to a lab in Boston," Ross continued. "I'm going to try to get it, but my chances won't be good. Using the helicopter is out of the question. They'll be scouring the area. I need to find another form of transportation. Any ideas? Oswald? . . . Oswald!"

Snapping to attention, Oswald complained, "This is your world, not mine. Can't believe Jay talked me into coming with her to this dirtball of a planet."

"Okay, okay, enough griping. Go find the closest town, or at least a nearby farm or something. I'll go back to the road and start following it away from the base. Hurry, we're running out of time."

"You know, just because I have wings doesn't make me the go-to bird every fu . . ., sorry, every time you need to find something, or the patsy for a risky job."

"Oswald, now!" Ross shouted.

* * *

Ross peered around the side of the puddingstone boulder, about three feet higher than him. Looking across the small, granite-strewn cow pasture, he saw the old, well-maintained farmhouse. His eyes moved to the lime-green, faded early '70's Volkswagen Beetle sitting in the driveway. "That's your idea of transportation?"

"It's got wheels," Oswald replied. "And it's a pretty color."

"Jay should have gotten a bird with a bigger brain."

"That's it. I've had it with you. Find your own transportation."

Ross smiled and stroked Oswald's feathers. "Easy friend. We're on the same side here. I'm just tired."

Oswald's ear tufts pulled back against her head. "We're both getting edgy. Sorry comrade."

Moving from behind the stone, and into the field, Ross asked Oswald to circle above and warn him if she spotted any of the residents. Maintaining a crouching position, he ran in spurts between the granite boulders, vigilantly keeping his sight on the front door of the house.

When he touched the handle on the car, the front door burst open, and a farmer in blue coveralls rushed out onto the porch, a side-by-side shotgun already shouldered. Attempting distraction, Oswald swooped in front of the man, as Ross retreated at a full run. Two rapid-fire blasts violated his eardrums as he dove behind the puddingstone outcrop. Looking back, he saw the man reloading, and a couple of reddish-brown feathers floating down through the air.

A strange rasping sound interrupted Ross' thoughts, followed by, "I'm dying," and then a choking noise. "I'm behind you. Hurry, I can't hang on much longer."

Heartbroken, Ross spun and dashed into the woods in pursuit of his critically wounded friend.

"Not that way you fool, to your left."

He moved to Oswald collapsed on a bed of leaves, her feathers ruffled, her head listing to the left, she appeared to be shivering. He fanned the air in front of her to help her breathe.

"I'm a goner." She scraped out the sound, convincing Ross of her imminent demise.

Finally his fingers slid in to separate the layers of feathers for signs of blood or other damage. When he found nothing, he asked, "Oswald, where were you hit? I can't find anything."

"Really, no blood? I think I'm feeling a little better now." Oswald stood, swiveling her head side to side. "Maybe it was that electrical wire I flew into then."

"You are a drama queen," Ross said, his face betraying happiness.

"Did you see how I scared that guy and saved your life? Make sure you tell Jay. Courageous, don't you think?"

"Yes, you were very brave, Oswald. Thanks for your help."

She perched on Ross' shoulder, and asked, "So what is plan B?"

* * *

Standing at the edge of the grassy field, Ross watched the single engine Piper land, probably the most graceful touchdown he ever witnessed. After making a turn, the small two-seater jiggled across the uneven ground, coming to a stop only a short distance from them. Ross grinned at the lettering on the fuselage that read, "So You Think You Want To Learn To Fly? Montpelier, Vermont."

The pilot was shorter than Ross had imagined, about five-seven he estimated. His grey hair, with a few remaining strands of red spoiling the uniformity, was cropped in a military buzz cut. He wore faded jeans, an Air Force T-shirt, and western boots. Approaching Ross with a friendly smile framing gleaming white teeth, he stretched out his hand. "Hi, I'm John. Did you know there's an owl on your shoulder?"

"Ross Barton. No, I hadn't noticed."

He saw the headband on Ross' head, but chose not to say anything. "My good buddy Ernie in Indy tells me you're a good guy and need a little help. Something to do with the strange shit that's been goin' on around here. I told him it was true. Doesn't usually ask for favors, so must be important."

"I need to get to Logan in Boston as soon as possible," Ross said as Oswald flew to the ground. Turning to his feathered companion, he silently communicated, "I want you to take the headband to Jay so she will understand you. Tell her that I have discovered where the transmitter is located, but that my chances of getting it are not very good. She knows I'll risk anything to get it for her. If I don't come back . . . well . . . tell her I love her."

He lifted the headband from his head and placed it at Oswald's claws.

Puzzled by his passenger's interchange with the owl, John shook it off. "Ready when you are."

Ross watched Oswald fly away, and then circled the plane to the passenger door. Once seated and buckled in, John throttled up the engine until the propeller roared. They bounced down the field, building speed, and took off, the wheels clearing the top of a pine by a couple of feet.

When they attained the flight altitude, John said to Ross, "Like to hear about what you saw and what kind of trouble you're in. Have to be in trouble to need a ride from a field in the middle of nowhere."

Ross hesitated, and weighed the value of bringing him into his predicament. "You have to understand that if I tell you and you continue to help, you'll be considered my accomplice. It may mean trouble for you."

"Why don't you let me decide? Get started. I'll tell you to stop if I feel it's too hot for me to hear."

"Not sure if you'll believe this, but I saw aliens from another planet," he said.

"I knew it. I knew it. Told everyone strange shit goin' on here. I knew it. What they look like?" No skepticism or disbelief or sideways look at the wacko sitting next to him.

"Something resembling squid," Ross answered, watching the pilot for a reaction.

"No shit? Did they attack you?"

"Quite the opposite. They are friendly. Just children on a field trip. Military shot down their ship and dissected one."

"No shit? So that's what's been goin' on. Why you goin' to Boston?"

Ross hesitated. "Here's where it gets tricky for you. You'll be taking a big chance if you agree to help. Actually, it could affect your livelihood, even your freedom."

"Let me decide."

"There's a signaling device that was sent to a place in Boston for study. That device would enable them to get back home. As I understand it, it's used to contact a rescue ship in orbit waiting to return them to Jupiter. I'm trying to get it back for them. I'm not exactly one of our military's prime enlistment candidates."

"No shit? Jupiter, huh?" He was silent for a few minutes before asking, "How did you talk to these squid aliens?"

Ross thought, *Wonder how this one will come across?* He answered, "There's this woman who actually is one of them. Some kind of body switch. Oh, and that owl was one of them too."

"I see. Like that movie *The Body Snatchers*. The owl talks?"

"Not exactly, they communicate with each other by a kind of telepathy. That headband you saw allows whoever wears it to read thoughts."

"You mean to tell me you knew what that owl was thinking?"

Plunging on, he answered, "Yes, if I was wearing the headband."

"Aren't owls kind of stupid? Shouldn't they have chosen a dolphin or something like that?"

Grateful Oswald could not hear the disparaging "owl" description, and anxious to pull the conversation away from any philosophical discussion on the aspects of alien host body selection, Ross shrugged his shoulders. "Hell if I know."

"Okay, then, let's get you to Boston as fast as we can." John throttled up the engine speed.

Chapter 15

Bright late morning sunshine flooded the cockpit as they flew over the Massachusetts border. While John plotted the course and checked the instruments, Ross' mind turned to the task of hammering out yet another plan. This one would require greater thought than the others because the challenge was substantially larger. He could not just wait for some last minute inspiration to pop into his head. To succeed, he needed to develop the details of this plot beforehand. Implementation would require great care. Anything as simple as crashing through a roof or having an owl start a bonfire would not be adequate for this operation. Rudimentary elements of the plan had been worked out in his mind by the time they approached Logan Airport.

"Thanks for your help, John. I don't know where'd I'd be without you picking me up. Certainly hope you don't draw trouble from this."

"Naw, got my story worked out. Just got a job to pick you up in a field and deliver you to Boston. Nothing illigit about that. As far as I'm concerned, you weren't the talkative type. You've satisfied my curiosity about all the strange shit going on back there. Always knew there was somethin' at the bottom of it. Just wouldn't have guessed alien squid and a talking hawk."

"Owl," Ross corrected.

"Same thing. Just give me your email and I'll send you a bill."

Although Ross understood his plan was risky at best, he could think of no other, and so checked the flight schedules and purchased a temporary cell phone. He found a relatively isolated sitting area by a small fly-by-night airline deserted ticket counter.

He called Marsha's phone number apprehensively, realizing if he could not reach her on her cell, this particular plan ended instantly. After the fourth ring, he heard her seductive, sleepy voice. "Hello?"

"Hi Marsha, it's me."

"Ross?"

"I need your help."

"I don't understand, how . . ."

"Just listen," he interrupted. "There's a flight leaving for Boston in an hour and I'd like you to be on it. Use my credit card in the nightstand drawer at my place. I'll be waiting for you."

"But why? And I couldn't be ready that fast. I need to dress, and decide what to bring, and then pack."

"Please do me this favor. It's difficult to explain over the phone, but I found out that a government agency has been doing research in the same subject matter as me. It is important that I know the results but they're not willing to release it to me."

"You want me to help you steal it?" she asked incredulously.

"It's not exactly stealing. They've made the information available to some other universities they treat as favored children and it's not equitable. I just want to discuss it with the person in charge but can't get an appointment."

"Why not get it from one of the other universities given the information?"

"The project leaders at those schools know I'm way ahead of them with my work and see this as a golden opportunity to close the gap."

"I didn't know professors got involved in such covert goings-on."

"Will you do it?"

"For you, yes," she answered sweetly. "We'll have such a wonderful time together. There're some stores in Boston I've always wanted to shop. You could buy me some special lingerie and we could spend the night in a classy hotel. I would wear it for you and . . ."

He cut her off, abruptly changing the conversation to fill in the details she needed to know once she landed. He emptied his head of any guilt he may have for lying or entangling her in his illegal plot. He rationalized she would be innocent of any real premeditated wrongdoing. The authorities would consider her a pawn in the whole affair and release her with nothing more than a reprimand when it was over . . . or so he hoped. At least she would get a trip to Boston at his expense.

He phoned information, got the number for the Air Force base, and then tapped another set of digits, thus beginning his next lie in a series to come.

"Mary Delante please." Ross waited as he heard two clicks, and then another phone ringing.

On the eighth ring an elderly woman's voice asked, "May I help you?"

"Major French for Mary Delante."

"Sorry, she's not in this morning."

"What? She guaranteed she'd have some information for me first thing this morning."

"It's not her fault, Major," the woman defended gruffly. "A maniac held her at gunpoint this morning and stole her car."

"That's terrible! Is she okay?"

"Just shaken up. They gave her the day off."

"How did this car thief get off the base?"

"He crashed through the front gate," the woman said, her voice rising.

"Ohhh-nooo, Mary's new Mustang."

"Yeah, she's heartbroken," the woman confided. Any reservations about talking to the stranger on the telephone were obviously gone. Thoroughly warmed for conversation, Ross now learned about her husband, grandchildren, neighbors, and her opinion of the shoddy manner in which the base was being run.

Ross seized a pause in her oratory while she caught her breath. "Speaking of the way those jerks run the base, I'm going to get in hot water by not having the information Mary was instructed to give me, but . . ." He paused with a pathetic sigh and continued, "it's not her fault. She couldn't have foreseen being involved in a crime." He waited, anticipating.

"What information was she going to get for you?"

"The telephone number and address for the government's contracted scientific research lab E1530 in Boston."

"That's easy. I'll get it."

The lady's voice, happy to help fulfill poor Mary's obligations, returned within minutes with the needed data. Ross thanked her and asked her to say hello to Mary for him when she returned.

Immediately Ross touched the numbers for the research lab.

"NAC Industries. May I help you?"

"Yes Miss. My name is Steven Harley from CSD, and I am responsible for the installation of future computer system upgrades. Who is in charge of your IT systems?"

There was a silence while the woman presumably referred to some organizational chart, then answered, "Mr. Apost."

"Okay, and who is responsible for the building floor plan? You know, desk arrangements, who gets which room, etc., etc."

"I am."

"Your name?"

"Bonnie Rentler."

"Okay, Bonnie, I'll be contacting you and Mr. Apost later this month to discuss the installation of some new printer stations just approved."

"Oh? I didn't know anything about this."

"Oh really. Who normally informs you of potential changes required at E1530?"

"Why our director, Mr. Wiley," Bonnie answered as if insulted.

Ross, actually beginning to enjoy his charade, continued, "No, not him. Who from the outside?"

"Oh," she brightened as if she just remembered the answer to a million dollar quiz. "You mean Margaret Beamsley at the Facilities Engineering Department in Washington."

"Yes, she's the one. She was supposed to have notified Mr. Wiley that your operation would be equipped with additional printers."

"Well she didn't and I don't know where they expected to put them," she said somewhat irritated.

"We can work with you to arrive at the best solution. Glad I checked. I'll give Margaret a call and make sure your operation is notified properly in the future."

"Thank you, Mr. . . .?"

"Haley, Steven. Good day, Bonnie."

Ross swept up his notes and cards, and walked briskly to the terminal front doors. Glancing at his watch, then the sky, he discovered he was ahead of his own schedule and that it looked like rain. He slid into the first cab and asked the driver to take him to the nearest department store. Within a short time he exited the store carrying a large shopping bag.

After arriving back at the airport, he paid the driver and scrambled through the driving rain into the terminal. He emerged from the men's room fifteen minutes later, transformed from a grubby hiker to a clean-shaven, neatly attired businessman in dress shoes, navy blue blazer, red striped tie, and gray slacks. Ross checked his watch then returned to his private phoning area and again spread out his notes.

"NAC Industries. May I help you?"

"Yes, I'm trying to reach Bonnie Rentler."

"That's me."

"Hello Bonnie, my name is Peter Garub with Office Greening. My company has been contracted to place and maintain plants at your location. I was told you are the one I should contact to set up an appointment."

"By who?"

Ross shuffled some of his notes for audible effect, then answered, "Let's see . . . a Margaret Beamsley."

"That woman!" Bonnie said angrily. "Second time today."

"Is there a problem?"

"Nobody tells me anything," she complained.

"It won't take much time."

"What is it you want?" she huffed.

"My assistant and I would like to meet with you at say, one-thirty. We would like to discuss the type of plants you find suitable and identify acceptable locations."

"But I don't have time to water a building full of plants," she puffed.

"Oh no, Ms. Rentler. We'll make recommendations for your approval and once in place, we'll maintain and care for all the plants as required. You just need to select the plants you want and designate locations. Shouldn't take long."

"Okay, but you should know, I'm no interior decorator," she relented after a minute's silence. "See you at one-thirty Mr. Garub."

"It's pronounced Gaar-ube," Ross corrected.

"Mr. Gaar-ube," she repeated.

Ross ended the call and patted his pocket for the camera memory card. "My luck may finally be changing," he murmured. The toughest part of it would still be getting his hands on the transmitter, but once he had that, everything else should work out. Marsha could drive him back to the forest, enabling him to get the transmitter to Jay in enough time. Then he could get copies of the photos he took of the alien exploratory vehicle to some of his trusted professional friends. Publication of that photographic proof, along with sworn testimony of his knowledge about the aliens and the government actions, would provide enough of a threat to those in power to give him the bargaining ability to preserve his freedom. The only flaw in his plan was it would leave him without Jay.

He looked at his watch again and hurried off to meet Marsha, surprised to see her standing at the baggage pickup area, waiting. A flight fifteen minutes ahead of schedule was a rarity.

When her eyes caught his, she smiled, more beautiful than ever. Inwardly he recoiled as she clutched him in an "Oh, I missed you so much" hug. He returned her embrace, hoping she did not feel his wave of uneasiness. Grabbing her luggage, he went into each detail of her intended role as they clipped through the airport, relieved she readily agreed to everything. In fact, she appeared giddy to comply.

As he handed her the shopping bag and watched her prance off to the nearest ladies room, he acknowledged, with shame, her willingness to do anything for him without question. In his mind, that she was using him did not justify his corresponding treatment of her. He considered laying out the truth when she returned. But his thoughts went to Jay and the children. No, he would do nothing that might increase the risk to their safety, or failure of his mission.

Heads turned as Marsha strutted from the restroom, across the aisle to Ross. He had selected the sexiest dress he could find in her size, but he never imagined that any real body could fill it in so wonderfully. The style of the white, clingy garment might be considered as appropriate business wear on some. However, on Marsha, with her shapely figure, unbridled breasts, and sleek, tanned thighs flashing through the side slit the outfit could register as obscene. Catching the glint of appreciation in Ross' eyes, she beamed with feminine confidence as she pirouetted around, asking, "You like it?"

What a seductress, he thought. He nodded and said, "It'll do."

Ross flipped through a plant catalog lifted from the flower shop as Marsha drove the rental car on Route 128 through the downpour. "Why did you put this car in my name?" she asked after a long period of silence.

As he turned to answer, his eyes drifted down to her right thigh showing through the parted slit in her dress, pleased his emotional bond to Jay eradicated any personal interest in Marsha's sensuality.

"Keep your mind on business. We'll have time for that later."

He responded with a smile. How could he tell her she was there only to be the ornament in his plan, merely a distasteful necessity?

"Ross?" she broke in on his thoughts.

"Sorry, just daydreaming. When we're finished here I'm going to have you drop me off back in Vermont so you'll need the car to get back to the airport."

"Are you serious? I thought we could . . . you know," she said and gave him a quizzical look as she folded back the front of her dress to uncover both legs.

Ross moved his gaze to the wiper blades. "Just one more day and it'll be all over."

"You give me the chills when you say it like that. Is that the building?"

He followed her eyes to the right and saw a building set in a wooded hillside. A sign reading "NAC Industries" stood prominently in front of the square structure. "Yeah, this is it. Take this exit." Marsha guided the car to the right while he pulled his thoughts together, silently rehearsing the exact words he would use in response to the variety of potential scenarios he could face, and so he was startled when Marsha shut off the engine.

As he reached the door handle, Marsha's hand touched his shoulder. He looked at her warily.

"Maybe we should forget it, Ross. We should just drive to a motel and spend the day making love."

Her words struck him as sincere, so he smiled, patted her hand and told her softly, "I have no choice."

"I think I understand," she answered.

He squinted through the rain-blurred windshield up at the single level building sheathed in copper-colored glass, elevated above the ground. His eyes followed a stairway ascending up three flights. His heart scrambled. "Ready?" Together they bent their heads against the rain and darted up the stairs, to the entrance, to the one-inch-thick plate glass lobby doors.

A woman with vibrant, reddish-brown hair and a face peppered with faint freckles lifted her eyes from a magazine on the desk and smiled. "Are you here about the plants?"

"Bonnie Rentler?" Ross queried as they strode toward the young woman.

"Yes," she answered, standing to greet them.

"Peter Garub of Office Greening, and this is my associate, Marsha.

"Pleased to meet you," Bonnie replied, unavoidably eyeing Marsha's superior feminine attributes. "So where do we start?"

"The ladies room," Marsha requested. "It's been a long ride."

Bonnie nodded understandably, "Follow me."

While he awaited their return, Ross paced. *What's keeping them?* When they returned, both appeared suspiciously nervous. Two revelations struck him. One, he discovered he retained a minute portion of his ability to communicate mentally even without the benefit of Jay's headband. And two, that same residual talent allowed him to perceive their uneasiness, like they had formed a partnership that did not include him.

Ross manufactured a polite smile to camouflage a gut feeling that something was out of order. "We'd like to tour your building so we can suggest suitable locations. Please point out all the rooms and areas in which you would not permit plants."

"Sure. Follow me," Bonnie said. "I've done some homework."

Marsha paused to withdraw a note pad and pen from her purse. Ross prepared to ask her about her discussion in the ladies room, but stopped. He read her aura as dangerous and she was not to be trusted. He chose to say nothing to her.

As the three moved through the corridors and adjoining rooms, Marsha, as he expected, drew the attention of every man who chanced to see her. Word spread of this dazzling woman in the building. Soon she was the Pied Piper of NAC Industries. And she played her part well, pausing to smile and answer ridiculous questions like "Did they predict rain today?"

That elation collapsed when Bonnie halted at a closed door and announced, "This room is off limits. They're investigating some kind of strange object they found out in Vermont."

Bonnie's voluntary declaration about the type of research occurring behind that closed door left no doubt; this was a trap. For all practical purposes, she had told him the transmitter was in that room. They were baiting him with information, so clear only a complete fool would miss its innuendo. Trap or not, he had to play the game out. Even if his chance of success had been reduced to a billion to one, he had to try.

The tour ended back in the reception area. Ross glanced up to see a small cluster of men around the front desk. A few others at the copy machine. He informed Bonnie he needed a break in the men's room and suggested she and Marsha begin to review the plant catalog for possible choices.

Ross braced against the bathroom wall, struggling to stay alert. His tired mind could not understand what was going wrong and why his plan failed; unclear thoughts coiled around every idea he conjured up. What had he seen between Marsha and Bonnie? Was he just paranoid about the unveiled tip from Bonnie? Marsha had proven a worthy decoy. With or without her at his side, he knew he could walk into any room and be accepted as "that plant guy with the voluptuous blond."

His time for review had run out. He had no choice but to step quietly into the hall and follow his memory to the "off-limits" door. His hand poised midair for a moment before reaching for the lever. Taking a deep breath, he twisted the handle and the door fell open. As half expected, the room was not empty. In the center of the room, three men stood at a table littered with electronic equipment. A fourth man, a security guard, stood off to the left, training the barrel of a revolver at Ross' chest. "Aaah, excuse me. I was just surveying for sunny locations for plants that . . ."

"Oh, come on Mr. Barton, I think we're all too intelligent for that game." A man in the center of the three addressed him first; his ID badge read Wiley, the director of the building. "Don't be shy; come in."

Ross took a few reluctant steps into the room; his eyes quickly settling on the glass rod resting on two notched wood blocks on the table.

"That's what you're here for, isn't it?" Wiley smirked. When Ross did not answer, he continued, "Air Force MPs will be here shortly to take you off our hands. They tell me you left quite a trail of destruction."

Ross remained silent.

Wiley tapped the transmitter with a finger and asked, "What is this thing?"

Ross only blinked.

"Don't be such a pain in the ass, Mr. Barton. We'll find out sooner or later. Why don't you make it easier for us and we can put in a good word for you?"

Ross stared at the paunchy man.

Wiley snapped, "Frisk the bastard."

The guard obediently moved to Ross and patted him thoroughly through his clothing, shoulders to toes, then stepped back and shook his head.

"Put that gun away," Wiley spat at the guard, and then looked back to Ross. "What if I break it?" Wiley threatened, and brightened when he saw Ross' instant concern. "Bothers you, huh? Is it some kind of explosive?"

"No," Ross finally verbalized. "Be careful with it."

It should not have surprised Ross when Marsha walked into the room, but it did. All conversation stopped until Wiley offered his hand and said, "Miss Cooper, glad to meet you. We are indebted to you for your cooperation in this matter." Wiley grinned when he caught a sad expression cross Ross' face. "Oh, how insensitive of me," he consoled Ross facetiously. "You didn't know, did you?"

Marsha was plainly on the verge of tears. She edged tentatively to Ross and placed a sympathetic hand on his shoulder. "I did it for your own good," she told him, looking into his resigned eyes. "They called me, thought you might contact me. And you did. They explained you were in serious trouble, and they might be able to arrange it so you could be freed and we could be together." Her eyes begged for understanding, but his returned with impassive indifference. Her speech ended in a flood of tears and she fled from the room.

"Touching," Wiley placated.

Slow crawling hate for the man added more fuel to his restrained anger. He stared out the wall of tinted glass at the trees. His thoughts repeated the words, *must escape.* "I'll help," he agreed, stalling for time.

"Gooood, gooood," Wiley praised.

"Give it to me," Ross said softly.

Wiley raised the rod loosely and smirked before handing it off to Ross.

Clutching the treasured object of his quest, Ross gazed blankly at the window, watching rivulets of water stream down.

"Get on with it Barton," Wiley prodded anxiously. "Show us what it does."

Giving no warning for what he was about to do, Ross was halfway across the room, sprinting at full speed toward the glass wall. Seconds before impact, he leaped with a twist, so that when he was within inches of the glass, he was tucked in a ball, face down, knees at his chest, feet poised for contact, head trailing, and the transmitter held safely against his stomach. His legs suddenly exploded into an extended position, driving his feet through the thick plate glass and shattering it into a nebula of fragments. The four, paralyzed onlookers watched in astonishment as Ross' body sailed through the cascade of glass and dropped from sight.

The soggy, moist earth, combined with a well-practiced bending of his knees, cushioned Ross' impact so that he sustained no leg damage in the landing. The slick soles of his shoes caused him to slide and fall across the slippery soil, but all things considered, he could not have hoped for a better execution of the dangerous escape. Ross scrambled to his feet and bounded into the woods, gripping the glass rod like a baton in a relay race. Darting between trees, the heavy rain wetting his face produced a sharp stinging sensation on his right cheek, and he soon tasted something like iron in his mouth. Gasping for air, he put his fingers to his cheek, and winced at the searing pain. The glass had opened a large gash on his face. A small price for the object in his hand, he resumed his dash, curving to the right down a treacherous path cluttered with twigs, leaves, and broken branches from the increasingly heavy gusting wind.

Shivering and coughing, he continued to surge forward with driving intensity, finally breaking out of the trees and onto the shoulder of the expressway. Getting back to Jay seemed hopeless. His mind thrashed around in chaos; as much as he tried to pull his thoughts together, he could find no clarity. He had planned to have Marsha drive him to Vermont. The simple image of her brought a rush of wasted anger and he struggled to purge his picture of the traitorous woman.

With all potential avenues seemingly closed, he resigned himself to hitchhiking and moved to the breakdown lane. If Ross had a mirror, he would have fathomed the unlikelihood of any passing motorist offering him a ride. Besides being drenched head to toe, his slacks and jacket were torn; mud smeared his shoes and pant legs. Thick streams of crimson blood flowed to his neck and onto the open collar of his newly purchased dress shirt.

Many unsuccessful minutes later, he abandoned all hope of acquiring a ride when the sound of helicopters rose above the noise of the speeding tires on wet pavement. Looking at the transmitter clutched in his hands, tears indiscernible from the drops of rainwater, streamed from his eyes. Despair, mingled with his need to be with Jay, caused his mind to call out for her. The world darkened while his quasi-conscious brain raced over the most recent events. He relived his crash through the Air Force base gate, his actions at Logan Airport, the drive to the research lab building, the incidents in the building, his leap for freedom, and the seemingly endless running. A replay of the moment when Jay told him they were married according to her people's customs was the last vision his mind held as his overwrought brain slipped into unconsciousness.

Chapter 16

Eerie lighting blanketed Ross' reclined body, forcing him to open his heavy-lidded eyes. He gazed curiously up at the transparent domed roof above him, and tried to bring clarity to his thoughts. Memories of his escape gradually congealed, and then he remembered blacking out under pouring rain on the side of the road. A searing jolt of reality brought him to a sitting position. He had no vocabulary for what he was seeing.

The words, "You are awake" formed in his head but emanated from a small group of creatures before him, looking oddly familiar.

"This is real?" he asked mentally in response.

A large squid-like life form waved its tentacles in affirmation, telling him telepathically, "It is."

Ross scrambled to his feet to examine his surroundings. His body swiveled 360° to take in his captive enclosure: an enormous, see-through cylinder with hemispherical domes capping the ends above and below him. A flat, circular plate, with matching transparency, served as the floor he stood on, the inside of the lower dome cap visible below it. As a means of exit, a tube, large enough for a man to stand upright, ran horizontally from his cylinder sidewall. The cylinder's interior was separated into a few compartments, all with transparent walls, and in each were human amenities one would normally have expected in a small apartment. The complete cylindrical living space hung suspended in a liquid or gas with a faint brownish-red tint. Three Ruthra, like the children he had witnessed, floated just outside the curved side nearest him. He studied the closest and concluded these were adult versions of those Jay had allowed him to see. They were about twice the size, but displayed identical features and coloration.

"You are not frightened?" the male Ruthran leader inquired.

"No, I'm not," Ross answered offhandedly. "But how did I get here? And where is here?"

"You beckoned us with the transmitter. We brought you aboard our ship. How did you gain possession of our transmitter, and where is our scout?"

"Oswald and Jay? You don't have them? And the children? Didn't you get the children?"

"We have no knowledge as to their location. When we received the signal we thought we had recovered them, but instead we found you, Earthman, and decided to probe your mind."

"I don't know how I signaled you. Jay never told me how to use the transmitter."

"It is activated by a mental link. We do not understand how you managed to use it, or how you are communicating with us now. Humans do not have this ability."

"I didn't think I had the ability either, at least I didn't before. Jay allowed me to use her amplifier, but I sent it back to her with Oswald."

"She should have never permitted a member of your species to gain the knowledge about its operation, and especially allow it to be used. Or did you take it from her by force? We are very familiar with your undesirable flaws."

Ross felt the loathing for human beings in the Ruthra's last sentence. This he accepted as justifiable, but the insinuation about Jay's incompetence in her task elicited an immediate emotional response. "She did not betray your people! She knew I could be trusted with her secrets, and I can. I would rather end my life than divulge any information to my people which could possibly threaten Jay or her mission."

A lapse in the exchange between beings of different worlds occurred while the leader pondered the human's strange reactions. Finally, the leader observed, "I detect a strong affection for our scout in your thoughts. The one you call Jay. There must be a defect in our link. Please explain why she trusted you, one of the beings that murdered our people."

Ross hesitated, not knowing what this creature's reaction might be to the truth. "Look, just accept that I have great affection for her."

No direct response came from the Ruthra after Ross' admission, but his growing aptitude for mental linking allowed him to pick up the peripheral revulsion the alien felt. Why not? To him Ross was an ugly, loathsome member of a species that had inflicted senseless killing on his kind. And they murdered innocent children. The thought of one of these horrible, barbaric people actually having the audacity to profess affection for a female of his society was just incomprehensible. Ross knew the leader would have found it easier to accept a confession of guilt for her murder than a declaration of love.

This was not the time to tell them of her love for him or that they married by Ruthran custom. That additional information could certainly precipitate a reaction that could not be taken back. Instead, he outlined the events that led him to the possession of the transmitter.

The lead Ruthra did not fully embrace Ross' story, but asked if he would be willing to give them Jay's location. Ross quickly agreed, and then watched one of the other two swim away.

Seeing one of the creatures move for the first time, the unique method of locomotion awoke his scientist's curiosity. The ten, long tentacles encircling the head of the being were apparently not rigidly attached to the adjoining tissue as he first supposed. He noticed a thin line or crevice at the juncture of each tentacle and the head. This nearly undetectable discontinuity became readily apparent only because each of the tentacles rotated. Each took on a corkscrew shape and this configuration, combined with the rotation, created a kind of liquid screw, pulling the creature forward along its axis. The slight upward tilt axis of the spinning tentacles obviously compensated the buoyancy of the trailing air sack.

Ross contemplated about what fascinating wonders of natural engineering were hidden inside a joint that permitted rotation while providing the necessary sealing of body fluids. Even more difficult to imagine was a mechanism providing power to the extremities for both tasks of gripping and propulsion. The animal kingdom native to Earth derived the forces required for movement from systems of muscles and tendons, but those types of living systems, if applied to the rotating appendages before him, would sustain damage within a few revolutions.

Although Ross' interest in learning the workings of the Ruthran body stirred his inquisitive mind, he did not ask the leader for enlightenment since he was certain that such curiosity would only aggravate the existing resentment toward him.

More stray fragments of thoughts from the leader manifested themselves in Ross' head, alarming him. His ability to link was growing beyond what Jay had indicated as being normal for her people. He was receiving thoughts he knew the leader did not intend to transmit. Those private thoughts Ross overheard, told of the leader's increasing dislike of the alien Earth creature within their midst. Ross' claim of affection for one of their own only confirmed the Ruthra's initial opinion of humans. The leader felt certain that emotions of love were plainly impossible between such different beings and suspected Ross was setting a devious human plot to harm his people.

The other Ruthra returned, clutching an octagonal, faceted, crystal globe in two tentacles, propelling himself with the other eight. The alien released it a foot or two beyond the transparent wall to hang motionless in space, its hazy, yellow center starting to glow.

Ross retreated a safe distance when a three-dimensional, topographical, holographic map of a portion of the New England area materialized to his right, waist level. Familiar labels of state names and cities were not evident, nor were reference longitude and latitude grids. Recognizable features of cities, rivers, lakes, mountains, and the coastline quickly allowed him to identify Boston and the Appalachians. Ross reluctantly approached the holograph when his eyes met the landscape of Vermont. He pointed to the area on Long Trail where Jay remained stranded.

"Touch it," the leader commanded.

Ross did. A new map encompassing an area of a fifty-mile radius around the point his finger indicated, instantly replaced the old one. Comprehending the operation of the system, he studied it again then placed his finger slowly into the glowing image. The map repeated the magic, showing a small area in minute detail, even depicting the government's forest encampment, indicating recent updates. "Here," he said, pointing to a rock formation barely visible through the carpet of trees. Lines of a coordinate system popped up over the surface and a bright yellow dot pulsated at the point he had indicated.

Abruptly, Ross lurched toward the wall, his arms flexing to brace against it as the ship accelerated with a flash of speed.

* * *

Following another surge Ross attributed to deceleration, the leader swam up to his cylinder chamber. "Do you think us fools, human? The murder of our children and scout were not enough. You wish to make the atrocity complete by the destruction of this ship and all aboard, even at the sacrifice of your own life. The mockery . . ."

"Murder of your children and scout?" Ross interrupted, his eyes wide.

The leader could not help but read the intensity of despair the human's mind transmitted, but his rage was too deep to care. "Do not feign sorrow, it was of your own doing. They are lost and you would have us subject ourselves to your people's weapons."

He felt acid rise to his throat. "They are lost? She's gone?" He had already begun to accept the inevitable loss of Jay to her home planet, but her death was unthinkable. His mind played a quick series of snapshots as if through a viewer: the rays of sunshine playing off the highlights of her glossy black hair, the traces of a loving smile on her full lips, her vibrant violet eyes which showed as a road map to her thoughts. He remembered back to when he knew he loved her; it was when she told him: "You do love me."

"How did she die?" he finally asked.

The Ruthran leader's brain grappled to make sense of the intensity and seemingly sincere outpouring. Straining to decode this human's reactions to determine their truthfulness, he missed Ross' question. He had been so certain of this human's part in a plot to harm his people, that he left no room for the possibility he could be wrong. And now, studying Ross' response over the deaths of his scout dwarfed his own sorrow, so much so in fact that he saw this strange being's desire for his own death. Such devotion to another individual was difficult to imagine, but he acknowledged its reality. The Ruthra's anger metamorphosed into pity as he watched Ross move to folded women's clothing on a shelf.

"She used this room?" Ross asked pointlessly.

"I did not believe your claim of love for our female scout. I believe now. How did this come to be?"

"I don't know. She certainly didn't encourage me. She was without emotion and asked me to leave her alone at every opportunity. I convinced myself I wanted to be with her out of fascination with her strangeness until she told me of my true feelings before I, myself, was aware of them."

"And yet when you discovered her true identity, you retained this attachment?"

"It was too late by then. I could no less stop loving her than stop breathing. There is a beauty inside her that stands her apart from anyone I've ever known."

"And she explained she would return to Jupiter and her Ruthran body would be restored?"

"Yes, she did."

The leader considered Ross' statements, and then followed, "And what were her feelings toward you?"

Ross hesitated to answer, and then remembered nothing mattered anymore and he said, "She loved me."

"How do you know this?"

"She explained your customs. How a Ruthran female is destined to love only one male during her existence, and how I was the one she selected. She allowed me to comprehend her love through the amplifier." Ross again paused. The reality of his loss snaked through his core, driving pain to his every nerve as he struggled to connect the gap between his brain and his body. "We mated. She said that by your customs, the act made us united. She was my wife!"

"I understand," was the only response that came from the Ruthran leader's mind.

"Please tell me how she died," Ross reiterated. "I want to know."

"She is not dead, but will be soon."

"What?" Ross shouted aloud, the word reverberating off the room's walls and causing the leader to flinch at the unexpected sonic waves striking his skin. Ross jumped to his feet and bellowed, "She's alive!"

"Yes but the situation is hopeless. It is only a matter of time."

"Why can't you fly down and save her?" Ross hounded.

"We would be attacked."

"Use your weapons," Ross pleaded, almost incoherent with frustration.

"We have no weapons," the leader responded, surprised at Ross' willingness to take action against his own kind in order to preserve Ruthran lives. "We do not believe in the taking of any being's life. It is not our way. We only have surface exploration vehicles, similar to those used by the children. They are larger for adults, but essentially move in the same manner on articulated legs. They are used solely for observation and have no weapons."

"Then teleport or beam them all up. You know, like on *Star Trek*."

"We must land to pick them up."

"Shit!" Ross summarized.

"Define shit."

"Never mind. Can I see what's going on down there?"

In response, the Ruthran retrieved the globe previously used to provide the maps. Once the live image formed, Ross saw the helicopters swarming over the rocky outcrops, soldiers poised for attack around the landmark, and more equipment and soldiers being ferried into the government's clearing by large, twin rotor cargo helicopters. "Christ, a military offensive against innocent children, an owl, and a defenseless woman," he mumbled.

"You see, there is nothing we can do," the leader explained.

Nevertheless, Ross' eyes found two pieces of newly arrived military equipment especially interesting, smiled and asked, "Can you put me down there?"

"But why? There is no chance."

"I think there is. Can you do it?"

The image of the area below disappeared from Ross' container and reformed directly in front of the leader. After a few minutes of examination he announced, "We can land here," pointing to the location with the tip of a tentacle. "After landing, it will be necessary to ascend back into orbit in order to avoid attack."

"That's fine, but could you monitor Jay's position so if I succeed in moving the soldiers you can pick up her and the children quickly?"

"Yes, but I do not understand how you can distract so many."

"I'll give it my best shot. It's better than sitting here watching them die. How are your exploration vehicles controlled?"

"Mental link."

"Good. Can they be controlled from the outside?"

"Yes, a link can control the vehicles from inside or out."

"Could Oswald direct them?"

"Yes, but . . ."

"How many do you have on board?" Ross interrupted, his enthusiasm building.

"Ten."

"I'll need them all. Do you have anything which could be mistaken for a weapon?"

"No."

"Think. Something that makes sounds like gunfire, shoots projectiles, makes explosions . . ."

"How about intensified light?" one of the Ruthra suggested, catching the Earthman's fervor.

"A laser. Great! How powerful?"

The leader described the surveillance equipment that beamed enough energy to hole a thin piece of Ruthran metal at close range. Its effect on common Earth materials was unknown.

"Can they be mounted to the vehicles?" Ross continued.

"Yes, but we have only four," the leader responded almost apologetically, becoming more and more infected by Ross' determination to rescue the Ruthra below.

"Activated by mental link?"

"Yes."

"Good, mount them."

The leader signaled one of the other Ruthra and with renewed vigor rattled off a series of instructions. "All will be ready in ten of your minutes. Anything else?"

"Yes, don't fail to get them up if I do my part."

"Do not be concerned. If you succeed, we will bring the children, our scout, and her parrow aboard."

"And get them back home safely," Ross prompted.

"Yes, we will take care of your wife."

Ross let out a sigh of relief.

"I understand completely now," the Ruthran leader said.

"Understand what?"

"Why the one you call Jay chose you for a mate."

"But she should mate one of her own kind when she returns. She deserves a life of happiness. Her return to her planet would establish a new start for her."

"I have learned enough of you and know enough of her to confirm her love would never allow another. You, my friend, will always be her choice. I know the ways of our people, and to suggest another would only shame her."

The whole topic regarding Jay began to unsettle Ross. He knew his chances of forcing the conditions that would make her rescue feasible were slim and he sought to forget it for a while. And so he turned to his curiosity as a means to distract his thoughts by inquiring, "May I ask a question about the function of the Ruthran body?"

"Certainly."

"I noticed that your locomotion is accomplished through the thrust created by the rotation of your tentacles. This type of joint movement is unparalleled in the higher forms of life on Earth."

"I am familiar with the internal structures of many of the Earth species, including yours, and can therefore appreciate your inquisitiveness relating to the Ruthran physiology. The animals of Earth have evolved utilizing central nervous systems that conduct electrical pulses sent by the brain. Your senses, organs, and muscle tissues are directly wired to your brain. Most animal species on Jupiter evolved without central nervous systems, the signals to organs and senses being transmitted from the brain without physical connection. A wireless system if you will. In the Ruthra, movements you would think would be affected through the employment of muscle tissue, given your experiences, are instead accomplished with pressurized fluid."

"Hydraulics?" Ross summarized in fascination.

"Yes, precisely."

"But how is the force generated to move, one of your tentacles for instance, in a particular direction?"

Simple system of pressurized and depressurized internal chambers, each controlling its pressure level by valves, which are in turn controlled by the signals broadcast from the brain. Since you are particularly interested in our tentacles, I will use one of them for an example.

"Pressurized fluid enters the tentacle through a hollow core at its axis. The wall of the tentacle, beneath the outer skin, is a tube comprised of thousands of individual chambers. These chambers have inlet and outlet orifices than can be constricted to a completely closed position or completely open. If a chamber is to be pressurized to full, the inlet opens and the outlet closes. If it is to be depressurized, the inlet closes and the outlet opens until the desired pressure is reached. A low pressure return system carries low pressure fluid back to the central pump, our heart. Now, if the tentacle is to move to the right, the chambers on the left increase in pressure and those on the right decrease, thereby allowing the elastic tissue to stretch on the left and shrink on the right. Then the tentacle moves right. This is a great simplification, but I think it is adequate to describe the fundamental principles of the system. Additionally, the base pressure of the complete system can be increased or decreased to counteract the differences in atmospheric pressure as an individual seeks different altitudes. The fluid is also the primary method of maintaining body temperature."

Ross was dumbfounded, and although the extraordinary living system just described to him seemed to be a hydraulic engineering nightmare, he could understand why it might be an efficient evolutionary solution for the atmospheric conditions on Jupiter.

The leader sensed he had impressed his pupil and began to ask if Ross had further questions, but one of his shipmates interrupted. All was ready. Landing was imminent.

As instructed, Ross moved through the horizontal tube and waited against the ship's metal hull.

Chapter 17

The ship touched down for a long agonizing minute before the panel in front of Ross opened to fresh air. His eyes found the rungs of a ladder and he stepped out. As he clamored down the twenty feet to the ground, his eyes traversed the surrounding meadow for signs of the military's presence. When his feet contacted the weed-matted earth, he caught sight of the tan, seven-feet-tall, bullet-shaped Ruthran surface vehicles and his mind called out, "Oswald!"

"Been on vacation?" came a familiar reply.

"Ross, you are alive!" Jay cut in on the bird.

"I missed you Jay."

"Cut out the mush," Oswald reprimanded.

"Ross, I am frightened," Jay responded. "We are trapped. There is no way that you can reach us."

"Jay, just pay attention. I must hurry. I am going to try to draw the military away from you. As soon as they move away, your ship will pick you up. You and the children must be ready. You will not get a second chance."

"I do not understand. How do you know . . . ?"

"Jay! I don't have time to explain. Just be ready. Oswald, I need you with me."

"Not again," the bird objected. "War is hell. I'm on my way boss."

"Your people will explain, Jay. Goodbye." Ross blocked any further communication from Jay to concentrate on Oswald, giving her his location and what he wanted the bird to do. Ross glanced up at the Ruthran ship as it began to rise, comprehending its shape and size for the first time. It was an immense silver sphere, the picture of simplicity. In a flash, the huge ball soundlessly became a speck against the bright blue sky, and then vanished altogether. Ross began to run toward the military camp.

As he ran zigzagging between the densely packed pines, maples, and birches, Jay pleaded with him repeatedly to link with her. Regardless how much his heart wanted to communicate with her, he was set on taking the action necessary to save her life. He would allow nothing to preempt complete and total focus on that goal.

Finally his ears picked up voices mixed with helicopter engines that clued him to the close proximity of the government encampment, but he did not shorten his strides. Time for caution had past. He pushed ahead even more furiously, spurred by another unanswered entreaty from Jay. He clambered up to a bright sunlit area showing through the trees ahead. Once he reached the open area, he prepared to be subjected to the first of several tests of fire.

His feet leapt high into the air, vaulting over a fallen tree trunk, and landed him in the clearing. He quickly found the Black Hawk helicopter gunship positioned among the military soldiers. He veered to a path directly for it. The noise of its whining turbines told him that if he had been there minutes later, an empty field would have greeted him.

The flight crews gathered in a small circle to finalize the briefing on the positions of the presumably dangerous children. Ross still had a thread of a chance. But angry shouts reached him, followed by rapid gunshots and the corresponding zings of projectiles, narrowing his window of success. Plumes of dirt erupted from the soil around him. When he felt a sudden searing pain in his right side, he staggered, nearly collapsing to the ground. Jay's insistent concern reverberated through his brain giving him the will to detach his agony from his consciousness.

Diving into the cockpit, he latched onto the controls and started a wild ascent before he was even in the seat. Shots began to riddle the fuselage, producing an increasing myriad of new ventilation holes in the metal skin. Shreds of stuffing from the seat aside him exploded up into the air, filling the interior with a cloud of debris that brought on an uncontrollable coughing spasm. To escape the barrage, he pushed the stick forward prematurely, abruptly throwing him forward when the helicopter jerked violently. Ascertaining a strut had caught in one of the high branches of a white pine, he tried to grab onto something to brace himself for a crash.

The tension eased when the helicopter surged upward, abruptly free of the limb. Looking below, Ross glimpsed the detached skid dropping from branch to branch of a tall tree. Concerns about the difficulty of any landing without it did not cross his mind since landing was not the issue at this point. Life to him only had to last long enough to get Jay and the children on their ship. He deemed the blood saturating his clothes and the operational worthiness of the aircraft as trivial. His obsession to save the one entity holding ownership of his existence consumed him completely.

Undaunted by offending gunfire, Ross opened the turbines to maximum, increased his altitude and raced toward Jay's position. He grabbed for the radio headset; he needed to arm himself with information about the military's actions.

". . . set it down or I'll blow you out of the sky," threatened the first voice he heard.

The initial oddity of the military speaking to each other in that manner, gave way to comprehension when he recalled two gunships existed. He had one, which meant the other was out there somewhere. Ross was about to congratulate himself on such a profound deduction when a burst of machine gun fire angled across the sky only feet ahead of him. *I think I found him.*

"Found what?" Oswald answered mentally.

"Just thinking," Ross replied.

"I'm busy, keep your thoughts to yourself," Oswald complained.

"I repeat," the other pilot's voice resounded in Ross' ear. "Put it down or you'll have more holes in you than a twelve point buck that trots into a hunting camp on the first day of open season."

"Colorful delivery," Ross murmured as he banked to his right and caught sight of his pursuer. As the follower banked to match his movements, Ross returned his attention to his own flying and initiated a series of evasive maneuvers, which successfully prevented easy target shooting for the attacker. Ross, however, soon concluded that something more elaborate than defensive patterns was required if he was going to be of any support to Jay before either he or his friendly sky chum ran out of fuel.

Changing his tactics, he swooped down to treetop level, skirting the sides of hills. He took to weaving in and around the tallest trees, picking out the narrowest valley, and negotiating the precarious depressions as his flying skills would allow. Regardless of his maneuvers, the other chopper drafted on his tail. After a series of profanities, Ross surrendered the role of rodent in the cat and mouse game, reasoning that since he was a virtual novice at flying, he was no match for the seasoned, well-trained, combat-ready military pilot. He pulled back on the stick in disgust, increasing his altitude.

Loud laughter assaulted his ears, followed by, "Ready to put'er down Bunnyfluff?"

Confused about what steps to take next, Ross called out to Oswald, "Status?"

"About in position. Things not going well?"

"No, not very well. But I'm working on it."

"Seems I've heard that before," Oswald teased. "Did that guy call you Bunnyfluff?"

"Get off my back you overstuffed parakeet."

"Not very original. Jay is worried about you. She wants you to forget them and save yourself. She says there's no point . . ."

"Shut up and let me think!" He resumed his evasive tactics, trying to buy time until he came up with an idea. A light suddenly began glowing on the panel, and after a cursory study of the graphics, he figured out it was the onboard warning system indicating the launching of an enemy missile. Abruptly, he dropped in altitude just in time to see the missile vapor trail streak by, seemingly inches above. The incident did not frighten him since he anticipated an attack sooner or later, but it did remind him that his helicopter was also armed. If he could only get into position for a clear shot at this adversary, he could possibly disable a turbine with some well-placed cannon fire.

Ross slowed, then pulled up, finger ready on the fire button. His opponent expected his move and was already looping back for another try at "Bunnyfluff." Astutely, Ross reinstituted defensive flying patterns while his mind again grappled for solutions. There had to be some advantage in the situation to gain the upper hand; however, his training in botany and gymnastics did not include the skills he needed to get out of this tight spot.

He began wondering if his latest talent, telepathy, could provide an advantage. Could he perform the trick on just anyone? Even link with the pilot? In other words, could he use the link to command another being to act against his will? *What the hell.* What could he loose in the face of nothing else. He moved to a higher altitude to concentrate fully on the link without the distractions of low-level flying.

Ross first attempted a small test by willing the tailing pilot to veer right, disappointed when he did not. He repeated this concentrated effort many times, all to no avail. After reviewing his tactics, he theorized that *suggesting,* rather than willing, might be more effective. This, he thought, would be more like remote hypnotism, and at a minimum seemed plausible.

In spite of the persistent cannon fire clouding his concentration, Ross repeatedly suggested to his subject to relax. Holding his breath, he then proposed to the pilot that a sweeping right turn would be nice, make him feel good, prepare him for battle. Incredibly, the subject obeyed, turning in a gentle arc to the right. "Very cool!" Ross whispered as his opponent continued the turn until he executed a complete circle. He subjected the military pilot to a few more tests until Ross became a believer of his own powers.

Having finished the trial, he set about preparing the pilot for his next set of instructions. He spied a tiny break in the trees below which gave him the germ of an idea, and after suggesting the pilot follow, dropped down for a closer inspection. The ideal size of the small opening in the continuous carpet of hardwood and conifers brought a smile to his lips. "I see smoke coming from your engine." Ross began painting the imagined scenario. "It doesn't look good. It looks like it could go at any time. Set it down in that small clearing below and I'll pick you up. See it?"

"Yes, it's not big enough," the pilot replied in monotone.

"The chopper is as good as gone, and you'll never make it to a larger clearing. We don't train you guys just to have you killed. Play it safe. The helicopter can be repaired; you can't. Just keep it in the center of the opening and everything should be okay."

"Initiating landing," was the obedient response.

Still not fully believing the pilot would actually go through with it, Ross hovered, waiting expectantly. When the other gunship neared treetop level, Ross, still suspicious of the pilot's submission, prepared to fire his cannon while he had him in such an indefensible position. The need for armaments soon receded when Ross watched in awe as the Black Hawk lowered between the trees. A cloud of shredded green vegetation mingled with chips of brown wood misted around his adversary's chopper. The tips of its rotor blades chopped a swath through branches, limbs, and leaves before the rotors broke free of the spinning shaft, instantly vanishing from sight. The helicopter seemed to hang in the air for seconds, the shaft mechanism whirring senselessly before dropping to the forest floor. Sounds of the metal-crunching impact reached Ross fractions of a second later.

Ross shortly heard, "What the hell!" The crash, obviously, had broken the spell.

"Bunnyfluff here. Sorry to leave you like this, no rotors and all, but I've things to do. Over and out." He chuckled, thoroughly enjoying his victory.

* * *

Spotting helicopters in the distance ahead, moving forward in the air like bees around a hive, Ross called, "Oswald. Status?"

"In position. Hurry."

Ross flew directly toward the swarm, reasoning he could make at least one unchallenged surveillance pass and gain an overall perspective on the military's deployment. His assumption proved to be accurate; the soldiers actually welcomed his arrival with all types of encouraging clichés. The radio messages from and between the soldiers allowed him to discover, not only the positions of the men on the ground, but also the fact that they would initiate their seizure of Jay and the children now that airborne firepower was on the scene.

Ross circumnavigated the area one more time to get a better estimate of the number of troops and types of hardware utilized. The soldiers, positioned equidistantly, spread out in a circle around the outcropping of rocks. He determined their armaments to be only of the handheld variety, evidently not having managed to bring in any cannons, rocket launchers, tanks, or battleships. The several airborne helicopters, amongst which Ross was flying, were unarmed, apparently there only for observation and ostensibly transporting their future prisoners. He tried to glimpse Jay through the foliage, if only to gain a degree of comfort that she was there and still alive, but the green awning obstructed his line of sight entirely.

Ross peeled away from the cluster of flying machines, heading in a path back toward Oswald's hidden line of alien marauders.

His gunship's unexpected reversal precipitated a flood of questions calling out for explanation. The ship's silence launched a flurry of pandemonium. "What the hell is going on with that jerk?" the soldiers' field leader bellowed. He followed up with an outbreak of vehement, X-rated commands.

Ross switched off the radio to drum out the cacophony disrupting his need to study and formulate what he needed to do next, which included uninterrupted contact with Oswald.

"Okay, Oswald, you're on. Fan them out and start moving toward the military. When you get a little closer, begin firing the lasers now and then. I'm depending on a good show."

"Great!" the bird answered sarcastically. "I do all the work again and risk my feathers while you flitter about in that contraption."

"You know, I liked you better when I didn't know how to communicate with you."

"And you've become a real pain in the ass," Oswald sparred.

There was a long pause of private contemplation, and then Ross said, "I may not see you again. I want you to know I'll miss you. Please take good care of Jay. Don't let her forget that I'll always think of her."

"Me too; I will, and she won't. Good luck and may the force be with you."

A sharp pain jabbing at his side cut Ross' spontaneous laugh short. He glanced down at the crimson mess on his clothing and seat beside him. He smiled to himself as he switched on the radio and considered the idiocy of the speech he was about to transmit; but when he thought of the mindset of those below him on the ground, the charade seemed more plausible. He reasoned they had blindly assumed an evil intent of beings from another world without substantiating evidence, he figured facetiously that it was his responsibility that they should see death ray wielding monsters where they expected. "Self-fulfilling prophecies," he mumbled aloud.

"People of Earth," he started into the mouthpiece giving his best imitation of a hostile, English speaking alien. *God this is corny.* "Abandon your siege on our people and retreat from this locality and we will leave in peace. If you do not, you will be destroyed," he continued. *This is pure nonsense; no one with an IQ over three would swallow this fairy tale.*

"You have five of your minutes to comply before we attack," he warned. *They'll begin laughing at me any moment,* he thought. *Who would believe in alien beings pirating a single*

213

military helicopter? My blood loss must be affecting my thinking.

After five minutes, they still had not budged. Another two seconds passed and Ross' earphones blared to life. "We are not intimidated by your threats," the military mouthpiece stated proudly. Assuming his fantastic ploy had not worked, Ross slumped into the seat but perked up again when the voice resumed, "We are prepared to defend ourselves if it means the death of every single one of us. You will discover that to underestimate the resolve of the people of the human race will reap grave consequences for your kind. We advise you to return to where you came from and never again tread on the people of Earth."

My God, Ross thought, astounded. *Underestimate you? I certainly underestimate your stupidity. I had no idea.* He realized of course, the soldiers below were not stupid men, just gullible, and assuredly frightened of the unknown. They were so wrapped in being magnificent, brave guardians of the American way that they never paused for thought about the incredulity of a supposedly intelligent alien race hijacking a solitary helicopter in order to spearhead an attack on a group of soldiers. Surely, if they reflected on the events, they would be able to comprehend with clearer heads that any self-respecting alien aggressor would choose the more sophisticated death ray. Shaking off his inane mental rumblings, he cried, "Fire!" to Oswald and set up for a strafing run.

He could not see anything of Oswald's troops through the trees as he banked, but he did notice that the soldiers who were previously surrounding Jay's position were regrouping in a line to present their full force to the ten oncoming empty Ruthran surface exploratory vehicles. He grinned, dove, and pressed the cannon's fire button. His gunfire tore into the ground in a line several yards ahead of the military front, and then he pulled up, banked and sped back to the direction from which he had come. He noticed a wisp of smoke rising from a tree, indicating his ground support was putting up the show he requested. "Oswald, can they see the vehicles yet?" Ross checked.

"Yeah, they're shootin' them full of holes, but I think the lasers really have them worried."

"Great!" Ross responded. "Retreat."

"Retreat? We got the bastards shaking in their boots. We're going to push them to the sea. We have not yet begun to fight. Give me liberty or give me . . ."

"I said retreat! We need to get them to move away from Jay and the children so your ship can land."

"Comprende amigo; we retreat."

Ross began flying in a tight circle, observing and hoping. He noticed the military beginning to creep from their positions in cautious pursuit of the Ruthran decoys. Satisfied with the behavioral pattern consistent with their aggressive mentality, he abandoned the continuous banking and took a line perpendicular to the path of the troops so as not to give away his destination. He maintained that course until he judged there was little chance of discovery, gradually turning until Jay's location was between him and the ensuing foray, and then banked sharply. He sped toward the rocky outcrop. "Status Oswald?"

"They've destroyed half the vehicles and they're gaining on me. And look, they're starting to whoop and holler like drunks at a picnic. They must know something's up. After all, we haven't inflicted any damage on them."

"Stop and put up a fight. Maybe they'll dig in for a while."

"It won't work, Ross. They're getting too cocky."

"We need time Oswald. Do it."

"Aye, aye captain," the bird replied.

Ross feverishly searched the heavens for the appearance of the Ruthran ship, but saw only blue sky and a few wispy clouds. "Jay, how are you and the children holding up?"

Her thoughts gushed into his mind like water suddenly free of a constraining dam. "You are wounded. Come down and let me help you. Please."

"How are you and the children?" he repeated, ignoring her concern.

"They are all frightened; but no one is hurt."

"Your ship should be there soon." His subdued voice was meant to bring confidence in spite of deep doubts twitching in his head. Now that all he had fought so hard to achieve, seemed to be in ready, he began to dwell on possible, last minute glitches. He wondered if the Ruthran leader had reconsidered the risk to his spacecraft, or if his helicopter gunship would be mistaken for one controlled by the military, or if the current state of readiness could be accurately discerned through the trees. "Jay, there's a clearing about one hundred-fifty yards due south. I want you to move to it as fast as you can."

"Are you sure that is wise?"

"Yes, hurry," he prodded.

Placing complete faith in Ross, she gathered the children, and then guided them from their protected area, out into the open. Without the cover from rocks and trees, she understood full well their vulnerability to easy capture or worse. She also knew Ross was sacrificing his future freedom for hers and would do everything in his power to ensure their safety.

Ross flew to the area above the open field and looked up impatiently. Seeing nothing obvious at first glance, he took to inspecting each patch of sky more intently. After a while, he began seeing spots of light where none existed. To clear his vision he rubbed his eyes, blinked, and looked down to the clearing. The sight of Jay walking out onto the field, her face upturned toward him, precipitated immediate emotion, tightening his throat.

"Big shot commander, faithful scout calling," Oswald spoke, preempting Ross' contact with Jay. "The soldiers got all our vehicles," she continued, then added, "and they've discovered that it was a trick. They're pissed off. You thought *I* swore, well you should hear some of the filth coming out of their brains."

"Get back to Jay. I'll try to hold the military back."

"Nooo!" Jay's thoughts wailed in his head. "Ross, land. I need to see you one more time."

A projectile punched a small hole in the helicopter bubble. Ross' eyes jumped to the damage and caught sight of an enormous sphere slightly above. Another shot rang through the airframe somewhere behind him, pushing him into action.

"I love you," he told her as he opened the throttle and swung the helicopter around to face the oncoming soldiers. They were closer to the field than he had estimated and moving fast. He passed over, made a complete circle, and on the next approach, fired a missile at the ground in front of their path. His speed carried him through the blast, momentarily obliterating his view. After he again set up for a pass, he could see that the military had abandoned their charge and were clinging to the forest floor awaiting another strike. Not wanting to disappoint them, he fired the cannon as he swung the chopper side to side. Trees splintered, rocks pulverized, and clumps of soil flew into the air on either side of the soldiers. They stayed put. Assuming the military would remain in position for a minimum of a few minutes, Ross banked hard and hurried back to the field.

The Ruthra made good progress. The children shuffled aboard, but as Jay placed her foot on the first rung of the ladder, Ross' helicopter passed overhead. Jay hesitated to look up, perhaps to wait for Ross if possible; but the rapid staccato of sniper fire raining from the trees hit their target. Ross watched in horror as she fell face down into the grass, a patch of bright red traveling from her spine across the jersey he had given her.

Pushing through layers of pain, he retained enough presence of mind to turn the helicopter. His eyes immediately picked out the soldier who shot Jay crouched at the edge of the forest, apparently anxious to go in for the kill. Overcome by hatred, he dove straight for the man. He leveled off only feet above the ground, sighted with ultimate concentration, and fired a missile at the sniper. Before it reached the unfortunate target, Ross executed an impossibly sharp turn. He cut the power and let the helicopter drop to the ground. Supported by only the remaining strut, it listed to its side causing the spinning rotor blades to disintegrate on contact with the earth.

Unimpressed by the spectacular landing, he raced frantically from the helicopter, even before the rotor pieces hit the ground, to the woman lying motionless on the grass. He sprinted clumsily to the ladder.

A chilled gust of wind blew over him as he cradled Jay against his chest with one arm and gripped the side of the ladder with the other. He struggled up to get her to the safety of the ship. She was unconscious, but how unconscious he did not want to consider. By the time he reached the opening in the ship's side, his wound had reopened, and began bleeding profusely. Disregarding his blood and pain as only superfluous distractions, he hurried into the entrance tube and scurried to the chamber that he had used on his ride in the Ruthran ship. With great tenderness, he laid her down on the small bedding, and touched his lips to hers.

"They will do what they can for her."

Ross glanced up to the owl perched on one of the struts supporting the bed, unable to answer.

"I'm sure she will be all right," she encouraged more positively. "But you must leave now, before it is too late and we'll all be stuck here, including the children."

His every second delay brought the military within closer range to disable the ship. He turned from his wife, and ran to the tube's exit, and clamored down the ladder. As his feet touched the grass, he looked up and saw the ladder retract into the opening and the hatch slide closed. The spherical craft rose slowly at first, and then accelerated rapidly until only blue sky remained.

Ross fell to his knees, placing his hands over his eyes.

Chapter 18

Ross smiled and said his usual "Good morning" to Louise. She was the only nurse to care for him since his incarceration at the hospital three days before. She had a touch of lightness to her personality that interrupted his gloomy disposition, occasionally forcing a smile from him. His repeated stabs at serious conversation were always met with a patronizing smile and a soft pat on the arm. It was obvious she had been told he was mentally deranged and should not engage in any heart-to-heart talks with him. Slightly overweight with a broad, malleable face that bounced into a variety of expressions he was learning to interpret, he thought she just might be persuaded to converse were it not for the omnipresent MP. Often, when he asked about his location or his fate, she would flash her eyebrows over to the MP sitting in the chair by the door, and then answer with some profound statement like, "My, it's nice out today," or, "You look much better, Mr. Barton." He delusionally came to believe her words as code. She would then proceed to show interest in his comfort and disposition, like a squatting mother hen. Eventually he gave up and accepted her animation and good intentions for what they were: animation and good intentions.

"Good morning, Mr. Barton," she said cheerily, moving to the windows to open the blinds. "How are we feeling today?"

"Wonderful," he answered dully, gazing out the same window at the same trees a distance away. He wondered if nurses were trained to use the word "we" in speaking to patients at the University of Cute and Endearing Hospital Talk. His eyes moved to the MP, so rigid he appeared to be more stone than flesh.

Ross considered asking him a series of questions but decided it would be a fruitless exercise because up to that point, any words directed at Mr. Military or any of his duplicates had not even elicited a grunt of acknowledgment.

"Come, come now, Mr. Barton," Louise rebuked. "It's not all that bad now, is it?"

"Yes it is," Ross responded, a blank look in his eyes.

"Well, you'll be happy to know a visitor is on his way," she said as if presenting him with a treasure in gold.

"Oh, who is that?" he questioned without care. The lasting image of Jay wounded was still much too vivid for him to be concerned with much else. He was curious about his circumstances, but could not worry about any punishments they were planning, and would even welcome death. Incredibly, how could it be that in such a short time, Jay had embedded herself into his core? He grieved for her so deeply; not much else mattered.

Louise answered with an "I can't tell you" grin, waved goodbye to him as one would to a six-year-old, and walked out.

The door opened again several minutes later. Ross turned his head and contemptuously muttered, "Earth's savior."

The major strutted into the room, puffed up with godliness and rolling the same stubby, brown cigar to the corner of his mouth, his round shoulders slumped down, making his body seem as wide as it was thick.

The word "buffoon" came to Ross' mind.

The major brought his shoulders erect, and placing his hands on his hips, blared, "You're going to talk Barton. I don't care if we have to torture you, but you are going to talk." He paused, glanced around the room as if checking for appreciative spectators then returned to Ross. "You killed one of my men. That's murder. You helped them monsters escape. That's treason. You destroyed millions of dollars worth of military property. You're deranged." His passion in that last accusation made Ross believe the major considered that the greatest crime of all. "Deranged or not, you're not going to get out of this with some pussy lawyer claiming you're insane. No, you'll never see the outside of a military prison for the rest of your life."

"But I'm not in the military and . . ."

"Shut the fuck up!" he yelled, nearly spitting his unlit cigar out. He rushed to Ross' bedside, his face bursting with rage. Bending down, he enunciated through clenched jaws, "You-are-going-to-answer-each-and-every-one-of-my-questions! Capish!?"

Ross saluted with satirical belligerence, then watched the major's cheeks puff up to the size of small balloons.

Unleashing the pent up frustration, the major suddenly lashed out, striking Ross' jaw with his fist. The force of the blow knocked his head aside into the pillow and then, as fast as Ross could manage, he rolled it back to face the major.

A grin spread onto Ross' face. "Feel better now?"

This deprecation fueled the fury inside the major and mutated him into an unthinking beast. He swung uncontrollably again, this time so wildly his knuckles contacted Ross' forehead instead of the target jaw.

Unflinching, Ross closed his eyes during the hit, but otherwise showed no fear. He smiled.

That pushed the major over the brink and he began pummeling Ross' head and upper body savagely with both hands. Most of the impacts were glancing since he threw them with no control whatsoever. Ross lay stationary, accepting the pounding with little reaction. The major had no way of knowing that Ross' apparent bravery was not a result of his exceptional inner fortitude, but rather to the absolute despair over the loss of Jay.

The expenditure of such unleashed energy in such a short time drained the physically unfit major. He stopped.

Ross' tortured face and neck throbbed in pain. In spite of this, he smiled again at the confused major, and then glanced at the MP, who quickly avoided meeting his eyes by blindly staring out the window.

Breathing heavily, the major stood stationary and silently glowered at Ross until his adrenaline settled back to normal levels. He rolled his cigar to the opposite corner of his mouth and said in a passably controlled voice, "That's just a small sample of what's in store for you unless you answer my questions, Barton."

"Careful, Major. Ever hear of a stress-induced mini stroke?"

The door swung open and three men dressed in business suits strutted into the room. One of them approached Ross' favorite major and said, "We'll take him off your hands now."

"Who the hell are you guys?" the major reacted with characteristic diplomacy.

"CIA," the man answered.

"Well, we'll just see about that. If you think you posies are going to walk in here and take charge, you're sadly mistaken. This guy blew one of my men to smithereens, and he destroyed military property, and he . . ."

"We know all about his actions, Major," the man interrupted.

"I'm not going to let him go until I get some answers."

One of the three suits evaluated the damage done to Ross' face. "Appears as if you have already started interrogation. Get anything?"

"No, nothing. The bastard doesn't understand, but he will."

"Sorry Major, he's ours now. I think we can find more civilized methods to get him to talk."

The major stormed from the room, threatening to return after he straightened out his superiors. The new man in charge then motioned to the door at the MP, who then obediently obliged and left. He dragged the chair that the MP had vacated to Ross' beside and lit a cigarette as his two companions stood stoically on either side of the door.

"My name is Frank Drew."

"Don't tell me you're here to ferret out my foreign connections," Ross said with disgust. "Not suppose to smoke in public buildings, you know. It's against the law."

Frank grinned widely, exposing his over-perfect white teeth. "Come on Mr. Barton, you are not dealing with the military now. We know all about you and are confident you harbor no foreign sympathies and are a patriotic American citizen."

"Let's not get too carried away with the patriotic stuff. I don't go around waving American flags. If you have no misgivings about my political bent, then why are you here? What interest could the CIA have in my, shall we say, recent activities?"

"We are with the extraterrestrial branch."

"Extraterrestrial branch? I never knew such a thing existed."

"Has for many years, but you couldn't have known about us. Classified, hush-hush, top secret."

"Why are you permitting me to know of your branch if . . ." Ross began, but paused and said, "Oh yeah, I forgot for a second. I'm not going to be a problem because I'm going to be locked up for the rest of my life."

Frank snubbed out his cigarette on the bottom of his sole, dropped the butt in the wastebasket under the no smoking symbol and observed, "You don't seem to care."

Ross shrugged.

"Why, Mr. Barton? The reports I've received would lead me to believe you are the opposite of what you portray. You've been resourceful, fearless, and completely committed to your goals. And now? Care to tell me about it?"

"No point in it. No one with a government mentality would ever believe the truth."

"We're pretty experienced at this sort of thing."

"You mean at listening to crackpots describe their alien encounters?"

"Some crackpots, yes. Some very respected."

"And you believe them?"

"Yes, of course. We even have proof of the validity of some reports."

"You do?"

Frank nodded.

"And you've managed to keep it secret?"

"Yes."

"Why?" Ross questioned, wondering if he should believe this guy, hoping to hide his eagerness.

"It's not our decision. Seems whichever president happens to be in power sees some good reason to keep the reports under wraps. I think it gives them a feeling of insecurity and impotency to acknowledge the existence of beings capable of landing on U.S. soil without their permission. I don't profess to comprehend their rationale; I just do my job. Quite an interesting job, I might add."

Ross' opinion of Frank rose.

"Would you care to describe your actions for the past several days?"

Ross wavered at the request, finally concluding nothing was gained by keeping his knowledge secret. There was even the remote possibility some good could come of the government learning the whole truth about the Ruthra. "Yes," he finally answered, leaning back into his pillow.

Frank withdrew a micro recorder from his jacket pocket and asked, "Mind if I record your statement?"

Ross shook his head. Frank switched the recorder on and Ross began his account in fine detail, trying to maintain as much objectivity in the telling as possible. The mental images of Jay that manifested in his head caused portions of the story to be very difficult for him, and at times his throat tightened, making speech hard. Most troublesome of all was reliving the final minutes when the soldier shot Jay. Ross omitted all references concerning his bond with Jay and his experiments with mind control.

When Frank switched off the recorder, the agent had a gut feeling Ross was holding back. It had to do with the woman. His body tensed during any segment relating to her. Frank smiled warmly and said, "Interesting."

"I didn't expect you to believe it. I don't know why I bothered."

"Oh, I believe it," Frank said nonchalantly and poked another cigarette between his lips.

"Do you guys always react so calmly to stories of beings from Jupiter landing on Earth?"

"After you have listened to several, the novelty wears thin."

Ross sat up attentively. "I know you said you've investigated others, but they must have been just sightings. This is different. Isn't it?"

Frank, finally lighting the cigarette dangling from his lips, let out three puffs and watched ringed clouds form in the air above the "Smoke Free Building" sign. "Somewhat," he said. "You've just given us many facts we weren't aware of, but we did know about the Ruthra existence, the description of their ships, and what they look like. We didn't know where they came from, how they communicate, their social behavior, and the intent of their recent visits to Earth. We have you to thank for that."

Ross shook his head in annoyance, "If you knew that much, then why? Why did you attack them? Why did you kill them? Why did you destroy one of their ships? And why were you trying to do it again? If you knew they are intelligent beings, intending no harm, why in God's name didn't you try to communicate with them rather than capturing them? Frank, I just don't understand." He probed the agent's face for understanding.

Frank looked at Ross' partially beaten face and, fully aware his explanation would not appease Ross' anguish nor answer him satisfactorily, he sighed. "I didn't have anything to do with it. *We* didn't have anything to do with it. The CIA didn't know about it until two hours ago." He leaned forward, lowering his face only inches from Ross, and confided, "We got caught up in our own game. We've been so damned successful at secrecy that almost nobody in the military knows we exist. Normally, incidents related to UFOs reach us through either the media or key people in various government agencies. The military did an outstanding job of keeping these recent incidents classified and knowledge of them restricted to as few people as possible. Word never reached us."

"They must have reported something to someone on the presidential staff. I can't imagine anyone in the military getting involved in anything that significant without wanting some kind of approval from the White House."

"They did and that's what is so ironic about the whole affair. Everyone that was privy to the information and knew of our function assumed our group must have been involved because the events were so damn big."

"Okay, even if I swallow your story, why the hell did the military take the action they did?"

"We will probably be investigating that one for years and may never find out where the responsibility lies. Seems someone got the brilliant idea that they were defending our great nation against an invasion. Probably watching too many old sci-fi flicks."

"Then if you understand and believe the peaceful intent of the Ruthra, will the government make all of this public?"

Frank sat back and tapped a long ash into the trash basket. "No chance. This story would be absolute political suicide to anyone even remotely connected with it. Collectively, our government made a complete mess of the affair. Not only would our own population want our necks, but we would be laughed at or humiliated by every country on the face of the Earth, especially by those begging to see our country's image tarnished. This would become fodder for propaganda against us for a decade. No, this is one case in which consideration of going public won't be mentioned once."

"So nothing has changed," Ross mumbled, moving his eyes to the window.

"Not true," Frank answered cheerfully. "We will improve our alert system so this can't happen again."

"Do you honestly think they would ever want to visit this planet again after what we did to them? I wouldn't be surprised if the Ruthra instructed their scientists to develop weapons so they could protect themselves from us."

"We are going to recommend that the government establish a task force to attempt communications with them."

"If I were them, I'd never answer your phone call. I'd expect it to be obscene or a trick."

"They trusted you, didn't they?" Frank questioned. "Why did they trust you?"

Ross maintained a vacant stare out the window.

"Come on, Barton, what didn't you tell me? Is it the girl?"

Ross nodded.

"You were friends with the girl?"

"More than friends," Ross confessed.

For the first time Frank's face showed surprise, and he pressed, "What do you mean, 'more than friends'"?

"She was my wife."

Frank's cigarette tumbled from his lower lip onto his lap. A few seconds later, when the glowing ash burned through the wool slacks, he shouted and hurriedly brushed it off, stamping it out. "Married?"

"Ruthran custom provides that if a male and female have . . . never mind."

"But . . . but you said she was one of those creatures?" he stammered.

"Yes, I've already explained. Her life essence, her self, her soul was Ruthran, but her body was completely human. It doesn't matter. Whatever she was, I loved her."

"Now there's a new twist. Nobody is going to believe this. Shit. Really Barton?"

Ross nodded.

Frank repeated, "Shit," then added, "No wonder you were fanatic about helping them." The two sat silent for long seconds, each in their own thoughts until Frank shouted into the room. "Barton. How would you like to work for the government? It would be perfect," he emphasized, his eyes aglow. "You could be the one to make contact," he continued, energetically jumping to his feet and beginning to pace. He stopped, said, "This is a golden opportunity," and then resumed his movements, looking at his feet. "You could ensure nothing like this ever happens again!"

However, Frank's high exuberance abruptly fell into equally low despondency, like his pet puppy had been hit by a car. "Can't do it," he conceded, dropping into his chair. "I could get them to bend the rules a little, but you've chalked up too many violations. You would be considered too much of a security risk. Too bad, you would have been ideal."

"Don't feel bad Frank, I couldn't have helped. Please understand. She was dying in my arms. How could I assist the same government that did that to her?"

"Don't condemn all of us for what a few did," Frank answered.

"Maybe in time I won't, but today I don't have the inclination to differentiate."

Frank rose to his feet and said, "It will not be a problem soon anyhow."

"Don't be so cryptic. Why won't it be a problem?"

"You're not going to remember any of this conversation, your experiences over the last several days, the Ruthra, the girl . . . anything."

"I'm to be executed?"

"No, this isn't a police state. We don't go around solving our problems by eliminating them. We are going to erase your memory for the period covering your escapades with the Ruthra."

Frank had made the statement in such a casual manner that its implications did not register immediately. Ross' mind reconstructed the string of words moments later, and he replied profoundly, "What?"

"You won't remember anything that has happened from finding the empty Ruthran exploratory vehicle in the forest up to the time we release you."

"You are going to release me?"

"Yes. We can't very well just have you disappear from the face of the Earth without questions, and we don't like people probing into our business. Since you will not recall anything of your adventures, there is no benefit in keeping you."

"But I killed a man," Ross debated mechanically while his mind struggled to fathom all that was being said.

"I'd say your actions were justifiable at that point. The record will show the soldier inadvertently strayed into a missile target area during maneuvers. It happens and goes with the uniform. The CIA has already cleared you with the military authorities. You're a free man."

"How can only a select portion of my memory be eliminated? I am not aware of such a process."

"It's perfectly safe. We have used the treatment on over a hundred people with no damage to other parts of the brain and no loss of memory outside the programmed time period. It's precision induced permanent amnesia. And you'll be happy to know you'll be in some well-respected company. An astronaut on an Apollo flight, commercial jet pilots, military pilots, police officers, and also a Supreme Court Justice were some of those who have undergone the procedure over the years."

"How long has this been going on?"

"Oh, thirty-five, forty years."

"How is it done?"

"Unique form of hypnotism. It's computerized now so we don't need the services of a psychiatrist."

Ross' thoughts raced. It would be so easy to awake now from sleep and to accept all that had happened as just a vivid, incredible dream. Although seemingly incredible, the experiences were certainly real and he did not want to passively accept the loss of what he had learned. He desperately wanted to retain his memory of the love shared with Jay, however brief. His memories were his property and no government agency, regardless of how well-intended, would take those from him. "Whatever you say, Frank."

Chapter 19

Ross was told he would be fit to travel within two days and then would be transported to the mental rehabilitation center, as Frank called it. Through innuendo from inadvertent comments by his nurse, Louise, and the agents who took shifts sitting in his room, he had a fair degree of confidence he was in a small hospital somewhere in Vermont. He tried to extract information from the agents on the whereabouts of the rehabilitation center but never got a definitive answer, only that it was located on an Air Force base.

Considering his potential opportunities for escape, he knew he would have to make his move prior to his departure from the hospital, reasoning that the tight security at an Air Force base would substantially reduce the likelihood of success. Settled on the when, he contemplated the how. His eyes moved to the butt of the semiautomatic barely visible underneath the unfastened suit jacket on the agent who was sitting against the wall, reading *Guns & Ammo*. Given the danger of the whole affair to many powerful government officials as indicated by Frank, Ross assumed the agent would not hesitate to use his weapon to prevent an escape and the resulting publicity.

When Louise extinguished the lights for the night, leaving only a dim glow from a single, low wattage night-light, Ross was still deep in thought about a means of breakout. Over the past several days his problem-solving had been exciting, dynamic, daring, and dangerous, but now he wanted a more sedate, easygoing plan because the aches and pains he endured hinted that his body could not sustain much more punishment. If only his guardian angel would fall into a deep slumber. *Sleep. Hypnotism. Mind link!* he congratulated himself.

The conditions in the room being conducive to Ross' hypnotic link, the agent was lightly snoring within three minutes. Ross waited an additional five minutes to ensure the agent's sleep was not just a short nap, then uncovered himself, swung his feet to the floor, and stood. A dull pain radiated from his side at first, but then faded. He removed his johnny and quietly slipped into the pajamas neatly folded at the foot of his bed. Taking his slippers into his hand, he tiptoed to the window and slid the glass sideward. He pushed the heel of one of the slippers against the screen with increasing force until it tore. Then, sticking his fingers through the break in the plastic filament mesh, he began pulling at the screen. He slowly worked at expanding the small tear until a man-sized hole had been created, frequently looking back at the agent to see if the noise was waking him. First poking his head through the aperture to check the area below the ground-floor window, he then put one leg, followed by the other over the sill and slid out onto the crushed stone boarder that ran along the side of the building.

Once steady on his feet, he looked back through the open window at the sleeping agent. A mischievous grin spread over his face as he relinked with the agent's mind and then planted a posthypnotic suggestion. When finished, he turned and padded away in a crouch to the trees.

After traveling approximately one hundred yards through the woods, he stopped, leaned against a tree trunk, brushed grit from the soles of his feet and put on the slippers. "What the hell am I going to do now?" he murmured aloud to himself. He had no clothes, no money, no identification, no means of obtaining food, and nowhere to go. He had managed to keep his memories intact, but what of his life?

The issue was instantly forgotten when loud voices reached Ross from the direction of the hospital. Assuming he was the cause of the fuss, he resumed his getaway at a more urgent pace. The voices soon faded and Ross slowed to reduce the strain on his fatiguing legs. After another hour of almost blind travel, he stopped. He felt a soft bed of pine needles underfoot and laid down, the security of the darkness and the enormity of the forest to comfort him. He fell asleep with the aromatic scent of fresh pine filling his nostrils and the rescued memories of Jay filling his head.

* * *

He travelled all day, not really knowing where he was, or where he was going. Hunger began to nag at his stomach as he looked up at the summit of a small mountain near sunset. Ross climbed to its top, hoping to find signs of a road, house, or town. The ascent was much steeper than anticipated and he found himself winded when he reached the top. He stood on the rocky peak, the only vegetation being bushes, weeds, and several short, scrubby trees, and breathed deeply, enjoying the rejuvenation he felt as the clean, crisp mountain air flowed into his lungs. He turned slowly through a full circle. Forest greeted his eyes in every direction as brisk winds buffeted the loose-fitting pajama top and bottom against his skin.

Gazing fixedly over the countryside, he wondered if he could adapt to a life of exile from society in that beautiful place. If supplied with some bare essentials, he should be able to learn how to live off the land. He imagined spending his days freely studying forest vegetation to his heart's content, pursuing his chosen profession. But he accepted he would always be a fugitive. His other option would be to voluntarily submit to the mind treatment the government had slated for him. How could he willingly give up his knowledge that other living beings existed in the solar system? How could he surrender the feelings of the personal relationships that had blossomed with two from their world, one of friendship for Oswald, and the other of deep love for Jay? He knew the likelihood of the press or anyone believing his story without proof was slim to nonexistent. Frank and his kind would never stop trying to track him down like a hunted animal.

The swollen orange, oblate ball on the western horizon drew his eyes and he became aware that the air had become suddenly still. Resisting the temptation to stare indefinitely at the sun, he looked upward, seeing the residual image of a disk of light superimposed on the blue sky. Ross blinked repeatedly, encouraging the temporary visual defect to disappear but became alarmed when the spot in his sight became brighter and more distinct.

It soon became obvious what he had supposed to be the aftereffect of gazing directly at the sun, was not that at all. It was real. The silvery disk grew larger in size as did Ross' eyes. His pulse began to race. When the enormity of the spherical object became recognizable with its decreasing altitude, Ross yelled, "They're back!" and then began waving his arms furiously above his head. Disappointment followed by panic surged as the unearthly, huge ball continued straight down, not heeding his best energetic efforts to beckon them. "Jay, I'm here!" he screamed, leaping up and down feverishly. He tried communicating via the mental link but found it impossible to concentrate. As the ship continued its vertical descent, Ross noticed a clearing in the valley below at a point he judged to be directly under the Ruthran vessel. Concluding it was the only reasonable choice for a landing site, he sprinted forward.

After a few awkward strides, he realized the hospital slippers were more hindrance than protection, so he removed them and launched himself forward again. The steep grade down the side of the hill made forward speed effortless, the majority of his strength applied to retarding his motion enough to maintain balance. But the exertion it took to keep his speed under control was at the expense of severe punishment to the bare heels of his feet as they dug into the hillside on each stride. Fortunately, the trees in the area were spaced relatively far apart, with little underbrush. Not once, as he bounded down toward the valley, did he allow his mind to think about the question he had ignored since he last saw Jay; "Was she alive?" He simply refused to accept the possibility she had not survived her wounds.

Upon reaching level ground, Ross' anticipation became overwhelming. His body seemed detached from his brain as he dashed forward, completely impervious to the twigs, stones, and low, woody plants that battered the bottoms of his bare feet. His excitement built to a fever pitch when he saw the bright sunlight beyond the trees only two hundred feet ahead, and he nearly collided with the sturdy trunk of a towering sugar maple. Moments later, he broke out of the forest and pulled to an abrupt halt, gawking at the scene he had resigned to never witness again.

The Ruthran ship sat motionless on the tall grass at the center of the meadow, its shell aglow with the reddish illumination from the setting sun. A human form came into view from behind the craft and Ross took a few tentative steps forward. The person stopped, as if waiting for him to advance. The form before him was undoubtedly female, tall, with long black hair softly curling to her shoulders. Dare he believe what he was seeing was in fact real and not some cruel trick of his mind?

He began taking larger strides to the woman waiting for him. He wanted to run to her and smother her in his arms, but an uneasiness tugged at his will. He stopped. Reaching out with a mind link, Ross called her name. Receiving no reply, he probed at the woman's thoughts and sensed her tension. Absolutely certain this figure was not Jay, he waited for a move on her part, curious as to her identity and relationship to the Ruthra.

Her eyes remained trained on him as she slowly bent her knees, reaching with her hand into the grass. As she rose, a long dark object, he guessed to be a gun, cleared the grass, already leveled at him. He turned his head, quickly sweeping his surroundings. Two men in green camouflage clothing moved at him from behind with shouldered rifles. The readiness for explosive actions beginning to mount within him diffused. He looked back to the woman who was walking toward him, seeing that the only features she had in common with Jay were her height and black hair.

Ross stood waiting in a cloud of confusion as the three closed in on him. He watched the wind skid the Ruthran ship several feet across the grass. It was at trick; a hoax; a lie. He wanted to be angry but the energy needed for anger eluded him. He was beaten and drained instead. Ross' resigned, dull brown eyes moved to each captor's face, finally resting on the giant balloon he had mistaken for the Ruthran ship.

A helicopter emerged into the airspace over the clearing, and when it dropped for a landing, the balloon slid away from the churning air, bringing a faint smile of self-pity to Ross' lips. After the aircraft touched down, the door opened. Frank stepped out.

The CIA agent sauntered up to Ross, shaking his head with a grin, and said, "You have put us through a lot of unnecessary trouble, Mr. Barton." Frank motioned with his head over his shoulder as he pulled a pack of cigarettes from his jacket pocket. Smiling, he said, "Ingenious, huh? My idea." He pulled a lighter from his trousers, lit the cigarette, puffed until smoke chugged from his mouth, then added, "We had to make up seven of those things and scatter them within the section of forest we calculated you would be in. Since you didn't leave us a note on where you were headed, we needed something to get you to show yourself. I thought that the balloon and a tall woman with black hair would do the trick if seen from a distance."

Frank turned back and nodded to the woman. "You are fortunate that you found this one. Since we couldn't find many women that tall in our employ, five of the other decoys assigned to the other locations are actually men dressed as females. Some of them make fairly ugly women. They will be happy to hear their services as female imposters are no longer required."

Ross gazed blankly at Frank, offering not a single word of comment. *Did he want my approval for a job well done?*

Frank acknowledged his despair and said, "Come on Barton, it's not that bad. We are doing you a favor. When you finally go home, you won't recall any of this. You will no longer have to live with the pain of losing the girl. It will have never happened." Frank, hearing or seeing no reaction, grabbed Ross' arm and pulled him gently in the direction of the awaiting helicopter as he comforted, "Come, Barton. It will be over before you know it. It was all a bad dream."

* * *

Jay collapsed onto the ground. Ross sprinted to her and felt his chest tighten and his mouth instantly dry when he saw the scarlet liquid spreading through the blue jersey.

His eyes flashed open in horror to the empty seats ahead of him in the large jet. Looking across the aisle, he found Frank watching him with compassion. "Be landing soon," Frank said. "I want you to know I think you're quite a man, Barton. I laugh every time I think of the way you outwitted the military at every turn, especially that major. I don't like that ass. Seems to have the intelligence of a frog. Oh yeah, you'll be happy to know that one of my men popped him in the jaw."

"Why did he do that?" Ross asked, talking to Frank for the first time since capture.

"I don't know. It was the strangest thing. Larry, the agent who fell asleep in your room, just hauled off and hit him for no apparent reason. I just don't understand it. Larry has an impeccable record. But falling asleep on the job then striking an officer will cause people to question his stability. I'm sure he will have to go up before a review board." Frank chuckled, and said with some difficulty as he strained to control the laughter, "You should have seen the shocked look on his face when Larry laid a fist onto his mouth. Flattened his cigar."

"Don't be too hard on Larry," Ross said softly.

Frank's face took on a questioning expression.

"Sometimes people get an idea in their head that's not their own, like in a hypnotic trance or something."

Frank's eyes narrowed slightly; he leaned across the aisle, glanced back at the three other agents sitting further back in the plane, then asked, "You wouldn't happen to know how ideas could have gotten into his head, do you?"

Ross realized he did like this man. He was only the victim of requirements put upon him by the system. Under different circumstances, Ross could have thought of him as a friend. "Frank, hiding these facts from the general public is wrong. If our scientist had been informed and permitted the opportunity to try communicating with the Ruthra, the human race as a whole could have benefited. As it stands now, with all the secrecy, both the Ruthra and individuals here on Earth have been injured and killed. We could have learned so much from them. Frank, they're like us. They think like we do, they love like we do, and they die like we do. The only thing they don't do like us is harm other living beings."

"I agree with you Barton, but I'm in the minority and don't have enough power to do anything about changing policies."

"Then why do you stay in this racket?"

"The group will exist whether I'm part of it or not, and if I remove myself from it I'll just be turning my back on something that intrigues me."

"But you could change it," Ross charged. "With your knowledge, you could talk to the right people on the outside . . ."

Frank shook his head, ending Ross' plea. "Barton, if I quit I would get the same treatment you will undergo and I wouldn't remember anything."

Ross digested the information, and then asked, "But how can you live with yourself?"

"It comforts me to think that if I wasn't here, a person with objectives more in line with the military could replace me. I argue for my opinions every chance I get. Someday, someone may consider them."

Ross nodded comprehension, wondering what he might do if in Frank's shoes. Maybe his condemnation of Frank's philosophy was not as justifiable as it initially seemed.

"Did you do something to Larry?" Frank returned to the deserted topic.

Ross nodded and smiled.

"What?"

"It wouldn't serve any purpose by my telling you. It's enough you know Larry wasn't responsible for his actions."

"Knowing how you did it would sure satisfy my curiosity."

Ross leaned back against the seat, glanced through the side window and noticed the jet was dropping in altitude. "Looks like we'll be landing soon," he said softly.

Frank grunted, then leaned back into his seat, sulking.

"Don't look so glum, Frank," Ross said, actually feeling sorry for the agent. "The method I used is nothing to get concerned about. I'd tell you but I don't want to end up being a governmental guinea pig for the remainder of my life."

"I won't tell another soul," Frank promised.

Ross linked his mind and discovered the agent was sincere. "Okay. I'll tell you. What can it hurt? I told you the Ruthra communicated by mental links, like telepathy."

Frank nodded hurriedly.

"And I told you that I communicated with them by means of Jay's headband."

Frank nodded.

"Well, I gradually developed the ability to communicate without it, first with Jay, then with anyone."

Frank stared.

"Next, I discovered I could read the thoughts, or at least get impressions of feelings from people without their knowing."

"You mean that . . ." Frank began, but became silent.

"Eventually I attempted to place suggestive thoughts in the head of another individual, almost like a hypnotic suggestion, and it worked. I put Larry to sleep and suggested he had overheard the major making obscene remarks about his wife."

"I think you're right about my superiors turning you into a laboratory animal. Barton, that's incredible!" Frank stroked his chin, peering thoughtfully at Ross and eventually requested, "Could you give me a demonstration?"

"On who?"

Frank motioned with his head to the rear of the plane.

Ross snuck a glance at the three obviously bored men then shrugged and answered, "Why not." He stared at the headrest in front of him and began to formulate a demonstration his guardian CIA agent might enjoy.

Frank licked his lips expectantly.

A few moments later, Ross said, "Watch the one with the beard," and then stared blankly ahead.

Frank bristled with anticipation as he turned around to observe the subject. After four minutes passed, Frank's eyes moved back to Ross, concluding the odd professor either failed or fibbed about his ability.

Ross gave him a smug grin and turned toward the rear. As soon as Frank followed the direction of Ross' head, returning to look at the intended subject, the man rose and stepped into the center of the aisle. The other two men looked lazily at the standing man, finding any distraction a welcome relief from the monotonous flight. Attentions really perked when the bearded man casually unbuckled his belt and ran down the zipper to his fly.

One of the men said, "What the hell are you doing Carl?" but further comment died when Carl dropped his pants to the floor. He stood there with a dignified expression still on his face as his audience broke out into rollicking laughter. Frank pointed at the poor man's voluminous boxer shorts imprinted with small, green mermaid figures. He tried to speak, but was completely overcome by the hilarity of the scene, and instead rolled onto the aisle floor, laughing so heartily his eyes began to tear.

A "fasten seat belt" lamp chimed on. Carl blinked, and then looked down to the trousers gathered at his ankles. As he lifted his sight, seeing the grinning sets of eyes studying him, his face colored deeply. His hands lunged down for the waistband. He hurriedly pulled up his pants with a yank, and then slid into his seat, absolutely befuddled.

Frank crawled to his feet, rested a hand on Ross' shoulder and said, "You're all right Barton," truly impressed by the man's talent. He then moved to his seat and fastened his belt, imagining the possibilities of such a gift, and for the first time envying his prisoner.

Ross also sat back and buckled his belt while being absorbed with inward contemplations. His control of Carl's mind had been easier than his second attempt, as that one had been easier than the first. Jay never mentioned anything but communication through the mental link and he wondered whether she simply did not have the time or inclination to refer to it, or whether the Ruthra were not familiar with the technique. Was it possible the human brain had a greater facility for mental linking than the Ruthra, but never cultivated by need? Suddenly remembering the whole subject would be academic, he pushed the matter from his mind and peered out the window up at the dark blue sky.

* * *

Prodded ahead by Frank, Ross walked a few steps into the room, and halted. Everything about the cramped room was cold and sterile. The white polished flooring, glossy white walls, stainless steel table, and off-white computer console caused a chill to run up his spine. A technician, wearing a floor-length, squeaky-clean, white lab coat walked around him to the computer console and brought a monitor screen to life. He beckoned Frank with a finger, and then talked to him in tones too low in volume for Ross to overhear. Frank extracted a small notebook from his breast pocket and began to quote its contents to the technician, who typed and nodded as he listened. When apparently finished, Frank replaced his book, then asked Ross to lie on the table. Obedi- ently, he stepped to the dull, silvery platform, sat, then reclined and waited calmly.

The technician walked out of sight, behind Ross' head. The whirring sounds of the multiple small electric motors reached his ears, soon followed by the slight sensation of a bowl shaped helmet barely contacting his head. The techni- cian stepped to the side of the table, enabling Ross to see him and the black, fabric belt in his hand. The technician reached across his neck, and engaged one end of the band into a slot in the table, then ran it over his throat and snapped in the other end. The band tightened against Ross' throat until a light uniform pressure encircled the front half of his neck. Ross reacted as if being choked, but quickly real- ized that if he did not move, it merely rested against his skin.

A low continuous hum resonated from the enclosure that surrounded the upper portion of his head. Reflexively, he tried moving but was told to remain still. He felt the contact of a soft finger at the back of his skull, followed almost instantly by another, and another, until finally his head felt as though floating in a hemispherical chamber of small foam pins. Experimentally, he tried to turn his head. The pins in the direction he attempted to move exerted substantially more pressure, almost to the point of pain. He surrendered and relaxed, believing the pins and neckband were there for precise fixing of his head and the brain contained within.

Frank's smiling face came into view. "I am sorry this has to happen. I wish circumstances were different, but . . . Goodbye friend." The agent's face slid from sight. A tickling sensation materialized deep within his head, eliciting desires to scratch at the irritation, but he found his arms immobilized.

When did they strap my hands to the table? he asked himself, not recalling the restriction before. The tickle grew and Frank's face reappeared in front of him. He closed his eyes, but the face remained. Frank's face was supplanted by a replay of a vision of the bearded agent, Carl, dropping his pants. The scene shifted into a kind of fast rewind, soon replaced by a rapid-play version of the hoax with which they had entrapped him. Images of recent days in reverse sequence then streaked by so fast that he had difficulty recognizing the events or the participants. The pictures then grew into vivid bands of brilliant colors and began to swirl in a kaleidoscope of moving patterns. The cyclonic morass started funneling into a black point at the center of the scene. And then, the black point grew into a spot, then into a large disc, finally engulfing all light.

Chapter 20

The murmur of voices pulled Ross from the depths of an abstract, unsettling dream. When he succeeded in raising his eyelids, the faces of Marsha and a strange man in a white medical jacket met his gaze. Noticing the pensiveness plainly written on the face of each, he became worried and sprang to a sitting position. Taking a quick glance around, he saw that he was in a private hospital room. Marsha and the stranger both smiled warmly. Ross' mind shifted into high gear, seeking clues to place his surroundings into perspective. Trying to focus with greater concentration on the problem, he closed his eyes, pressing his thumb and forefinger on them, and then grappled to recall the reason for his incarceration. After again drawing a blank, his thoughts sought events he did remember, reasoning that a beginning on familiar ground would be instrumental in prying lose the circumstances that had landed him in a hospital.

The memories flowed easily. He remembered Marsha, their relationship, the discovery she was using him, the trip to Vermont, meeting a strange tall woman named Jay, and mounting his backpack to begin his journey, then absolutely nothing. Although he hunted for the next moment, it was as if it never existed. He could not remember anything beyond the minute he took his first step into the forest.

"Hi there," Marsha said cheerfully, ending Ross' mental turmoil.

"What's happened?"

"You had a little accident," she explained. She moved closer to settle a light kiss on his cheek.

Her touch created an inexplicable sensation, like being pierced by an invasion of stinging insects, and caused him to recoil. Ignoring this, he looked at her angelic face and asked, "What kind of accident?"

"You were caught in a rockslide," the strange man informed, and then asked, "Don't you remember?"

"No. Who are you?" he answered and questioned in a single breath.

"Your doctor, Frank Drew. You are fortunate, Mr. Barton. Other than a mild concussion and a stone fragment that penetrated a little flesh in your side, you have no damage to your brain. If this pretty young woman is willing to take you into her care, you can go home tomorrow."

Marsha beamed and spurted, "I'll take good care of him."

"What hospital am I in?" Ross queried.

"Indianapolis," Frank answered, then turned to Marsha and said, "Would you step out Miss while I conduct a few last checks?"

Frank watched her go and then withdrew a light scope from the white jacket pocket. "Lie down Mr. Barton." Once Ross' head settled into the pillow, Frank switched on the light, raised Ross' right eyelid, shined the beam into the pupil and murmured, "Uh huh." He repeated the ritual on the other eye, and nodded approvingly as he dropped the scope back into his pocket. "Marsha told me all about your research. Did you make any progress on your theories?"

"I don't remember. Did someone get my notes?"

"I'm told nothing of yours was salvageable. Sorry."

"What's the date?" Ross suddenly remembered to ask.

"August twenty-eighth."

"I can't remember two weeks of my life?"

"Do you recall finding anything unusual?" Frank asked casually.

"No, it's all a blank."

"Marsha is quite an attractive woman. Are you two in a serious relationship?"

"No, it's not that serious," Ross responded, the memory of the phone conversation he overheard still stabbing like a sharp knife.

"Oh, she led me to believe otherwise," Frank commented with surprise. "She mentioned a girl named Jay you met in Vermont," he added conversationally, testing for reactions.

"Yeah, a real nut!" Ross commented brightly, wearing a grin, suddenly cognizant of his lightheartedness at the mere mention of her name.

"Think you will ever see her again? Marsha sounded jealous."

"No, never learned her real last name or where she came from. The strangest person I ever met," he answered, still smiling.

"A military helicopter pilot found you," Frank said.

"I think I remember the ranger . . . Yes, the ranger told me something about military maneuvers in the region."

"Fortunately they were in the area, otherwise . . ." Frank took a deep breath, and then plunged into his boldest test. "One of my favorite movies was about the military covering up a UFO visit in Wyoming. Wouldn't it be something if that military group that found you were actually dealing with alien beings from another world instead of playing war games as they claimed."

Ross rolled his eyes, and said, "You do have some imagination, Doctor."

"Well, enough of this," Frank announced with satisfaction. "I have other patients in more need of my services than you, Mr. Barton. I will not see you again before you leave, so goodbye. If any problems crop up, Marsha has my card. And don't forget, don't worry if you never regain the memory for the time span around the accident. It's quite common in cases like yours." He opened the door, called Marsha and then whispered something to her as she passed that produced an instant smile and nod of comprehension.

* * *

During the weeks following Ross' release from the hospital it became evident his lost memories would never return, and although he did not know why, it bothered him. His relationship with Marsha resumed from the point he left it, and although he intended to break it off, they somehow drifted to an arrangement of living together. Aside from the seeming return to his life as it had been, some significant change had occurred inside him. A hollowness. A disposition once buoyant and optimistic, one certain everything would be all right, had been replaced by a sense of cold uneasiness. He was ambivalent toward his work, his life, and even Marsha's exceptional sensuality. He waited for that electric air that once passed between them; it never showed itself despite the appreciable effort she devoted to seducing him. Intimacy between them never occured. Not only did her motives weigh on his thoughts, even her touch struck him as inappropriate and manipulative. His thoughts, when not hazy or dull, brought him disquieting inner turmoil.

Ross' despondency did not go undetected, and by the second month of their cohabitation, Marsha's encouragement for sex play gradually diminished, until by the third month, she stopped trying to entice him altogether. There-after, Ross watched her leave the house most nights with no explanation. The development in their arrangement should have infuriated him, but he felt no jealousy or even loneliness regarding her absences. In fact, he welcomed those nights. They only underlined his opinion that continuing their relationship was a sham. He told himself he would discuss the matter with her, certain she would blame him for their dysfunction. So be it. It needed to be done.

* * *

"When you said we were going out, I thought you meant to eat, not walk across a football field in the dark," Marsha complained as she rubbed her hands together to ward off the late fall evening's brisk air.

"I want to talk to you about something important," Ross responded in almost a whisper, his eyes watching the barely discernible goal posts at the end of the playing field.

"Couldn't we do that in a nice warm restaurant?" she challenged.

"It's peaceful out here, and there'll be no interruptions. I'll take you to a restaurant when we're finished."

"Well okay, since we're here already. But hurry up, I'm freezing."

Ross stopped, and turning to her, asked, "Have you been with other men?"

"What are you talking about?" she questioned, stalling for time while her mind raced to establish a defense.

"You've been gone a lot lately."

"Just seeing girlfriends," she answered in a voice so unsteady she may as well have answered yes to the question.

"Marsha, you don't need to be defensive about it. I have no claim on you."

Her lips moved, poised to vocalize an argument, but instead she stood quietly, her head bowed. For once Ross sympathized, as he knew her thoughts were tangled and confused. She simply did not know how to answer.

"I think it would be best for the both of us if we broke up," he continued. Her tears glinted in the faint light; he touched her shoulder tenderly, and added, "Marsha, I know you don't love me. I overheard a phone conversation you had with one of your friends before I went to Vermont. You don't have to pretend." He looked up at the stars, escaping her eyes. "I don't even know why I stayed with you, but since . . ." He paused, gazing at the impossible expanse of the pinpricks of lights above, then resumed, "But since the accident, something has changed. I just let this happen with you, not caring for your feelings or my own. Hell, I'm not sure I have feelings anymore; either that or they're so deep I can't reach them. It's like my heart gave way in that rock-slide. It's buried beneath the rubble."

She wiped the tears with the back of her hands and pleaded, "I don't care. I'll make it work. I promise I'll never look at another man again. I'll make you want me again."

"But you don't love me," he argued.

She sniffled, caught a short breath, and then said, "I'll be honest with you. I don't love you, but I think I could, and I'm so lonely." She dropped to her knees, wrapped her arms around his legs, pushed her face into his thighs and sobbed uncontrollably.

He reached down and ran his fingers through her finely textured hair, and softly said, "Don't Marsha, I'm not worth that." After enduring another few minutes of the pitiful weeping, he gently stoked her hair. "You win Marsha. We'll give it another try."

"I'll make you happy, Ross." She kissed him lightly, and then draped her arms tenderly around his neck. "I promise," she said. Her voice carried a peculiar sincerity and serenity he had never heard from her before.

Ross brought his arm around her, and whispered in her ear, "Come on, let's go eat."

As they strolled back to the car, a night bird's eerie vocalization ended the near perfect silence. Automatically, Ross' eyes drew upward and rested on a bright point of light in the southern sky that mysteriously pushed his thoughts to the Vermont trip and his elusive memories.

"What are you looking at?" Marsha asked. When he didn't respond, she nudged him and said, "Hello there. I asked what you are staring at?"

"Jupiter."

She raised her head to the sky and wondered to which star he was referring since they all looked alike. "Something interesting about it?"

The question heightened his awareness of the tickling sensations now doing a boogie in his head. Suddenly the bird, Vermont, Marsha, Jupiter, Doctor Frank, and the strange woman, Jay, all filled his brain like a concoction of mulligan stew. He strained to catch the interrelationship between those images, but they drifted just beyond his ability to assemble. He struggled to lift these seemingly unrelated pictures over an imagined hurdle. On the threshold of placing the pieces together, however, the tingling sensation fled and with it, any hope of a common thread. What remained was a collection of isolated facts with no more relationship between them than a rock and a giraffe. His mind relaxed, allowing a tremendous tension to escape. "No, nothing interesting," he finally answered. "Just trying to imagine what the Earth would look like from there."

* * *

During the next week, Marsha's commitment to her promise became readily evident. She renewed her attentiveness with vigor, seldom going anywhere without Ross. Or if she went alone, she left him with a detailed account of where she planned to go and when she would return, much like a teenager with a curfew. He knew her fervor to please him stemmed from her determination to upgrade his interest in her. She would give him no excuse to end their relationship. For his part, he would never allow her diluted feelings for him be his excuse for behaving badly. He would give the relationship a try; he would stick with it only because he did not have enough interest in life to confront it.

Exactly one week following their reconciliation on the football field, a Saturday night, she announced her plans to prepare an elaborate dinner for them both. For the past three days she had busily cut recipes from magazines, placed random lists around the kitchen, and made frequent runs to the grocery store. "Ross," she called from the kitchen, "I'm running out for a few last items. Be back in a minute." The giddiness in her voice almost pleased him.

But, she did not return in a "minute," or an hour, or even two, or three, or four. Although increasingly cranky and tired, Ross continued his vigil on the sofa, vacillating between anger at her undependability, and worry about her being the victim of a crime or accident. He called her cell phone numerous times without an answer. Since she been in the middle of a grand dinner preparation when she left, the scales in his mind tipped toward justified concern. He decided to report her as a missing person.

"Indianapolis Police Department," a practiced voice answered.

"I'd like to report a missing person," Ross said, wondering what would happen next.

There was a click, and after two rings a new female voice said, "This is Sergeant Norris."

Ross repeated the missing person request, and then was led through a canned list of questions about physical description, like age, hair color, and weight.

"Sorry, my computer is a little slow tonight," Sergeant Norris apologized after fifteen minutes of data entry passed. "So what's your relationship with this woman?"

How do I answer this one? he thought. "Sort of a girl-friend," he answered quickly.

"Sort of a girlfriend? Don't you know?"

Ross hesitated, thinking, Yeah, that sounded stupid, then said, "We live together."

"Okay then," Norris continued. "How long has she been missing?"

Ross explained the dinner plans, Marsha's running out for some missing ingredients, did not answer her phone, and that she had been gone over four hours.

"Has she ever disappeared like this before? Sorry, but I got to ask this. Standard procedure."

"Well, not in the past week," he answered. Detecting a muffled snicker at the other end of the phone, he thought, *I shouldn't have said that. I should make coffee.*

"Soooo, she's disappeared before?"

"Sometimes . . . she'd go out to a club, or with friends, and not come back until dawn," Ross answered. "But this is different," he threw in assertively.

"Let me get this right . . . she's gone out before until dawn before without telling you?"

"Yes, spontaneous type of woman. But, as I said, this is different. She had these plans for a meal . . . and a week ago she promised to never do anything like that again. We had a talk."

"You had a talk . . . I see," Sergeant Norris said. "Thank you Mr. Barton. We have her description and the description of her car. Our officers will keep an eye out for her. We'll give you a call if we get any leads. Anything else I can help you with?"

Convinced the police would give the lowest priority possible to the report, he ended the call with a "No thank you."

When the first light of Sunday sun radiated through the window, sleep overcame him. He awoke a little past noon to discover Marsha still had not returned. He wolfed down cold cereal and juice, concluding it would be irresponsible of him not to begin a search for her.

As he turned the key in the ignition of his Escape, he considered where he might begin, but since Marsha had no relatives in the area and he did not know where any of her friends lived, he pulled out into traffic with no destination in mind. Patrolling streets selected only by intuition, he drove slowly while his eyes swept over oncoming traffic and parked cars for the sight of her familiar lime-green Honda.

Subjecting himself to self-analysis as he drove, he eventually understood the reason why her disappearance bothered him so much. While it was true he did not love her, he believed she had grown dependent on him. He was her social future, and although such a role just emphasized the weakness of her character and his current state of mind, it also brought out that feeling of responsibility in him. It was as if he had found a lost child crying for her mommy at an expansive shopping mall. He would become accountable for the feeding, entertaining, and protection of such a defenseless youngster until a parent could be located. Nonetheless, a noise in his head grew louder and more insistent: he needed to end their bizarre relationship. And soon. She was an adult, not a child.

Glancing from the low sun to the fuel gauge that read nearly empty reminded him of the hopelessness of his hunt, so he drove back to his home after having spent five hours of futile wandering. Perhaps Marsha had returned in his absence; he pushed the key into the lock with a rush of anticipation that she would be standing there with a bag of groceries in her arms. But the door swung open into a stone quiet room. He lugged his tired and hungry body to the kitchen. Looking into the refrigerator, the sight of food upset his stomach. As he poured himself a Coke, he asked himself if Marsha could have abandoned him, just up and left. But that did not strike true.

He set his glass on the table alongside his laptop and cell phone. He began searching for phone numbers. As he sipped the drink, he made inquiries with the clubs and bars she haunted, and then went on to call the local hospitals. The reality that something bad had happened to her increased with each negative reply he got regarding a female fitting Marsha's description. She could have been kidnapped or raped or even murdered in some back alley. Images of her lying helplessly on the side of some indistinct road, bleeding and crying for help played out in his head like a series of snapshots. Ross decided to try the police again. Maybe someone other than Sergeant Norris would answer.

Grabbing his phone as he pushed himself up from the table, he felt a tingling sensation in his head, much like one he had before, again followed by an excruciating headache. He made it as far the sofa, before collapsing and drifting into a light, twilight sleep.

* * *

The sound of the front door opening jerked him upright and alert in an instant. He exhaled a weak cry of relief at the sight of Marsha standing in the room, staring at him.

Time suspended as their eyes met. The clear, jewel-like, transparent blue eyes conveyed an unfamiliar sensation of connection at the deepest emotional level. When the odd feeling threatened to envelop him completely, he escaped by shouting, "Where the hell have you been?"

She smiled with a warmth that struck him viscerally, then said, "It is good to see you again Ross."

"I've been worried. Damn Marsha, why did you just disappear like that?" When he finally noticed the black and white cat she carried, he added, "And why do you have that thing?"

"You have been concerned by my absence? You claimed you did not love me."

"I don't, but . . ." he said, and then paused, wondering what was different about her. "But I was worried you might have been hurt. My imagination went wild. Where have you been?"

"There were some important arrangements that needed my attention," she explained. "I discovered this cat outside. It appeared lost and hungry. I will give it something to eat."

"But you said you were just going out to get last minute groceries. You've been gone almost twenty-four hours. You could have called."

"I will give you my reasons later. I promise I will not leave you again."

"You said that before. Marsha, this settles it, I won't continue this charade. The whole idea of us being together doesn't make sense. You don't love me and I don't love you." He waited for the flood of tears and exasperation to begin.

Her smile broadened into a full grin. "I do not care if you do not want me. I will never leave you. I love you."

I must have soap in my ears, he thought. "What?" he said.

Still smiling, she moved to the full-length mirror on the inside closet door and beamed at what reflected back at her.

Am I dreaming? "What are you doing?" he asked.

Lowering the cat to the floor, she pivoted on her toes, twisting her upper body to see the reflection of her bottom in her tight jeans. She giggled and said, "I think it will give you great pleasure when you touch this body."

His attention was distracted from Marsha when the cat padded softly across the floor towards him, and placed itself inches from his feet. It stared up at his face. Ross reached the top of the feline's head between its ears, and stroked the soft black fur with his fingertips, eliciting an immediate purr of appreciation. "Maybe we should keep it if it doesn't have a home," Ross proposed, a smile finally emerging from his lips.

With one swift swipe, the cat's sharp claws tore through his pant leg to puncture his skin. And then, as if the incident had never occurred, the animal sat placidly looking up and resumed its loud purr.

"What the hell!" Ross cursed, lifting the material of his pants to discover two small pinpricks of blood.

Marsha looked at the pair, a wide grin spreading across her face. She said, "Cannot you two get along for a minute?" Walking slowly to the couch, she said, "Naughty kitty," and then sat alongside Ross. Leaning over, she lightly touched her lips against his and then pulled back. "You remember?" she asked.

Ross was about to question the meaning of her inquiry when it struck him. He was wordless. Her lips had not moved when she had asked! The words had formed in his head. Complete confusion washed through him. He reached out to the only security within mental or physical reach— Marsha. He pressed his mouth more forcefully onto hers as his arms moved around her. He asked, "Remember what?" frightened by what her answer might be. His mind flew into turmoil when he realized he only thought the question and had not actually vocalized it. How could he have? His lips were still hard-pressed against hers.

The unspoken words, her words, "You will," filled his head.

He wanted to stop. Stop thinking, stop kissing her, and stop holding her, but her presence had a magnetic pull so powerful that releasing her was as incomprehensible at that moment as not breathing.

He tried to pull his thoughts together, but an image of a tall, black haired woman blocked his every effort. The image of her was followed by another picture, one of an enormous sphere, followed by an owl. Soon short-lived images, one after another, each increasing in intensity, emerged until a steady stream of memories tumbled into place. His eyes opened to the expectant face in front of him.

"Jay?" slipped from his lips.

She nodded through sparkling tears.

He pulled her tightly against him, putting his head aside hers.

They clung dearly to each other. They both trembled.

Still in each other's arms, serenity settled into Ross' mind. Peace relaxed his body. His thoughts were clear. He was complete.

Ross asked, "How?"

"My body . . . Jay's body, was paralyzed by the wound inflicted by your military. My people kept that body alive for transfer of my essence back to my Ruthran body. I refused, explaining that without you, a continuation of my life was inconceivable. I felt it my right to choose with the successful completion of my mission. Our ship commander must have been impressed by you, because he spoke in my behalf and proposed that a new human body be created so I could be returned to Earth to live with you as a human.

"Our leaders were not easily convinced, but eventually conceded that my reunion with you was a reasonable reward for our extraordinary sacrifices in securing the safety of the children. Their only condition was that I would replace the essence of an existing human and she could take my place on Jupiter. A swap. They believed my permanent placement on Earth without a historical identity could possibly lead to complications for us. Since your government will undoubtedly check on you and anyone associated with you from time to time, the concerns are probably justified. I suspect that if you married a woman with no traceable background, they might devote substantial investigative time into her, and you can imagine the possible consequences of such an investigation. You see, Marsha was ideal. They know Marsha. They trust Marsha. She helped them capture you. And they expect you to eventually marry her.

"My essence is the same in Marsha's body as it was in Jay's. My memory is a summation of my Ruthran life, Jay's life, and Marsha's. If you are sympathetic about the fate of the Marsha you knew, do not be. Her life essence was stripped of all memory and placed in my previous Ruthran body. She has been provided with fictitious Ruthran history that essentially will be as real to her as her life was here on Earth. She would think of the idea of taking on a human body with the same revulsion I initially felt, although I am getting the better of the trade for mating. Ruthran mating is pleasurable enough, but it is more of a mental gratification." Jay flashed a wry grin, leaned backwards and brushed a fingertip over his lips, giggled at his unmistakable enjoyment, then said, "You certainly like it."

"I love you."

"Do you still want to end our relationship?" she teased and snuggled into his chest.

"We're already married," Ross pointed out.

"No, you married Jay. I am Marsha. We will need to have a proper Earth wedding so there is never any suspicion about you. I will be able to tell your government that you are being a good boy and remembering nothing." She smiled and kissed him again.

"Will you two cut out the mush," popped into Ross' head. "I thought I was going to get some chow."

"Oswald?" Ross linked. "You're a cat!"

"Figured that one out all by yourself, did you now?" the black and white feline answered licking its paw. "I want you to know I did debrief Jay, I mean Marsha, about how you abused me. She said she would put you on probation, but I'm beginning to wonder if she cares about my beefs anymore. She seems more concerned about you these days."

Ross watched Oswald run a paw over its ear as Marsha cuddled back into his chest. "You are very catlike," he observed and then added, "Why did you claw me?"

"That was for shacking up with Marsha before Jay became Marsha," Oswald explained, lowering its paw, and then looking into Ross' eyes. "You know this body and name changing routine is getting very confusing. I think I'm getting another headache. You have any pain killers around?"

Ross stretched his free arm to the feline and petted its back. "Why did they switch you to a cat?"

"You know Ross, there are times when you aren't very bright for a professor," Oswald retorted. "How many humans you know keep a screech owl for a pet? I was given the choice between a dog and a cat. I chose the cat because I wasn't really into the butt sniffing scene." Oswald began licking his belly, then screamed, "Son of a bitch, I'm a male. This hasn't been one of my better days."

Ignoring Oswald, Ross put both arms around Marsha and rested his head on hers.

"Excuse me," materialized in his head. "I hate to interrupt you two again, but where's the litter box? I gotta go."

ACKNOWLEDGEMENTS

What is the point of writing if not for the people who read books? You are the judge and jury of what is good or bad, fun or agonizing, what tugs at emotions, or leaves one cold. If it were not for time spent reading and unleashing your imagination, we would all be less human.

My four children, Melissa, Donna, Ron, and Sandra, support my writing obsession, each in a different way. More importantly, they gift me with joyful experiences that spark my creativity and storytelling. As a parent, I am so proud of each of them. But I should also indicate that the sequence of their names is in chronological birth order and not favoritism.

Erin Eveland is a published author who has taken countless hours from her own work to critique, discuss, encourage, and support my writing. Acknowledging and thanking her does not even come close to the level of appreciation and respect I feel. She taught me how to put heart into my work, and I continue to learn from her. I cannot envision writing without hearing her voice say, "No, Ron. Not good enough."

Editor for Selladore Press, Judy Berlinski, is a gem. She is tough, relentless, and caring about her work, yet strives to understand and maintain a writer's style. A wonderful, pleasant woman without whom we would be lost.

The After Hours writing group was comprised of Erin Eveland, Lynn Parsons, and Shelly Towne when I joined. It soon grew to include Ted Zahrfeld, Jim Hodge, and Marlene Sophabmisay. That group gave the first critique of an early version of *The Field Trip*. Their input was invaluable in evolving the story close to the published version. After

Hours has since expanded, continuing to help and encourage all members. We are good friends who celebrate writing and life.

I am fortunate to live in an area near the Cromaine Library in Hartland, Michigan. It is an exceptional place with extensive programs for children and adults to encourage not only reading, but many forms of learning. Cromaine Library also helps writers with author speaking engagements, and hosts a monthly meeting for writers. That meeting is chaired by Shelley Ragnone at the time of these acknowledgements. Her enthusiasm and assistance for writers at any aspiration level has been an asset to those interested in this craft for the surrounding area.

Also Available from Selladore Press

One Girl. One Boy. And the Masters of Darkness.
See the Shadow Creatures. They are everywhere.
But you can't run from the shadows.
Or the Masters who control them.

By   Erin Eveland

Coming Soon

Second in the Darkness Series

SHADOWS
by
Erin Eveland

PIXLEY TO THE MOON
by
R. A. Andrade

The attempt to establish a second base on the
moon and uncover the fate of the five who
vanished on the first.

About R. A. Andrade

Ron writes from a small community in Michigan, sometimes at three in the morning when ideas wake him from sleep. He was born and raised in New England, sometimes drawing on those childhood and teen experiences for his novels. Driven to write, his goal is simply to entertain by bringing the reader the unexpected. Additional information can be found at raandrade.com.